D0912362

THE FINAL GOODBYE

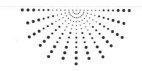

BRITTNEY SAHIN

EMKO MEDIA

The Final Goodbye

By: Brittney Sahin

Published by: EmKo Media, LLC

Copyright © 2018 EmKo Media, LLC

Extract, *My Every Breath* Copyright © 2018 EmKo Media, LLC

This book is an original publication of Brittney Sahin.

In accordance with the U.S. Copyright Act of 1976, the scanning, uploading, and electronic sharing of any part of this book without permission of the publisher constitute unlawful piracy and theft of the author's intellectual property. If you would like to use material from the book (other than for review purposes), prior written permission must be obtained by contacting brittneysahin@emkomedia.com. Thank you for your support of the author's rights.

Editor: Carole, WordsRU

Proofreader: Anja, HourGlass Editing

Proofreader: Judy, Judy's Proofreading

Cover Design by: Romantic Book Affairs / Images licensed through Shutterstock & Deposit

This book is a work of fiction. Names, characters, places, and incidents either are products of the author's imagination or are used fictitiously. Any resemblance to actual persons, living or dead, business establishments, events, or locales is entirely coincidental.

Print ISBN: 9781947717053

Sign up to receive exclusive excerpts and bonus material, as well as take part in great giveaways. Get alerted when books are released. Sign up at: brittneysahin.com.

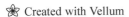 Created with Vellum

For our men and women in uniform.

PROLOGUE

ORANGE ROCKS JUTTED INTO THE SKY, SOME JAGGED, OTHERS smooth. They rose from the ground as if the earth had split open and given birth to the magnificent beasts. You'd almost think you were on Mars if it weren't for the greenery that dotted the landscape.

The Garden of the Gods: what an appropriate name for the towering rock formations in Colorado Springs.

But all Ben could think about was the way the porous, fragile sandstone felt beneath his palms.

He added more powder to his hands, shifted to the right, and reached for the next ledge.

"You good, buddy?" his best friend, Nate, asked from above.

"You're the idiot without a rope. Are *you* good?" Of course, Ben free climbed all the time but never at the Garden of the Gods —he was superstitious. Something about climbing there made him think the heavens might open and suck his soul straight up.

His mom despised when he climbed here. Hell, she hated when he climbed, period. But every year she gave in and bought him new carabiners, ropes, and everything else he needed.

They lived in Alabama, but ever since his fifteenth birthday he spent a few weeks each summer out west. And this year was no different.

In the fall, he'd be attending college on a baseball scholarship, and he wasn't sure if this would be his last summer climbing, for a while at least.

"Shit! There's a raptor nest up here. We need to reroute," Nate shouted.

"Everything okay?" Riley hollered from below.

Ben glanced down to look at his other best friend—the beautiful one.

She held her hand like a visor over her eyes as she peered up at them.

Nate, Ben, and Riley had been the three amigos since they were in diapers. When Nate and Riley started dating earlier that year, it had been a little rough. But Riley—or Ri, as Ben liked to call her, had refused to let her relationship with Nate sour her friendship with Ben.

"Did you hear that?" Ben called out to Riley, who was belaying him. Too afraid of heights, she rarely went up on the cliffs, but she'd learned enough to keep her guys safe.

"Yeah," she answered.

Ben's calves started to burn, and he craned his neck up to check Nate's position. It was prohibited to climb near raptor nesting sites, and if they were spotted they'd get booted or fined.

Ben asked Nate, "You ready to get your ass on a rope—"

The words died on his lips as his heart stopped.

Everything stopped at that moment. The moment Nate fell.

Time.

Stood.

Still.

Silence wrapped Ben up in a tight cocoon where nothing was real.

The years he and Nate had spent together chasing girls, rock climbing in the summers, ice climbing in the winters . . .

Kodak moments of the past shot through his mind, and he was stuck in a cyclone of memories.

His friend couldn't have fallen.

No damn way.

Nate's eyes had been closed, and he hadn't said anything when he'd dropped past Ben as if in slow motion like in the movies.

But this was real life, and there was no pause. No rewind.

Riley's scream shattered the sudden silence of Ben's mind. He scrambled to make sense of what had happened.

"No!" Ben's voice was raw, his eyes blurry.

It was too late.

Too damn late.

He couldn't save him.

His best friend was dead.

CHAPTER ONE

FOURTEEN YEARS LATER

"I HAD ONE RULE." BEN HELD UP HIS FINGER AND MADE A *TSK* noise. "One damn rule. Don't screw the client."

"Shit, she threw herself at me. What was I supposed to do?" Peter shrugged his massive shoulders. Too much bodybuilding was screwing with his head.

"You were supposed to keep your dick in your pants! You were paid to protect her, not to have sex with her." Ben tossed a file on the desk and straightened in the chair, irritation crawling through his body as he glared at his soon-to-be ex-employee.

"Come on, bro. I need this job." He folded his arms across his chest and stood in front of the desk. His green eyes narrowed as he waited for Ben to respond, and when he didn't Peter asked, "You're telling me you've never hooked up with a client?"

Ben scratched at his full beard. "First of all, my name is on the building. So, what I do is my own business. And second of all, you didn't just sleep with a client—your picture is all over the internet." He snatched his phone from his pocket and opened the

Instagram app. "You're trending. There's a hashtag that says #PeterhasabigPeter. If you're going to screw a famous pop singer at least do it behind closed doors so every teenager with a phone doesn't catch you in the act!"

Peter grinned as if impressed by himself and rubbed the dark stubble on his jaw. "Could be worse."

And this was why Ben should never have hired him last year. Too damn arrogant, and not in the ways that mattered.

Ben grunted in disgust. "How could it possibly be worse? You guys work undercover for me half the time. How the hell do you expect me to keep you on the payroll when your face—among other things"—he rolled his eyes—"is all over the place?"

"Well, at least they got a good shot of me. I mean, what if they had edited the pics and said I had a small one? Now that'd be some shit."

"Get out of my office." Ben shoved away from his desk, the chair wheels grinding down the already frayed carpet worn from years of stress.

"Man, you're supposed to be chill. What is wrong with you?"

"I am chill," he bit out, annoyed. "But when it comes to work, I don't screw around. Pick up your last check from Lindsay, and good luck. I hope the sex was worth it."

His firm, Logan Securities, wouldn't get paid by the pop star because of this incident, so Peter really didn't deserve that money. Hell, the singer wanted to sue the company because of the scandal.

Peter opened his mouth, but Ben held a palm in the air, demanding his silence.

"Go." He couldn't deal with talking to him anymore. "I need time to cool off."

Peter grumbled, turned on his heels, and strode across the room, slamming the door behind him so hard it rattled the framed pictures on the nearby walls.

Ben's head dropped back, and he closed his eyes.

Nothing had been the same lately.

The PI jobs, the bodyguard assignments—his adrenaline had remained tightly bottled up inside of him and hadn't been unleashed in months.

Protecting a bunch of bigwigs with money was . . . boring.

He missed the man he used to be. The Marine.

After eight years in the military, he never should've abandoned his career to pursue a childhood dream of playing pro ball. A dream that was short-lived after blowing out his shoulder.

Maybe he needed to shut down the company and go back into the service. Was that possible?

Probably not, but he still thought about it all the time.

A knock on the door had him opening his eyes. "Come in." He hoped to hell it wasn't Peter returning with his tail between his legs, begging for another chance.

It was his admin, thank God.

She shielded her eyes by staring down at her short black pumps as she walked his way.

He expected to see an I-told-you-so look on her face since she'd been against giving Peter a *third* chance last month, but he straightened in his seat when her hazel irises found his face.

A dark look overshadowed Lindsay's normally bright gaze, and her hand fanned against her collarbone.

Silence filled the room like a bubble that was growing too large and was about to pop. He knew in his gut there was only one reason why his chatty admin looked like she'd just read a Stephen King novel.

His abdominal muscles tightened, and he rose to his feet. Knuckled fists pressed to the desk as his head bowed. "Who died?"

It wasn't the first time he'd asked that question.

And each time, the same familiar sharp throb pulsed inside of him like he'd been punched too many times in the ribs.

"Your mom called."

It was enough to make his head fly up.

Dad?

Please, God, no.

"She, um, said Ralph Chandler died."

Ralph Chandler. Shit.

Lindsay was one of the few people who knew of Ralph, but it had taken a bottle of tequila on his birthday last year for him to spill the ugly truth about what had happened fourteen years ago.

Ralph had been like a second father to him. A man he hadn't seen since his son, Nate, died.

Ben's eyes flashed shut as memories hurtled to the forefront of his mind.

He'd send a card and flowers. That's what he'd do. And Ralph would understand.

It was a shit move, but he still didn't trust himself to go anywhere near Riley, even after all these years.

"He, um, he didn't just die."

"How does someone not 'just die'?" What the hell was she talking about?

"He was murdered."

CHAPTER TWO

"IT'S ONLY BEEN THREE WEEKS, AND I TOLD YOU ON DAY ONE THAT I wouldn't prescribe medicine for you if I didn't feel it would be beneficial. Nothing has changed." Riley shifted back in her worn black chair and set her ballpoint pen on her closed notebook, maintaining eye contact with Jeremy Stanton with each movement.

Every Tuesday and Friday morning, the man made her skin crawl and her body a little shaky.

She'd worked with some tough people, and she'd always done her best to help rehabilitate them—no judgment. A fresh start. But lately, some of her patients had been rubbing her the wrong way, this one included.

"All I'm asking for is a little Valium." A bead of sweat started to appear at his hairline, where his thin brown hair was slicked back with gel. His fingers tapped his knee like a child counting, *one-two-three-four*, forcefully repeating the numbers over and over again, never making it to five.

Riley preferred to sit directly in front of her patients, but when it came to Jeremy, she needed space. An entire room of space.

Her gaze darted to the polished wood of the desk, and her

nerves tickled her throat as she thought about the panic button she'd installed.

When one of her patients had wrapped his hands around her neck and tried to strangle her three months ago, she opted for extra security.

She wondered if she'd need to file a restraining order against Jeremy. It'd be her third in the last twelve months.

Was something in the Alabama water lately? The town had gone mad.

He stopped drumming his long, skinny fingers, leaving the index one pointed her way. He angled his head and chewed on his bottom lip. His eyes narrowed, the pupils so dilated you could barely see the dark green. "Tell me, Riley, do you take pleasure in seeing your patients suffer?"

"It's Dr. Carpenter, please." Her hand slipped under the desk, resting on the small button as Jeremy stood and approached. "I think we're done for the day." The words edged from her lips as if snapped by a mousetrap, and it was painful to say them.

She never did this. She never ended a session early because things got too intense for her. Well, except that one throat-throttling time.

She was a fighter.

She hated giving up unless absolutely necessary, and if she hit the button, it would signify a failure in her ability to treat Jeremy. So, she raised her hand back up onto the desk and maintained her confidence.

"If you don't get me that Valium when I see you next, I'll have Grandad pull that big fat check he sends you. I'll find someone else who cares about helping me." His nicotine-stained teeth flashed her way, and his yellowish-tinged skin tightened on his forehead as he, honest to God, snarled at her.

"There is no one else. Remember?" She crossed her arms. "If you don't see me, you violate the conditions of your parole."

Jeremy's rich grandfather had already sent him to every psychiatrist within a thirty-mile radius before sending him to her.

She'd been his last choice because she'd made it clear eight weeks prior she wasn't a pill-pushing psychiatrist. She mostly used talk therapy for her patients, and only when the situation was absolutely necessary did she prescribe pills.

She believed a healthy diet and the elimination of chemically processed food could do wonders for mental health. Of course, she was nicknamed the "Hippy Doc" and ridiculed by most of her peers, but hey—her methods were proven to work. People from the nearby cities had even trekked out to her small practice to get results.

"Do you want this to be our last visit?" She rose to her feet, refusing to remain sitting with Jeremy looking down at her with those glaring and sinister eyes. "No other doctor will see you, which is why you're here. So"—she shrugged—"you make the call."

He turned his back and started for the door. "Be back Friday."

Once he was gone, she released the breath she'd been holding and fell back into her chair.

Some days were definitely harder than others.

There was a quick tap on the frame of her already open door.

"You okay?" her friend Mandy asked, remaining standing in the doorframe.

"I don't know if I can keep doing this."

"I, uh, don't blame you. That's why I became a surgeon."

Riley glanced at her watch. "Shouldn't you be saving a life right now?" A smile found her lips but quickly disintegrated when she noticed a slight puffiness beneath Mandy's eyes.

She'd been crying.

Riley stood and rushed to her friend as fast as her black heels would carry her.

Mandy's hand went to her mouth as tears started trickling down her face. Her green eyes disappeared beneath her lids, and her long lashes splayed against her Alabama sun-kissed skin.

"Did you lose someone?" Riley placed a hand on her back.

Leading her by the elbow, she walked Mandy over to the couch near the window, where sunlight filtered through the partially open blinds.

"Daniel and I did."

"*My* Daniel?" She cursed under her breath. "I mean, my ex?" She sat next to her and reached for her arm.

"He was our patient. We were in the middle of performing an appendectomy, and things went sideways. He was my age. Only thirty-seven. Just had two babies."

Oh, shit. "Not Phillip Sanderson?" This was one reason why Riley had never gone into surgery. She couldn't handle a loss like that.

Mandy nodded.

"Oh, wow. I didn't know him personally, but he worked at the prison with my dad."

Almost everyone worked at either the prison or the hospital.

Mandy sniffled. "Daniel said it's my fault, but I did everything right. I-I don't know what the hell happened."

"I'm so sorry. Is there anything I can do?" She gave her forearm a gentle squeeze.

"Let me sit on your couch for a bit while I get my head together?"

"Yeah, of course. I don't have another patient for an hour." Riley stood and went to the small refrigerator on the other side of the room and grabbed a bottle of water.

The hospital was within walking distance of Riley's private practice, so Mandy usually made her way to Riley's couch anytime she'd had a rough day.

"Don't listen to Daniel. He's probably trying to pass the blame on to someone else." She crossed the office and handed her the water.

"Maybe, but sometimes he treats me like a child. It's tough, you know. I've only been here for nine months, and starting as an intern this late in life isn't easy." She kept the bottle tight between her palms and stared at it in a daze. "He doesn't treat the younger residents like this."

"Is it worse since we broke up?" Was Daniel that petty to take his anger about their breakup out on her best friend?

Of course, when Mandy had moved from Phoenix earlier that year, and Riley had met her at the hospital fundraiser, Daniel had been against their friendship. He didn't like her hanging out with his interns. He thought it'd be unprofessional.

The man was too uptight.

"He's been a bit more agitated with me lately." Mandy shrugged. "But, I don't know, he's like a grieving widow or something ever since you two split." Her long, sweeping lashes lifted, dampened by tears, and she met Riley's gaze as she positioned herself next to her.

Riley grumbled. "He's been relentless in trying to get me back, and I just don't have the energy for it to be honest." She sighed. "It's been over a month since we broke up, and he still sends flowers."

"You're lucky to have a man like him so in love with you," Mandy noted softly.

"Maybe, but I'm sorry if my breakup is impacting your work life." She made a mental note to talk to him the next time he called, which would probably be around 8 p.m.—like every other night.

"It's fine. The guy just misses you. He'll hopefully get over it."

"Hope so." Riley forced a stiff smile. "But, um, how are things with you and Bobby?" She wanted to take Mandy's mind off her loss, if even for a moment. "Or are you still contemplating one of the many other daily proposals you get?"

Five-nine, long brownish-black hair, a fit and toned body that would make twenty-year-olds jealous—Mandy had both staff and patients hitting on her all of the time, and it drove her nuts. She wanted to be admired for her brains and surgical skills, not because her boobs could barely be restrained by her double D bra.

Last week, Mandy had joked that they should quit their medical careers and go into modeling. She usually talked her off the modeling cliff for about a week before another handsy patient pissed her off to the point where she wanted to, in her words, use her scalpel on his penis.

The bad thing about their small town was there weren't a lot of single women, especially ones that looked like Mandy and Riley.

Riley hated thinking of herself as beautiful, though. She didn't mind being pretty or gorgeous, but *beautiful* was a word she'd stripped from her vocabulary fourteen years ago when her best friend had abandoned her.

He'd always called her beautiful, and after he left, she cringed whenever the adjective was used toward her. The word becoming like a knife to the heart.

"I don't think Bobby and I are going to work out."

Riley blinked away her thoughts. "Oh, no. Why not? Are you still worried about the age difference? Or, do you have issues that he's a paramedic and not a doctor?"

Riley would take a man with a great sense of humor over the MD initials any day. Daniel had fallen short on the ability to make her belly-laugh.

"Not really."

"So, what is it?"

"There are hospital rumors that he's sleeping with someone." She cupped the back of her neck and looked at the ceiling.

"Maybe that *someone* is you."

"Funny." But it did get her to smile. "Two nurses said they caught him making out in the supply closet with another doctor. And, for clarification, that doc wasn't me."

"Jesus. Are you on an episode of *Grey's Anatomy*?"

Mandy chuckled. "Sometimes I feel like it, although I'm still waiting for my McDreamy."

"Yeah, well, spoiler alert: that doctor died." Riley nudged her in the side. "We'll go for drinks tonight and get sloppy drunk. How about that?"

"Yes, that'd be—" Mandy cut herself off at the sound of the office line ringing.

Riley went over and checked the caller ID. It was her mom. It was doubtful she already knew about Phillip Sanderson's death, which meant it probably wasn't why she was calling.

The worrier in her could never transfer her mom to voicemail, so she shot Mandy an apologetic look and answered, "What's up, Mom?"

"You're going to want to sit to hear what I have to say," she said in a rush.

The last time her mom told her to sit was years ago when she informed Riley that her ex-best friend, Ben Logan, had been injured playing baseball. And it had been news that she didn't, in fact, need to sit for.

"Spit it out, Mom." She scratched her short pink nails against the side of her face, impatient.

"Ralph was killed last night. They found his body this morning."

"Say that again." Surely she hadn't heard her mom correctly.

"Murdered. He was murdered, baby girl."

She hated when her mom called her that, but . . . *wait—what?*

The room started to spin, and little black dots fell like snowflakes before her eyes. What was happening?

She was on her knees, palms to the floor, gathering oxygen into her lungs with deep breaths.

"You okay?" Mandy pressed a hand to her back.

"Shit. I—" Her eyes welled.

"Riley!" Her mother's voice sang loudly through the phone that rested near her hand.

Mandy snatched the cell off the ground. "Mrs. Carpenter, she'll need to call you back."

Ralph was dead.

Murdered.

But that wasn't possible.

Who would kill him?

"What happened?" Mandy helped Riley over to the couch, and this time, she was the one getting some water for her.

Riley polished off nearly the entire bottle before she could think again. She was still processing.

It'd been years since she'd gone through the stages of grief, and she wasn't prepared to do it again.

"Ralph's dead."

"What?" A sharp gasp left Mandy's mouth. "How?"

"Killed." The word sounded foreign on her tongue. It couldn't be true. It couldn't possibly be real. Her shoulders slumped forward. "I don't know how, but I sure as hell need some answers."

CHAPTER THREE

WHISPERED VOICES AND SAD EYES—IT WAS A CONTRAST TO THE bright sunflowers adorning the room.

Pops of white and yellow were arranged in elaborate bouquets all over the place. They were Ralph's mother's favorite flower, and so they'd been his favorite, too. At least, that's what he'd once told Riley, which was why she'd always brought them over whenever she had visited.

Most of the town had forgotten about Ralph after he lost his son, and it had broken Riley's heart.

She didn't regret her decision to forgo a great offer at a hospital in D.C. when her fellowship had ended. She'd turned it down so she could be near family, and so Ralph would know he had someone he could count on. Of course, Ralph never knew her decision had been, in part, because of him.

But now he was dead.

Murdered.

And for what?

He had a doctorate in psychology, but when Nate had died, he'd resigned from his professor position in Birmingham and taught at a local community college three nights a week.

The police still hadn't released the details about the murder, and Ralph's body had been held up for a week, delaying the wake until today.

As much as she wanted to know how and why he had been killed, she also couldn't stomach the idea of hearing the details.

He'd been murdered in his office at the college, but his home had been closed off by the homicide detective in charge, which meant they'd been looking for something. Maybe for answers.

She had planned on holding the wake at her apartment, but then the detective officially cleared Ralph's home. And in a mad haste, she decided it'd be more appropriate to have the gathering where he'd lived for the last thirty years.

She scanned the room, and goose bumps scattered over her skin at the sight of the urn, positioned alongside a framed photo of Ralph.

It was simple. Not too flashy. Pewter with a Grecian feel; it was crafted from solid brass and accented with three deep ebony lines. The urn could hold the ashes of a person who weighed up to two hundred pounds, she'd been told—and had wanted to throw up instantly.

"On sale for ninety-nine dollars, too," the elderly man had said when selling it to her as if price mattered. How much was a vase really worth if it held the ashes of someone you loved? Could you put a price on such a thing?

Her stomach knotted, and she looked at Ralph's picture, such a reminder of the boyfriend she'd once lost. The same blond hair and eyebrows as Nate. The same green eyes and freckles on his nose.

It had been difficult to spend time with Ralph right after Nate's death. They'd looked too alike; plus, it hadn't helped that every wall served as a memorial to Nate and that most pictures included herself and Ben.

Ralph had never spoken ill of Ben. He even wanted her to forgive him for leaving.

Cowardly—that's all she could think when she thought about Ben.

Sure, he'd taken off to join the Marines instead of going to college—and being a coward is a contradictory term related to the military, but still . . . he'd left.

Sudden chills skated down her spine when she realized her ex was standing next to her. His black hair was perfectly gelled and styled, his hard jaw tight like always, and his muscular body filled out the tailored black suit to perfection.

He was attractive, she couldn't deny that. And he was a genius, already on his way to becoming the chief of surgery. Of course, it was a step down compared to the job he'd said no to in Cleveland. Refusing to move with him had been the final blow to their relationship.

"You didn't need to come." She surveyed the crowded room, taking note of the people that had abandoned Ralph over the years only to show up too late.

"I'm paying my respects." Daniel's hand rested on the small of her back. "He was your friend, so I wanted to be here for you."

"Well, thank you." Sorrow thickened her throat, making it hard to swallow.

"How are you holding up?" He rubbed his hand up and down her back in soft strokes.

"Not great."

"You know I'm here for you if you ever need anything." His hand slipped up to her shoulder, and he gave it a gentle squeeze. "Like, if you want help packing up his home. Or you just want to talk."

She pressed her lips together in a tight-lipped smile. "Maybe."

And that's when she saw them—Ben's parents.

It had been excuse after excuse from them as to why he never came home.

Deployed.

Playing pro ball.

Running a security firm in Vegas.

Always busy. Always too important to be bothered with their small-town life.

His mom's long, brown hair was up in a bun, her brown eyes enhanced by dark black liner, her long lashes a reminder of Ben's. And his dad—he was a spitting image of her ex-best friend. Tall, broad-shouldered, fit, with short black hair and the same blue eyes.

In the summer of '85, Riley, Nate, and Ben had been born. On the same day. On the same morning. They'd shared some sort of special bond and had been nearly inseparable since the moment they'd left the hospital.

And when Nate's mom had died of cancer, Ben and Riley had been his rock. They'd helped a six-year-old through the roughest time of his life.

She blinked back more tears as the memories created a fresh wave of pain.

"Riley?" Daniel arrested her attention from her ocean-deep thoughts, saving her from drowning in the past.

God, Mandy was right, wasn't she? The man really did love her. Why couldn't she love him back?

Her drunken one-night stand two weeks ago proved she didn't have any lingering feelings for Daniel. Her only regret was choice in rebound. Patrick was a surgeon who worked on the same floor as Daniel.

She doubted Daniel had found out about it, though, or he wouldn't be so friendly right now.

Maybe it was time for her to move. To start over in a new city with new people.

With Ralph gone . . . why not? He'd been one of the reasons she'd turned down Daniel's request to move to Cleveland, but now, was there anything stopping her from leaving?

Sure, she had her parents here, but they'd always wanted more for her. They still had high hopes she'd become a big-city doctor in D.C. or Atlanta.

Riley caught sight of Mandy coming into the room, and Bobby trailed behind. He stopped to talk to a professor who had worked with Ralph.

"Could you be nicer to Mandy, please? Don't give her such a hard time." Her eyes landed back on Daniel's, and she lifted her brows, waiting for an answer.

His gaze hardened. "If I'm tough on her, it's to make her a better surgeon. She's ten years older than the rest of my doctors."

"So, she has to work twice as hard? That's bullshit, and you know it." She cursed again when she realized she'd drawn attention from the room. "I need some air. We can talk about this later, I guess."

She sidestepped him and approached Mandy. "Hey, you came with Bobby?"

"No, we just arrived at the same time. I didn't even know he knew Ralph."

She didn't remember Bobby ever hanging out with Nate back in school, but maybe it was possible. And then, Bobby had joined the military, just like Ben, after graduation. But unlike Ben, he'd come back home.

"Looks like Daniel came, too, huh?"

"Yeah, for support." The intensity of the day had been chipping away at her, and now she wasn't sure if she had the energy to make it until sunset. "But, uh, I need to splash some water on my face before I lose my mind. Sorry."

"Of course. If you need anything, let me know."

"Thanks." She took off toward the nearest bathroom. The door handle rattled as she gripped and shook it.

"Occupied," someone called out.

Shit. She'd use the upstairs one. She was too frazzled and impatient to wait.

Her heels clicked on the wooden steps as she went up the old, creaky stairs.

The bathroom was the first door on the right. She hadn't been upstairs since Nate's death, but she still remembered her way around.

She heard a faint sound coming from down the hall, so she paused outside the bathroom and continued to listen.

Her stomach folded in on itself when she realized she wasn't alone. Pivoting, she started in the direction of the noise, walking down the hall with careful steps, but her heels on the wood floors made for a bad combination.

Once outside Nate's door, her heart crawled up into her throat at the sight of someone inside.

What if he was the killer, and he was there looking for something?

But . . . the man was holding a framed photo. Although his back was to her, his head was tipped forward as if in mourning.

He had black hair that brushed against the collar of his blazer. Long legs were covered in dark slacks, and broad shoulders filled out the jacket.

She worked up her nerve and took a small step into the room, her heart pounding so loud it was in her ears.

"You should leave. Ralph wouldn't want you in here." Her pulse continued to quicken as a large hand set the frame back on top of the dresser.

"Been a long time, Ri."

At the sound of the husky voice, she staggered back into the hallway.

It was as if she were in quicksand and sinking fast.

Her mind blew to the past, to their shared seventeenth birthday.

"Friends, forever? No matter what?" she asked Ben and stared into his blue eyes.

"Ri, nothing could tear us apart. You, me, and Nate—they'll have to bury us together," he answered.

No . . . "Don't call me that." She hated that her voice trembled as the words nearly bled from her lips.

Her eyes squeezed closed, and her hands seized hold of her stomach as if she might fall forward and throw up.

"It's Dr. Carpenter, now," she said wryly after a minute of silence swept through the room, almost cooling her now flushed skin.

She couldn't open her eyes because then this would become real.

Ben Logan would be standing in front of her.

She wanted to edge back even more, but she couldn't get herself to move.

She was trapped in a sea of memories.

Pillow fights, stargazing, late-night swims in the lake, beach vacations, and to the very last time she saw him, which was seven years ago. Of course, Ben hadn't seen her then.

"You shouldn't be here." She loosened the words from her throat and hoped she'd delivered them with the necessary punch.

"I know," he said in a flat tone.

When her eyes opened, she couldn't stop herself from taking all of him in as if she'd never seen him before.

Fourteen years had turned him from a teenager into a man.

Muscles where there hadn't been.

A scar cutting along his right temple. His nose not perfectly straight as if it'd broken before.

Faint lines around his eyes and on his forehead. Maybe too much desert sun.

He looked strong.

Lethal.

But his hair—it was longer than normal, and his beard overgrown, like he hadn't seen a razor in a year.

"The least you could have done was shave."

He scratched the back of his dark head, a tight-lipped smile finding his mouth, which surprised her. It also made her uncomfortable.

His smile once had a magical effect on her. It'd pulled her out of whatever bad mood she'd been in. All Ben had ever had to do was take hold of her forearms, look her square in the eyes, and smile.

But this smile was different.

It was forced. It was uneasy.

He had changed. He wasn't her best friend anymore.

He was someone she barely recognized.

"I thought beards were in." His hands disappeared into his slacks pockets.

The blazer and dress pants didn't belong on a man like him. He'd never been a shirt-and-tie kind of guy. A baseball hat, jeans, and cowboy boots had always been his typical go-to.

"You missed the memo. Even Shaun White cut his hair." Okay, so that was the comeback of a fifth grader, and Ben's hair barely touched his shoulders, but she was in a foul mood and couldn't think straight.

A rumble of laughter found her ears, and a weird fluttering in her stomach had her shoulder blades pinching back.

"Since when are you into snowboarding? You could never keep your ass off the snow if I remember correctly."

"My ass is none of your concern." A breath of air whooshed from deep within her chest as he dragged his attention down, settling on her hips as if he were imagining what her derriere looked like.

They'd played strip poker in high school before she and Nate became a couple. And Ben had seen her in a swimsuit more times than she could count . . . but he'd never get another look at her again. Especially of her ass.

And why am I thinking about this?

"Maybe I had a shitty teacher back in the day. Maybe someone else could do what you couldn't." The mounting frustration continued to build as her arms crossed. Of course, she only knew who Shaun White was from watching past Winter Olympics, but she didn't need Ben to know that.

"Sure, beautiful."

Hell, no.

She was torn between tightening her lips into a hard grimace or opening her mouth to spew hot, angry words at him.

But nothing seemed to be happening as she focused on the quick curve of his lips that slipped into the briefest of smiles.

"It's not that long, by the way."

Riley whirled away, hating that she was now giving him a direct line of sight to her ass. She stole a look at him over her shoulder, and her brows knitted upon realizing her former best friend was staring at her glutes.

Years ago, he'd never given her so much as a sideways glance. He never had a remotely lustful gaze drift her way—well, minus that one incident right before Nate . . . *no, I can't think about that now.*

"Do us both a favor: get the hell out of here." The words left a bitter taste in her mouth as they rolled off her tongue.

"And you think you have the right to kick me out?" His voice dropped a few octaves, and it was different than she remembered. Deeper, laced with enough bite to cause most men to cower in fear.

It was enough to make her skin pebble as she faced him again. But what disturbed her the most was the sudden squeeze of pressure between her thighs.

She swallowed the short distance between them and jabbed a finger at his hard-as-a-rock chest, releasing a puff of air as if it were her dying breath.

His lips rolled inward, amusement flickering across his face as his gaze dropped to her index finger.

Ralph's face came to mind, and so she stitched her lips and tied a knot around her anger, trying to strangle it for the time being out of respect for him.

Ralph was gone, and they were at his wake.

"You're not worth my time." She turned away from him.

"Ri-ley." He dragged her name out as if the two syllables needed to be stretched for a mile.

There was a tight pinch of pain in her chest as if she were suffocating. She yanked her blazer off at the top of the stairs, trying to catch her breath.

"Go back to whatever cave you've been hiding out in," she rasped without looking back.

His heavy footsteps swallowed the space between them, masking her heels that clicked on the wooden steps.

Once she reached the last stair, his hand curled around her bicep.

She stilled as his mouth dipped down near her ear.

Her stomach churned, her nerves frayed.

Dealing with Ben was the last thing she wanted to do right now.

Her shoulders dropped forward, and his woodsy masculine scent floated to her nose.

"You'll never need to see me again. Promise." His words were hard around the edges, like an uncut diamond scraping against her skin, leaving a mark.

He maneuvered around her, and the beating of her heart became a dull thud as her insides shook, as if in protest to his departure.

"Mr. Logan? Dr. Carpenter?"

Ben clutched the front doorknob, but instead of turning it, he cast his eyes over his shoulder and to a man off to the side of the stairs in a tailored suit.

"I've seen a lot of pictures of the two of you," the man said and pointed to one particular framed photo that hung by the door.

Ben shifted to face him as Riley draped her blazer over the banister. She tucked a loose strand of hair behind her ear, trying to remember how she knew the man.

"I need to speak with both of you." The man's attention winged between Riley and Ben. "Can we talk in the office? I'm Stephen

Atley, Mr. Chandler's attorney. I'm sorry to do this now, but I'm on my way out of town."

Ben dropped his focus to the lawyer's outstretched hand. It took him a moment, but he finally clasped the man's palm.

"My condolences." The lawyer looked to her next.

She jerked her thumb Ben's way. "Why do you need to speak to him?"

"I think it'd be best if we discussed that behind closed doors." Atley pointed to the dining room which led to Ralph's small office. He'd obviously been in the home before.

Her eyes darted to Ben's face for a brief moment, but he was fixated on all of the other pictures near them.

The entire wall that followed the line of the steps was dotted with moments of the past.

Baby pictures, photos from climbing trips, high school events, and so forth served as a memorial to Nate's memory.

There was visible movement in Ben's throat as if he were swallowing his emotions.

So, he still had a heart. She hadn't been sure until now.

It didn't matter, though. Nothing could change history. And besides, history was meant to be learned from, and hopefully never repeated.

Her eyes followed the distressed oak floor as she walked behind the two men. She almost expected Ben to be wearing baseball cleats or combat boots, instead of the dark loafers he sported.

Once they were tucked inside the small office, the lawyer motioned to the chairs in front of the desk. "Please, sit down."

"I'll stand." Ben turned his back to them, roping a hand around his thick neck and over the black mass of hair.

God, had he always looked like he'd been carved by a Renaissance sculpture? Or was this a product of the military?

Riley's mouth pinched tight, and she hated herself for trying to drag up memories of Ben. She needed to stop creating a side-by-side comparison of him as a teen to the man before her now.

It wasn't only wrong because they were at Ralph's wake—thinking about Ben's looks was like a betrayal to her anger.

"Well." Atley popped open his briefcase and glanced her way. "Let's make this quick, shall we?"

"Wouldn't want to get in the way of your trip to Fiji, or wherever you plan on going." She wanted to hate the snarky tone that rolled off her tongue as smooth as butter on warm toast, but she couldn't find it in herself to.

Ben faced her and gave her the once-over, starting at her black pumps and traveling up her nylon-covered legs, to the hem of her black silk dress. The material was loose enough not to give away her shape, but it suddenly didn't feel appropriate without the jacket on top.

The dress was high-necked, so it didn't reveal much. And surely her bare arms weren't sexy . . . but there was something in Ben's eyes that had her wanting to cover her chest.

"Ahem." Atley held an open folder in his hand.

The room still held a hint of the vanilla cigars that Ralph had enjoyed on occasion.

His wife had died of lung cancer. Ralph had promised Nate he'd quit smoking after that, and he did. But when Nate passed, he had stopped caring about his health. It had been one of the reasons why she took a year off after high school before going to college; she refused to lose Ralph, too.

Why had Ben bothered to come back for the funeral? It was the burning question on the tip of her tongue, but she knew it'd be pointless to ask.

"Let's get this over with." Ben tugged on the cuff of his blazer as if the fit was uncomfortable, even though it looked frustratingly perfect.

"There's not much money, but he did ask that what he had be

divided between the two of you." The lawyer's pale blue irises met her face.

She found it hard to believe Ben would care about Ralph's money when last she'd heard he was rolling in dough and doing rather well for himself in Vegas.

As many times as she told her mom she didn't want to hear a word about the man, her mom always found a way to sneak him into conversations.

Her mom had announced Ben was dating a model this past summer, only to have her dad begin an immediate Google search, wanting to know which one. And when Ben and the Miss America lookalike broke up, her mom had called to break the news.

Riley wondered if the model left him because he'd stopped shaving.

However, looking at the man right now, she had to admit he had the rugged and sexy look on lockdown. He was smoking hot, and she wanted to kick her own ass for the thought.

"Did you know about the will? Is that why you're here?" she asked, unable to tolerate the idea.

"Of course not," Ben snapped back.

"There must be a mistake." She kept her hands tight at her sides to resist the impulse to rudely snatch the folder from the lawyer's hand.

"It's all right here. The property deed, and so forth. My secretary will get you squared away next week. But there's one more important detail I'd like to discuss."

The lawyer stepped forward and handed a small sheet of paper to Ben.

Not to her . . . but to Ben.

What the ever-loving hell?

Ben read it, taking noticeably shallow breaths. And then his eyes became dead as he stared at the wall while handing her the note.

Her stomach squeezed as she read it.

BEN AND RILEY,

ALL I WISH IS THAT WHEN I PASS AWAY, YOU BRING MY URN, AS WELL as Nate's and Maureen's, to Nate's favorite mountaintop in Tennessee. Please scatter us together over the peak. I'm sure that's what he would've wanted.

I'LL NEVER FORGET WHAT YOU'VE BOTH DONE FOR ME. I HOPE THAT you've found each other again before you read this letter – but if not, be honest with each other. Please. Life is too short to waste.

LOVE,
Ralph

EVEN IN HIS DEATH, HE WAS TRYING TO BRING HER BACK TO BEN, but why? She folded the paper in half, walked over to the desk, and set it down.

She could visualize Ralph sitting there, a red pen in hand as he graded essays about Freud's theories on psychosexual development.

"I won't let you go to the mountains alone, so before you try and argue, you should know you'll be wasting your time."

When she didn't say anything, Ben released a ragged breath.

"Riley . . ." He threw her name into the air as if she meant something to him, which was ridiculous.

You don't leave the people you care about.

She, on the other hand—well, after he left, she'd spent years worrying about him.

The reports on the news about fallen soldiers during the Iraq War had always terrified her.

And when her mom called and told her Ben had been injured by an IED in Afghanistan, she spent two days in her dorm room, sick to her stomach.

She bent forward. It was as if her ribs were crushing her lungs. "You don't get to make the decisions. You—"

"Left. I know," he said and mumbled a few choice curse words under his breath.

She stood upright and pressed a closed fist to her chest.

"Can we have the room for a minute?" Ben asked the lawyer.

Atley gathered his briefcase, and once the door was closed, she bit out, "You're not coming with me."

"Fine. You stay. I'll go."

She balked. "Absolutely not."

He stepped closer, leaving scant room between them. His blue eyes, with a hint of gray in the irises, became darker, like steel, as he stared at her, clearly in no mood to back down.

Well, neither was she. She lifted her chin and met his hard gaze with her own. "I'm going," she said, even though the thought of going alone to Tennessee was painful.

A heavy guilt set into her bones in the space of a heartbeat.

She was acting like a child on the day of Ralph's wake, ignoring his last request.

He cupped his mouth, and there were faint scars like streaks of paint that ran down the back of his hand. "We'll do this together." His voice was tense and uncompromising.

She swallowed her unease, which tasted sour going down her throat.

For you, Ralph. I'll do this for you. "Fine. We can take a flight Friday night. Spread the ashes Saturday, and be home by Sunday."

"Ri?"

At the sound of her nickname on his tongue, her pulse sped up.

"What?" she cried, instantly regretting the weakness in her tone. She had to remain strong.

He heaved a soundless breath, his eyes dark, his expression weary, but no further words came from him.

And honestly, she didn't have it in her to hear any. And so, she opened the door and rushed from the room without giving him a chance.

CHAPTER FOUR

"BEN'S NOT WHAT I EXPECTED." MANDY ROLLED HER TONGUE over her teeth. "I've seen pictures of him at Ralph's, but wow—in person . . ." Her voice trailed off, her cheeks becoming rosier than normal. "How'd you two not—you know—back in high school?"

"I was taken, remember? And besides, he never asked." She curled her legs beneath her on the couch, clutching the stem of her wine glass with a hard fist.

"I can't believe he never made a move on you. You're hot. He's good enough to eat with or without the strawberry sauce, and—"

"Mandy!" She slapped her thigh, and her wine sloshed up and almost out of her glass.

Yesterday was the wake, and she'd remained holed up in her apartment almost the entire day today. She'd been mourning, but also hiding from her mother who'd blown up her phone with a million texts asking about both Ben and the lawyer.

It wasn't until Mandy came over with a cheese platter and wine that she bothered to put clothes on. Well, sweatpants and a tee were barely considered clothes, but hey, it was better than her grandma PJs as Mandy loved to call them.

"If you go back to Daniel, could I have Ben?"

Go back to Daniel? Did her mom put Mandy up to those kinds of comments? Everyone may have loved Daniel, but people needed to accept things were over for them.

She swallowed another gulp of wine, and it burned her chest a little. Aside from the cheese, she hadn't eaten all day. Wine on a practically empty stomach probably wasn't the best idea.

"So, it's a definite no-go with Bobby, then?"

"Well, the rumors were confirmed when I walked in on him and Lydia this morning."

Her eyes widened. "Doctor Harper? No way she'd hook up with him if she knew you two were together."

"She did know." She shrugged, not appearing too upset.

"You sure you didn't misunderstand what you saw?"

Mandy raised a brow. "He was peeling off her shirt."

"Maybe she spilled something, and he was helping her."

She scrunched her nose and waved her hand as if swatting a fly. "He's a player. I'm over it. Let's get back to talking about Ben."

Riley dragged in a hard breath. "I'm actually exhausted from hearing about him."

"Oh. And who else mentioned your Johnny Depp lookalike to you?"

She brought an image of the actor to mind, one when he was much younger than he is now. "They look nothing alike."

Mandy immediately pulled up a photo on Pinterest on her phone. "Oh, come on."

Riley squinted as she tried to find a resemblance between Ben and Johnny Depp. "You're exaggerating. Not even close." Ben looked a hundred times better, and she hated herself for thinking that.

"*Pirates of the Caribbean.*" Mandy pointed to the screen. "I bet Ben makes sexy noises in bed, too. A little growling."

"His longish hair and beard do not mean he looks like a—" She stopped herself, realizing the genius of her best friend.

Mandy was doing this on purpose, and God bless her. She was making Riley forget the pain. And even if it was for a few minutes, it felt good to experience a bubble of laughter expand in her chest.

Riley released the chuckle she'd been holding and polished off the rest of her drink. "You're good."

"What?" She casually lifted her shoulders and grinned.

Riley grabbed the bottle and refilled both of their glasses. It was only their second round, but the bottle was now empty, thanks to the heavy pours.

A few minutes of silence filled the room and a somber mood replaced the soft laughter. "You're really going with Ben tomorrow to the mountains?" Mandy asked. "I don't like you being alone with him."

"Really? And you just said—"

"I was joking, babe. This is serious. That man burned a hole in your heart."

Mandy's fierce loyalty was something Riley loved about her. It had taken her years to find a friend to trust again after Ben had left.

"I have to do this for Ralph."

Mandy set her glass down and crossed her arms. "No, you don't. Ralph probably wrote you that letter after he hit the bourbon too hard."

"Yeah, I don't think so." She'd gone back and forth on the decision to go all day and had finally ordered the ticket from her phone while still hunkered in bed.

"If I didn't have shifts all weekend, I'd be coming with you." She stood, walked over to the window, and pulled back the curtains. Dust particles floated in the air, a reminder that Riley hadn't cleaned her place since learning of Ralph's death.

"I'll message you every day."

Mandy dropped the curtains and faced her. "How about every few hours. He could be an ax murderer for all we know." Her hands became white-knuckled at her sides. "Speaking of, uh, murderers . . . any news on Ralph's killer?"

Her mouth went bone-dry at the mention of his death, and Mandy sat back beside her.

"My mom found out the sheriff called in a homicide detective from a neighboring city." Riley set her glass down. "The local department needed help, which was why it took so long for them to release Ralph's body."

"Yeah, well, we don't exactly witness a lot of crimes like this. I didn't think the sheriff could handle such a gruesome—"

Riley reached for her arm, cutting her off. "Wait, you know details?" Her heart raced, and her palms became clammy as she waited for Mandy to spill.

"I work at a rumor mill, remember? Of course, I've heard stuff." She pushed her long hair to her back. "I didn't want to say anything unless you asked."

Riley stood and started pacing her small living room, torn as to whether she did, in fact, want to know.

After a few minutes, she stopped and shook out the tension in her arms. "Tell me."

Mandy sat up straighter, pressing her palms to her light blue scrub pants, and expelled a deep breath.

"Don't sugarcoat it." Riley bit the inside of her cheek, fighting the urge to take back her words, because she knew, once she heard the truth, she'd be back in her PJs and in bed.

How the hell would she be able to leave tomorrow while Ralph's killer walked the streets? But what could she even do about it?

Mandy stared at her lap. It was obvious that eye contact would be too difficult right now. "It looked personal, from what I heard. His aorta and pulmonary arteries were damaged from a stab wound to the chest. And, uh, his throat was slit."

He'd died.

She knew that.

But . . .

The way he'd died—it didn't seem possible.

"Who would do that? Why?" She pressed her hands to her thighs, her chest rising and falling with quick inhalations.

"What would you tell your patients right now? Deep breaths, right?" Mandy stood behind her, rubbing her back.

She blew her cheeks full of air for a moment and stood upright. "I need to talk to Ben," she announced and started for the door in a hurry.

"Let's think this through. It's late, and someone was just murdered. You're really going to walk outside . . . and to Ben's, no less?"

She didn't have her purse, keys, or anything—but she was pissed, and she wanted to take her anger out on someone.

Her palm landed on the door as she bowed her head against it. "I'm going there to yell at him."

"Why?"

"Because he deserves it," she hissed.

"Riley."

"Please, don't try and stop me. He's at the local inn down the street." She knew Ben wouldn't stay at his parents' house—why would he? He'd left home and never looked back. "It'll only take me a few minutes to get there." Her chest began to tighten to the point of pain.

"How do you even know what room he's in?"

"My mom told me—who else?" She whirled to face Mandy, noticing the faint lines of concern darting through her friend's normally smooth forehead.

She huffed out an exasperated breath. "If you're going to go charging off into the night to take your anger out on your *ex*-best friend the least you could do is put some shoes on. Maybe even a bra?"

CHAPTER FIVE

"AIDEN TALKED, DIDN'T HE?" BEN ASKED, PRESSING THE PHONE TO his ear.

A low voice rumbled through the line. "You can't go back home for the first time in nearly fifteen years without me finding out about it," Jake said.

Ben plopped back on the uncomfortable bed. The mattress probably dated back to when Nixon was president. "Is the sun even up in London? Go back to bed, and don't worry about me." Ben pinched the bridge of his nose and squeezed his eyes closed, remembering the last time he and Jake worked together.

Jake had asked for an assist in taking down a terrorist, and ever since, the seed of doubt about running Logan Securities had been planted.

He wanted to do something more exciting. More important.

"Yeah, well, Aiden forgot the time difference when he woke my ass up." Jake laughed. "But I'm glad he phoned." There was a pause on the line, and he knew exactly what was coming—a lecture of some sort.

There were only a few people on the planet who knew why Ben had left Alabama after Nate's death. Ben had confessed the news one drunken night to his Marine buddies during his second deployment. Truths always poured out like free-flowing water whenever tequila was involved.

But now he was wishing he'd kept his mouth shut. Jake would feel the need to intervene because that's what he and his friends did. They looked out for each other.

They helped each other, even as civilians. Hell, especially as civilians. It was a brotherhood few outside the military could probably understand.

"Don't even start. I'm fine. Everything is—"

"Then why have Ava hack the local police department to get you a homicide case file?" Jake interrupted.

Ava was Aiden's fiancée, and not only had she once worked for Homeland, she was also brilliant with computers. So, Ben had called in a favor to Aiden, another friend from his Semper Fi days.

"I'm in over my head with this agency Alexa and I are setting up, so it'd be tough to fly back to the States right now—but say the word, and I'll make arrangements. Regardless, you should get an assist if you've decided to become a detective." His voice was serious, not a hint of sarcasm coloring his words.

Jake had once been a special agent for the FBI, and his current girlfriend, Alexa, had been the female version of Bond for MI6, working in the cyber terrorism division. She and Jake were both do-gooders who couldn't help but continue to fight the war on terror, even without badges.

And every time Ben thought about it, he wondered if protecting bratty pop singers or asshole billionaires was a waste of his time and his talent, even if the money was good. Jake phoned him every week asking him to join forces. Was it time to say yes?

"I don't need your help, but I'll be sticking around until the son of a bitch is caught. I'm at a hotel since my dad has a full arsenal at his disposal, and I know he can keep my mom safe. Hell, he's already polished his shotgun."

"Let me get this straight. You go back home for the first time and don't even stay with your parents?" A light chuckle rose and fell through the phone. "Man, you're as bad as me."

"Come on, if I give my mom even an inch of hope I'll move back, she'll turn my old room into a tribute to the nineties. Punk bands and supermodel posters and all."

"Could be worse."

Ben smiled and sat upright, blinking his eyes open. "You don't know my mom."

"But that's not really why you're not home," Jake said, peeling back Ben's shitty cover story. "You're near Riley, aren't you?"

Fourteen years had passed, and she looked even more beautiful in her thirties than at eighteen.

At the sight of Riley yesterday, his heart had slammed against his ribcage so hard it was as if he'd run twenty miles with his rucksack on.

"And how the hell do you still remember her name?"

"Steel trap. Well, you know, minus my amnesia earlier this year . . ."

He could visualize Jake smiling and tapping at the side of his head. "Yeah, sure."

"But, you need to stop deflecting," Jake said. "Have you seen her yet?"

"At the wake yesterday." Ben let out a frustrated sigh, hating how things had played out between them. He hadn't been sure what to expect when he'd arrived in town, and he hadn't worked out possible scenarios ahead of time like he should have.

"And?"

And we have to spread a families' ashes together. But he couldn't bring himself to say the words out loud.

His knuckles pressed down onto his thigh as his gaze flicked over to the open laptop. The screensaver was on, so he stood and typed in the password before staring at the image of Ralph. Ralph was sprawled out on the floor at his college office in a puddle of his own blood.

Bile rose thick in his throat. He'd seen a lot of bodies over the years, but he'd never become desensitized to it.

"She hates me."

"Can you blame her?" A dry laugh made its way through the phone. "You did take off and never even answer one of her goddamn emails. Kind of a dick move."

"And how come you never called me on my bullshit in Helmand?" They'd been one of the first battalions stationed at Camp Leatherhead in Afghanistan in 2009. Hundred-man tents and shitty chow halls at first before the base got its act together.

"And why would I bust your balls when you could have very well taken a bullet for me on any given Sunday?"

"Hell, any day of the week." Ben cracked a smile, but it faded fast when he thought about how much Riley truly hated him, and rightfully so. "But still, you had permission to rip me a new asshole, so why the hell didn't you?"

Jake cleared his throat. "Why don't we get back to the situation at hand. What happened to Nate's dad?"

"I overheard the ME talking about the murder at the pub last night. He was stabbed, plus took a knife to the throat."

"Fuck. Sorry, man. But, uh, what's your plan? I know you. You're like me. You won't sit and twiddle your damn thumbs and wait around for the locals to find the asshole."

A hard rap at the hotel door had his mouth tightening.

"It's me." Riley's voice, normally like silk, was heavy and weighed down by her loss.

But why the hell was she standing outside his room?

"I gotta go. I'll call you later."

"If you don't, I'll be sure to have someone fly in and check on you. Or I'll find a way to come myself."

"Yeah, yeah." Ben shoved the foreign feeling of nervousness so far down his throat he almost choked. "Later."

After ending the call, he tossed the phone on the bed and

started for the door. "Coming." He hated the sudden crack in his voice.

He swung open the door, and her brows darted inward as her golden-brown eyes traveled from his face down the length of his body. He was still in jeans and a faded Grateful Dead T-shirt. Had he changed into his nightwear—aka commando—she'd be staring at a six-foot-three naked body right now.

He tapped a fist against his mouth and sidestepped out of the way to allow her entrance. He'd be damned if he'd have her outside in the dark, only the twitchy lampposts to keep her company.

She didn't move, though. She remained like a statue, observing him now with heavy-lidded eyes.

Skinny jeans disappeared into short brown ankle boots and damned if the denim didn't look as if it were glued to her thighs, showing off the obvious tone beneath. Her long-sleeved white shirt shouldn't have been so sexy. It was high-necked and cotton, for Christ's sake. But still—she couldn't hide her perfect breasts without swapping her wardrobe out for some heavy-duty garbage bags.

"You do realize a killer is on the loose, and you, what, drove here alone?"

"I didn't drive. I walked." She finally came inside, brushing against his shoulder as she strode past him.

He shut and locked the door, sliding the chain in place, and faced her with crossed arms and a firm, square stance.

But he couldn't stop himself from focusing on her plump lips. "Being a doc and all . . . not too bright to walk here with a killer on the loose."

"Yeah, well, I couldn't drive because I had a few glasses of wine."

"Just great. Out in the dark and inebriated. Really fucking smart." He dragged his palms down his face, wishing he could lock her up in a secure location until the son of a bitch who'd killed Ralph was either dead or on death row. Option one was preferable.

"Watch your language." She swallowed.

"What? You have a side job as a Sunday school teacher?"

A breath of air rushed from her mouth, but no words came with it. She only stared at him with contempt.

Beautiful. Stunning. Exquisite. And those were the adjectives that sprang to mind when he thought about her looks. When it came to what he remembered about her on the inside—there were enough words to inspire a novel, and he wasn't even a writer.

"You shaved." She tossed her small purse on the bed and faced him again, anger glinting in her eyes. "And cut your hair."

"Don't go thinking you had anything to do with this." He smoothed a hand over his clean-shaven jaw.

A smile tugged at the edges of her lips, but it only lasted a fraction of a second. "Your mother, huh?"

He rolled his eyes, not wanting to admit he'd shaved and gotten a haircut because his mom had driven him crazy about it from the moment he'd arrived.

"Why are you here?"

"Because this is your fault."

He pointed a finger at his chest. "What is 'my fault'? And how much exactly did you drink?"

"If you had stayed in Ralph's life, maybe he'd still be alive," she said pointedly, but then her lip tucked between her teeth.

She didn't mean it, and he knew it. He couldn't blame her for wanting to take out her pain on someone. He didn't mind being the target if it'd help her, and he also understood why he was such an easy target. He hated himself for having caused her any pain, but at eighteen, he'd thought he'd been making the right move.

Looking at her now, he wasn't so sure.

"Shit, I shouldn't be here. I'm pissed, and I want to yell at someone."

He moved to stand before her. "Be pissed at me." His chest

tightened at the sight of her quivering lip and the sheen in her eyes. She was going to cry. It was something that had shredded him when he was younger, and it had the same effect on him now. "I mean it."

Her hands pressed to his chest, and she clenched her jaw. "I hate you."

"I know," he whispered.

She pressed her balled hands even harder against his pecs, but he could take it. He could take everything she had in order to spend just two minutes with her.

He missed her more than she could possibly know. More than he could ever allow her to know.

She lifted her hands, closed her eyes, and tapped her fists gently against his chest. "Harder," he commanded, and she barreled a few jabs that were more like featherweight punches.

And then she collapsed against him, a sudden sob seizing hold of her.

With his arms wrapped around her and his chin resting on her head, he closed his eyes and sifted through the memories of their past when they were sixteen and at the school dance.

"You're everything to me; you know that, right?" Riley asked.

"I couldn't imagine my life without you, Ri." Ben winked and stepped back when Nate appeared at their side. He allowed Nate to take over, knowing that his buddy was hopelessly in love with her.

And so, right now, Ben used all of his strength to tear his arms free of her and to step back, even though she needed him.

Even now, he couldn't trust himself to be the good guy.

Nate was the good man, the better man.

Ben couldn't be him.

Riley swiped at her face, trying to dry the tears still on her cheeks. "I should go." She turned to grab her purse off the bed, but then she stopped, and her attention focused on his open laptop.

Damn the twenty-minute time setting on his screensaver because that meant the image of Ralph was still there.

He rushed to the desk and snapped the laptop closed. "You don't need to see that."

She pointed to the computer, the sadness gone, replaced by irritation again. "How do you have that picture?"

He didn't know what to say. He knew she wouldn't back down now. Fourteen years or not, Riley was still Riley. Beautifully stubborn.

"Did the police give you access to the files?" Her mouth remained open even after she finished talking, disbelief in the faint lines of her forehead.

He turned his back and gripped the top of the desk chair. "Not exactly."

"What is that supposed to mean?" She huffed out a breath. "Ugh, never mind. Just tell me if there are any suspects."

He cleared this throat. "The police are working their way through Ralph's student roster. They're assuming it was a crime of anger. His home and office weren't touched."

"Who the hell kills their teacher because of grades or whatnot? Ralph was the nicest guy. It's not like he'd ever heckle a student or something. This is absurd."

He agreed, but . . . "Look at the world we live in today. It really shouldn't be all that surprising, unfortunately." When she didn't respond, he continued, "I checked into the detective the sheriff brought into town. He has twenty years of experience. He's good." Ben hoped she'd believe him. Hell, he hoped he could believe his own words. "This guy will catch the killer."

"Then look at me when you say that." She grabbed hold of his bicep, her fingers tightening around the muscle.

He didn't move. He couldn't face her and lie. She deserved more from him.

"I should take you home," he said, his voice low. "What kind of security do you have?"

"Look at me." Her plea was softer this time. "Why do I need

security? Why would I be in danger if the police think it was a targeted kill?"

"Because nothing is for certain." He glanced back at her. "And I'll be staying until the killer is caught."

"And how can I trust that you won't leave?"

He released his grip on the chair to confront her. "First, we can't speculate, so we need to assume everyone is a suspect." He edged closer. "And second, I'm not eighteen anymore. I won't take off."

"And what was your excuse at twenty-five? Or thirty?"

The truth was uncomfortable, like hot wax on his skin. It burned.

He sidestepped her and grabbed his hotel keycard then phone. "Come on. I'm walking you home."

"I can manage on my own."

"Not on my life are you walking out there by yourself." He heaved out a heavy sigh. "Until the killer is caught, I don't plan on letting you out of my sight. Hate me all you want, but that's the way it'll be."

"Didn't you just promise me the other day I'd never have to see you again?" She screwed her eyes tight for only a brief moment. "But you don't exactly keep your promises, do you?" She captured a deep breath and allowed it to slowly roll out.

Her expression hardened. "You promised me we'd always be together. Remember?" Her words sounded like glass that had been run over—broken and sharp. They cut into every crevice of his body that had already been damaged from the time he'd spent away from her.

"Listen, Ri."

She held her hand up. "You have to stop doing that. You can't come here and pretend we're the same people."

"That's not what I'm doing." He looked up at the ceiling and pinched the skin at his throat, searching for clarity.

"Then what are you doing?"

"I don't goddamn know," he snapped and faced her again, his stomach muscles tightening.

Ralph was dead, and he couldn't fix it. He always fixed things, but he sure as hell didn't know if he could fix what was broken between him and Riley.

She wet her lips and cocked her head. He was pretty sure this was her third attempt to get a read on him tonight. He knew she'd only hit a dead end. No one got into his head unless he wanted them to—his training in the Marines had seen to that.

"Being around you is confusing." Her candor almost had him falter a step, but then she delivered a jumbled string of curses and spun around, pressing her palms to the wall by the door. "You see what you're doing to me. You're making me swear."

"Well, *shit,* we wouldn't want that."

"Blow me," she said over her shoulder, glaring at him. Her sudden potty mouth had him biting back a quip, knowing it'd only add fuel to the fire.

"You make me feel like a kid again." Her shoulders relaxed as she looked back at the wall.

His gaze dipped down her back to her hard ass. "Is that such a bad thing? Feeling young again?"

"There's a difference between immature and young."

"Why is being around me confusing?"

"Because I don't want to hate you. But I also want to punch you in the face."

A low hiss whistled between his parted lips. "You should hate me, and I don't mind if you need to punch me again."

She faced him, pushing her sleeves to the elbows as she closed the distance between them. Her height of five-five made it harder for her to look him square in the eyes, but that didn't deter her from trying.

He wondered if she really was going to slug him clean across the jaw. Hell, he wouldn't even turn his chin if she really wanted to go for it.

Her darkened eyes pulled him in, and he almost forgot where he was—even who the hell he was. With parted lips, a light pink crawled up her throat and took over her cheeks.

They were in some sort of staring match now like they were waiting for the other to blink.

"Honey, I can do this all day," he said after two minutes, diffusing the tense silence. "And before you say *don't call me honey*, I've already taken a mental note to skip it the next time."

She was fighting a smile, and damn hard. "I know what you're doing."

He raised a brow. "What?"

"Distracting me." She shook her head. "You're not protecting me, though. You can walk me home tonight, but when we get back from the mountains, there's no way in hell I'll let you become my bodyguard."

He was breaking through her stubborn walls, she just didn't know it, yet.

But what if she knocked his down, too?

He couldn't let that happen, though.

"We'll agree to disagree. Now, come on." He tilted his head toward the door. "Unless you want to stay here tonight."

She gasped. "Ben . . ."

His tongue swept over his bottom lip. "I didn't mean to have sex. Jesus, Ri."

Her well-timed eye roll, and the way her pouty lips pressed together, was too damn hot. A sarcastic and annoyed look shouldn't turn him on. "Let's go."

The walk to her apartment would take five minutes. He'd timed it when choosing his hotel. But five minutes was still too long in his mind to get to her if she were in danger. Of course, there was no indication in the police report that there'd be another murder, but the sheriff didn't have a Magic 8 Ball, so how the hell did he know whether or not it was a one-time kill?

"You never answered my question, by the way." He stuffed his hands in his pockets as they walked down the cracked sidewalk. "What kind of security do you have?"

"A lock."

He stopped and faced her. "No alarm? No camera?"

"It's an apartment. And nothing ever happens here." Her eyes closed for half a second. "Well, nothing ever did."

He blew out a breath. "The prison is two miles from here. What if a convict escaped and decided to take up residence at your place?"

"That's ridiculous." She started walking again.

"You're not being smart."

"I'll get an extra lock," she said once he was at her side. "Satisfied?"

"Hardly." But he stitched his lips together for now and kept his attention focused on the houses along the way. Stucco and brick homes where there had once been only wood. It was far too overcrowded now, as if contractors tried to stuff every square inch of space with livable square footage.

His town was different than he remembered. When he'd driven around earlier, it had somehow felt even smaller, hemorrhaging from too many stores, including the new Walmart.

And as they continued to head toward Riley's, he nearly halted as they came upon Joe-Joe Pond. Memories flickered to mind as they crossed the little six-foot wooden bridge, which looked about as unstable as it had when they'd been kids.

He and Riley used to tug a tackle box and his dad's fishing rods down there, acting like they were big stuff when they had barely been tall enough to reach the railing. He'd put his ball cap on Riley backward, and even as a kid, he'd loved to watch her smiling as the sun caught in the long blonde strands that hung straight down her back.

He blinked away the memories of the past as they tried to settle like a hard weight in his stomach. He needed them gone if he were going to survive his trip. He couldn't have flashes of his childhood skipping into his mind every minute, or he'd never be able to focus on finding Ralph's killer. All he'd be able to focus on would be Riley.

"Where's your key?" he asked once they were outside her front door. She lived in a complex that hadn't existed when they'd been younger, and he was pretty sure it now occupied the same space where his childhood barber had once been.

"Didn't bring one. My friend's waiting for me inside."

"Boyfriend?" He cleared his throat, willing away the unwelcome feelings swarming him like a storm of bees after a fallen hive. "It'd make me feel better knowing you had a guy staying with you." His hands became white-knuckled at his sides.

Her attention skirted to his fists, and then to his face. He felt the pulse in his neck throb. He wasn't sure how to explain away his weird behavior. Of course, when they'd been friends, he'd always been protective of her, basically rejecting every guy who came within ten feet—well, until Nate had the balls to ask her out.

Nate's name crawled through his mind, and his body stiffened. *What the hell am I doing?*

"No. My friend Mandy's inside. She's a surgeon. Tall, pretty fit. She could probably throw down, even with you." Her sudden smile took him by surprise. "Does that make you feel better?"

"It does, actually."

"Well, before she sees you and plays the twenty-questions game, I think I'll go inside." She turned and gripped the knob. "I guess I'll see you at the airport tomorrow."

"Yeah, okay."

"And, Ben?"

"Mm-hm?"

"I've decided I don't want to punch you." Her eyes met his over her shoulder. "But I think I'll stick to hating you."

He swept a hand to the back of his neck and cupped it. "Fair enough."

He waited until he heard the click of her lock once she was

behind the door, and then he did a detailed perimeter sweep of the building. There were no security cameras in the twenty-room, two-story apartment complex. And he didn't like that she lived on the second floor, with only one exit route, which involved using a stairwell with shitty lighting.

He glanced at the moonless sky. A dark cover of blue-black clouds hung above as he walked back to his hotel.

He wasn't sure how he was going to make it through a weekend with her in the mountains. But he had no choice. He had to do this for Ralph. For Nate. And he had to keep his screwed-up thoughts and desires for Riley stuffed so far down inside of him that even he'd start to believe his feelings weren't real.

CHAPTER SIX

Ben had been her first kiss. They were eleven, playing spin the bottle at a birthday party, and Nate had been home, sick with the flu.

When the bottle had landed between the two of them, she saw the pulse in his neck, like his heart was beating harder than normal.

It had been a quick touch of the lips, and her friends had giggled . . . and her cheeks had become warm. And when the ketchup bottle had matched her with another guy, she'd faked a stomachache and run out of the house.

Ben had offered to walk her home, but instead, they'd ended up sitting outside on a blanket to study the stars. They used to find constellations and create new names for them since they could never remember the real ones.

And then, seven years later, Ben had kissed her again.

Only, that time, she'd been in a relationship with Nate—and Nate had only been a tent away.

Stargazing, yet again, they'd stayed up all night talking, and then Ben had rolled to his side and just stared at her.

She remembered the exact moment when his eyes had dropped to her lips, and he'd leaned forward and pressed his mouth to hers.

Like the first time it had been quick.

But the second time it had been a mistake. Ben had jerked away from her and jumped to his feet, dragging his palms down his face.

She hadn't known what to think or to say at the time. And he hadn't given her a chance. He'd taken off down one of the trails, and she hadn't seen him again until the sun had risen and a new day of climbing had started.

That'd been the morning Nate died.

The day her world had ended.

Now, looking at Ben as he walked down the aisle on the airplane, she found herself staring at his mouth, wondering how good of a kisser he was at thirty-two.

"Guess we're next to each other." A man shoved his bag into the overhead compartment.

She smiled and shifted back to allow him easier passage to his seat.

Ben was on the other side of the aisle, stowing his bag.

Her lip wedged between her teeth as she found his denim backside.

Carved by steel? Titanium, maybe? What the hell were those glutes made of?

She knew the sudden pulsing sensation between her thighs had nothing to do with the good-looking man in the leather jacket next to her, and everything to do with Mr. Baseball. The town had started calling Ben that when he was sixteen and had pitched a perfect game.

Ben nodded at her once he was buckled and shifted his ball cap down, pulling it lower to cover his eyes.

She hated herself for feeling anything other than anger when thinking about him.

She'd stayed awake most of last night because every time she shut her eyes, she'd found herself picturing Ben's muscled frame on top of her, kissing every inch of her body.

It wasn't the first time she'd had that fantasy, but it needed to be the last.

"So, what do you do?" Leather Jacket asked.

She glanced at him as she finally strapped on her belt. "I'm a psychiatrist."

The guy rushed a hand through his brown hair, which had silver streaks at the sides. He was probably in his late forties, and although he was attractive in a polished, pretty kind of way, she'd never been into pretty. No, she liked a man like . . .

"I'm a doctor, too."

Of course, you are.

"I work at a hospital in Atlanta, though. Is your final stop Atlanta, or are you catching another flight?"

"Just a layover there."

He extended a palm, but she barely noticed since she couldn't stop focusing on Ben out of the corner of her eye.

"Name's Nate."

Oh, holy God.

Ben straightened in his seat and tipped his hat back.

"Riley," she said softly and finally took his hand.

"Isn't that a man's name?" The light wrinkles in his forehead deepened as he continued to hold her palm.

"Goes both ways."

"Huh. Well, it's nice to meet you." His green eyes cruised over her black, silky blouse and her fitted dress pants, which narrowed at the ankles and were matched with short ankle boots.

"Mind if I switch, buddy?"

Riley pulled her hand free at the sound of Ben's voice over her shoulder. He was standing with his hand on the top of her seat, his head dipped down to make eye contact with the man beside her.

"I'm good, thanks." Nate lifted his shoulders in a way that read *back off, man; she's mine.*

"My wife gets a little motion sickness when flying, and I'd hate for her to throw up on you."

"Wife?" Nate looked at Riley's ringless wedding finger and met Ben's cold stare.

As much as she hated whatever macho thing Ben was doing right now, she wasn't in the mood to have trivial conversation with a stranger on the flight. "He's right. I'm already queasy, and we haven't taken off yet."

Ben's hand shifted to her shoulder, and he gave it a squeeze. "Sorry, beautiful."

Beautiful. Did he have to go there?

She unbuckled and stood, prompting the man to finally relinquish his spot.

Once Ben occupied the guy's seat, she sat down and tried to ignore the close proximity. She tilted back her head, trying to remind herself that he was seriously off-limits, even in fantasy mode.

"You okay?" he whispered in her ear, and his breath had her skin breaking out into goose bumps.

"Mm-hm." She surrendered a quick murmur because she was anything but okay.

"He looked like a douche, so . . ." he said, clearly not caring if the guy overheard.

"Yeah, and the man I'm sitting next to now? What is he?" She couldn't stop the words from pouring from her lips.

"He's sorry" was all he said before tugging his hat down to hide his eyes.

* * *

"So, YOU ASSUMED THAT I'D LET YOU RIDE WITH ME?" SHE leaned back against the Ford Explorer in the Asheville airport parking lot and tried to remain casual, crossing her arms.

Although it was December and colder in Asheville than in Alabama, it wasn't that bad out. She figured once they entered Tennessee and drove deeper into the mountains the weather would change.

"Yeah, I did." He opened his palm. "Keys, please."

She shook her head. "I can drive."

"How many times have you driven on icy roads?" He adjusted his faded Dodgers ball cap, giving her a better look into his eyes.

"Who said they'll be icy?"

"I did my homework," he was quick to respond.

She smirked. "What? The Weather Channel app on your phone?" She turned and opened the driver's side door, but at the feel of his hand on her hip she stilled.

"Hon—" He paused for a beat. "I've driven in all kinds of terrain, even while being shot at with M4s. So, why don't you leave the driving to me?"

She knew he was right. She rarely even drove. Period. "Fine." She shoved his hand off her body. Even though his large palm had rested on her wool peacoat, she could still feel a singe of heat on her skin beneath.

She lifted her bag, but he reached for its handle, trying to take it from her grip. "Let me."

"Chivalry is dead."

"It doesn't have to be," he said dryly, and she looked back, tilting her chin up to catch his eyes, which had become darker as if taking on some of the colors from above. The navy sky disappeared into purple-tinted clouds that threatened a storm.

She'd already secured her suitcase of clothes in the trunk, but this bag was important. It held the ashes of Nate and Ralph. Ben had the urn of Ralph's wife in his bag, which was sitting by his brown mountaineering boots. She didn't have her boots anymore. She'd probably need to pick some up in town before they hiked to Nate's favorite spot tomorrow.

She finally released her hold of the bag, giving in to him— again. "Be careful."

"Always."

She circled the car, got inside, and strapped in. "Should take us less than two hours to get to the lodge. Tell me that you got your own room." Her eyes widened when he stared at her blankly from behind the wheel.

When he still didn't say anything, she said firmly, "You're not staying with me."

The sudden pat of his hand on her thigh did something strange to her stomach. It created a warm, fluttering sensation, like hummingbirds inside her core. She kept her eyes locked on his hand, the same hand that had the scars, and it had her whistling out a low breath.

She hadn't been there for him when he'd been hurt in the Middle East. He hadn't let her be there for him, at least. And she really hated it.

"Of course not." His paw of a hand lifted, and he tapped at the controls and powered on the heated seats. "But we used to sleep in the same bed."

Well, that was true, but only until they'd turned fifteen, and then things had become a little too gray.

"We were kids." She looked out her window as he began to drive, exiting the airport terminal.

She needed to remind herself of the relaxation techniques she taught her patients, or she'd never get through the weekend.

"Shit," she said and groaned a minute later.

He slowed the car a hair and glanced over at her. "What's wrong?"

Her shoulders slumped. "I forgot my essential oils, and I really wish I hadn't." They did wonders for easing her tension.

He picked up speed again, but he couldn't hide a grin.

She shifted in her seat to get a better look at him. She wasn't sure when he'd unzipped his black North Face jacket, but she noticed a chain around his neck, partially tucked beneath his dark cotton shirt. She wondered if they were his dog tags from the military. Ben had never been into wearing jewelry, but she assumed this type of metal was different.

"What's so funny?" she asked.

"Nothing."

"Then why are you still smiling?"

"I'll do my best to stop promptly, ma'am."

Oh, he was trying to rile her up even more, wasn't he? But she refused to let him. "Just get us there in one piece, please. My patients need me on Monday."

"Will do."

She reclined her seat and closed her eyes, hoping the drive would blur by so she could get into her room and not deal with Mr. Baseball until tomorrow.

"Riley?" Her name off his tongue twenty minutes later had her stomach knotting.

She shifted her head to the side to look over at him. "What?"

"I meant what I said on the plane back there; I just need you to know that." Gone was any hint of humor in his eyes.

"Sometimes it's too late for apologies."

He looked back at the highway, his shoulders arching back, his spine going stiff. "Is that what you'd tell your patients?"

She looked up at the car ceiling and pressed her fingers to her throbbing right temple. "No," she answered honestly and left the conversation at that.

CHAPTER SEVEN

THE MOUNTAIN LODGE, NESTLED IN A FOREST OF RED SPRUCE AND Fraser firs, looked like something out of a Hallmark movie. It was a few weeks until Christmas, so she wasn't sure why she hadn't anticipated the decorations.

Strings of golden lights, fresh pine wreaths, and red satin ribbons made the place almost majestic. But it also felt too festive and romantic for the purpose of her visit.

"You good?" Ben removed his hat and scratched his head before putting it back on.

"Um." Her gaze fell upon the massive stone fireplace at the center of the lobby. The flames roared, dancing and licking the air as if trying to escape. She felt the same. "Uh, yeah," she lied.

She had planned on booking a room at the cabin where Nate and his dad had always stayed. She and Ben had gone on a lot of the family trips, too. But those cabins weren't available. And honestly, she was relieved. She didn't know if she could handle the prickly feel of the past nipping at her skin quite that much. She was already getting a heavy enough dose of it with Ben at her side.

"You want to grab a bite to eat before we put away our bags?" he asked.

"I think I'd like to shower." She smiled and immediately regretted it. She didn't want him to misinterpret her slip of emotion.

"You look fine to me."

She reached out and tipped up the hat bill to better view his eyes. They'd already checked in, but they were still standing off to the side of the front desk, and she couldn't seem to get herself to move.

"I don't know how to do this," she whispered, her hand still touching the rim of the cap.

He cocked his head, and she started to lower her arm, but he captured her wrist, holding it between the two of them. "Do what?"

She could've sworn his voice faltered, but she was too dazed to be sure. It wouldn't matter anyway, she had to remind herself. Even if Ben was emotional about all of this, too, she needed to ensure she kept her walls up. She didn't want to get hurt again.

Her heartbeat kicked up, and he'd be able to feel her pulse escalate in her wrist. "I, um . . ."

Why wasn't he letting go of her?

Why didn't she want him to?

"Water," she sputtered and blinked. "I need some water."

His eyes tightened to thin slits as he assessed her—it was the same look he used to get standing on the pitcher's mound before he reeled back his arm for the pitch.

She had never missed even one of his high school games. She and Nate had been his biggest fans. Of course, Nate had always been more of an extreme sports kind of guy, but Ben's talents had spanned every sport. The man was frustratingly good at everything.

Well, almost everything.

Singing, dancing, writing, and anything involving acting . . . not so much. She used to always laugh whenever he'd had to act or share a poem in class. One thing he had been good at was making her crack up, though.

So. Many. Memories.

And that's all she had left—memories.

And it was like a slow burn traveling up her chest as she thought about how much she'd lost when both Ben and Nate had disappeared from her life. She'd become so empty, and as much as she loved helping people in her job, she'd spent years trying to replace that dull hollow feeling in the pit of her stomach.

"You want to let go of me now?" She swallowed. "There's probably water in my room."

He released her arm and went for her bags.

Chivalry, huh?

Riley followed him up the cedar steps that were behind the fireplace, careful not to study his glutes on the way up. He was carrying three bags and making it look effortless.

He waited for her to join him at the top of the stairs. "I think we're this way." He tipped his head to the right.

"Is your room near mine?"

"Next door."

She side-eyed him as they began to walk. "Coincidence or . . .?"

"Or what?" He stopped before a door that was trimmed in red lights. "This is your room."

"How'd you manage to get a room by me? And a seat on the plane next to me, for that matter?" She lifted a brow, but he simply smiled and cocked his head to the door, motioning for her to open it.

She wouldn't be getting anything out of him, apparently. Not too surprising. And so, she removed her key from the envelope and stuck it in the lock. It was a traditional key, not an electric swipe card.

"Well, uh, thanks for the baggage assist," she said after they'd entered the room and she'd set her luggage on the bed.

"Do you want to get something to eat after you shower?" Hesitation passed through his words.

Her stomach burned with hunger pains. She hadn't eaten all day or even touched the in-flight snack on the plane.

"I think I'll order room service." She moved to the window and parted the drapes to get a view of the outside. "The mountains are even more beautiful than I remember."

In the reflection, she saw him approach from behind. She forced her attention away and toward a couple down below, building a snowman. They were probably not even of drinking age, and they looked so carefree and happy. And she was jealous.

Riley gave him a quick look out of the corner of her eye, and he pressed a palm to the glass. "How'd you get those scars? Was that from the IED?" Her eyes fell shut. She was disappointed in herself for even asking the questions. Acknowledging she'd kept up with his health over the years—even if by force from her mom—wasn't something her stubborn self wanted to admit.

"No. The scars on my hand are from an animal attack earlier this year. I was rescuing someone, and a guard dog got the drop on me."

She could almost feel his smile—it was that strong.

"Can you believe that?" He chuckled lightly. "Damn dog bit me and ripped his claws down my hand and arm."

"What happened to the dog?" She opened her eyes and looked at his hand.

"I'd never kill a dog. He's fine."

"And what happened to the person who owned the dog?" She faced him, suddenly forgetting about the happy couple below, losing any lingering feelings of envy.

"Not so lucky." He flashed her a quick, confident smile, pushed away from the window, and headed to the desk next to the bed. He reached for a pen and scribbled something. "If you decide you want to eat, call me. If not, ring me when you're up tomorrow, and we can head out."

He was giving her his cell number. She didn't want it, though. What if she had a drunken night and a moment of weakness a few months from now and called him up, begging for answers as to why he'd never once returned her emails years ago?

It'd be too risky to save his number in her phone. Seeing him here, being near him, it felt like home, and she knew, once he was gone, it'd hurt so much more. The temptation to call him would be too great.

"Okay. I, uh, need to grab some shoes in town before we make the hike."

He faced her and glanced down at her ankle boots. "You can't hike in those?" His lips curved at the edges.

"Funny."

"I guess I should go." He lifted his own bag and started for the door. "Goodnight, Ri." He stilled. "Riley," he corrected and left.

She collapsed onto the bed, her energy spent. It was exhausting wrestling with her current kaleidoscope of emotions.

She eyed the minibar and chewed on her lip. She probably shouldn't touch the little bottles, especially since she had Ben's number now.

Pushing to her feet, she started to undress. As her hands went around to her beige lacy bra, the door swung inward, and she shrieked.

Her arms shielded her breasts, and Ben stared at her with parted lips.

"Jesus, Ben. What the hell were you thinking?" She grabbed her shirt off the bed and held it in front of her, thankful she hadn't taken off her bra yet.

"I was making sure you locked the door. I didn't expect it to open when I turned the handle, and when it did, I was pissed that you'd be so goddamn careless as to leave it unlocked."

Without thinking, she marched toward him with the shirt still clutched to her chest. "Are you really swearing at me? You just busted into my room without so much as knocking. What if I had been naked?"

His eyes dropped below her collarbone. "Lock up when I leave." A gravelly undercurrent swept through his speech.

"Is that really all you have to say for yourself? Not even an apology?"

"Yeah, you're right. I should be yelling. Always lock your door." He found her eyes once again, and there was a pulse in the side of his jaw as if he were clenching his teeth too tight.

"I can't believe you." She stepped back, bumping into the wall alongside the bathroom door.

He closed the gap and placed a palm on the wall above her shoulder.

"Why are you still in here?"

"I'm angry."

A humorless chuckle fell from her lips. "You're angry? Are you out of your mind?"

"You need to think about your safety. When I go back to Vegas, I can't be worried about whether or not you're locking your damn door at night."

He wasn't wearing his jacket now, and so she could see the hard planes of his well-defined muscles beneath the long-sleeved shirt.

Maybe he was the only one who actually posed a threat—to her mental well-being, at least.

His last words finally hit her, though, and had her shoving at his chest with her free hand.

"Worry about me? Are you kidding? That takes a lot of damn nerve." She pushed harder, but he wouldn't budge. He was made of steel. "Get the hell out of my room."

He finally dropped his hand from the wall and backed up. "Lock your damn door," he said and left.

* * *

IF SHE'D THOUGHT THINGS HAD BEEN AWKWARD LAST NIGHT, THEY were brutally uncomfortable now.

Ben had only managed to spit out a *good morning* and a formal *hope you slept well* when they met in the lobby that morning.

Now, inside the shoe store, her jaw went slack as he knelt before her and brushed away her hand. "You're doing it wrong."

She reached down to slap at him, but he caught her wrist, just like last night, and held on to it. But this time, he didn't make eye contact. "If you tie it too tight, you could lose feeling in your toes. Too loose, and you could twist your ankle. The trail isn't going to be easy, and I'll be damned if I'm carrying your ass two miles to the car and taking you to the hospital for a sprained ankle."

She glared at him, but he still wouldn't look at her. Instead, he released her hand and began working at the laces.

"First, I'm not that heavy. And second, I remember how to hike and can lace my own damn shoes!"

He smothered a quick grin before shoving upright. "There. Stand and let me know how they feel."

She rolled her eyes but stood. She wanted this day over with.

He pinched the skin at his throat, and she walked past him, testing out the boots.

"You, uh, still hike and climb?" she asked.

"I've only climbed if it entailed scaling a building to go after some scumbag or rescue a hostage."

"Hm." She wasn't really sure what to say to that response, but she'd always wondered if he had given up climbing after Nate's death. She'd never so much as gone near the side of a mountain ever since.

Why the hell couldn't Nate have used a rope that day?

She winced as her mind replayed the images of him falling. She had been holding on to Ben's rope, but she had wanted to reach out for Nate—as if she could have actually caught him—but if she'd let go, Ben could've been hurt, or even killed, too.

She knew she couldn't have possibly saved Nate by trying to

catch him, but the guilt of doing nothing other than watching him fall was still unbearable, even to this day.

Ralph had said there'd been nothing she could have done, but still . . .

Ben hadn't spoken a word that dark and gloomy day at Nate's wake. And before he'd left town to join the Marines, he'd simply whispered *goodbye* in her ear, given her a hug, and hadn't even bothered to meet her eyes before turning away.

"How do they feel?"

"It hurts." She gripped her chest.

"Too tight?" He crouched down and worked at her laces, and without meaning to, she placed a hand on his shoulder.

He looked up at her for a brief moment, and his mouth tightened.

"No, I wasn't talking about that." She blinked. "The boots are fine. We should buy them and get on the road before the storm hits."

"You're sure?"

She lifted her hand, and he stood.

"Yeah, I'm sure." She walked toward the register.

They didn't speak again until they'd reached Sugarlands Visitor Center.

He parked the SUV. "I don't think we should go all the way to the summit. There's a tough rock scramble near the top, and in these weather conditions, I think we're asking for an injury."

"You mean me, right? Because you've never backed down from a challenge before."

Except for the challenge of staying after Nate died . . .

She opened the door and zipped up her jacket once outside. She was thankful for the thermal leggings beneath her pants. The wind whipped harder than she'd anticipated. But the snow had yet to fall, and thankfully, the normally low-hanging fog had already lifted.

"It's two miles up and two miles—"

"I can count. Four total. Got it." She carefully slung her bag that held the urns over her shoulder.

Ben came before her, his mouth doing that tight-lipped thing again, which he'd clearly mastered. He could win an award for the scowls she'd witnessed so far.

"I'm going to the summit, with or without you."

"Are you always this stubborn?"

"When it's important." She started past him and headed for the trail without another word. The parking lot was empty, but had it been any other season it would have been bustling with cars.

"Go right," Ben said a little later when she'd started to go left at the fork in the trail.

She hesitated at the crossroads, and that's kind of how her life felt right at the moment.

"I'd prefer you stay at my side or in front of me, so I can keep an eye on you." Ben stood next to her, glancing at her out of the corner of his eye.

"You need to stop worrying about me." Her heartbeat quickened, and she was almost grateful because it helped warm her up a little.

"I've never stopped, and I never will."

"And that's pretty damn hard for me to believe. More like impossible, actually." A cold swirl of air blew from her mouth with her last breath.

Why was he making this so difficult for her? And why couldn't she hold on tight to her anger? Of course, she hated admitting it, but she'd always worried Ben had left town, in part, because of her—because of what she'd said to him after Nate died.

When he'd been deployed, had he even bothered to open any of her emails that had asked for forgiveness?

Eventually, she had stopped apologizing.

Eventually, she'd stopped writing altogether.

And shortly after that, she'd decided to place the blame for

Ben's absence squarely on his shoulders, it was easier than placing the burden on her own.

But standing there now, as they literally walked down memory lane—the same trails she, Nate, and Ben used to hike—all she wanted was the truth.

"Did you read my emails?" She tucked her gloved hands in her jacket pockets as the wind whipped her hair into her face and a bitter chill settled in her bones. "Look at me," she cried, and he finally did.

"We need to hurry before we get trapped out here" was all he said, and he jerked his head to the right, commanding her to walk ahead.

"Sure. Avoidance. Let's go with that. It worked just fine for you all these years." She tore her gaze from his face and walked past him. "But, Ben, don't worry—"

"Careful!" he shouted, but it was too late.

She tripped and fell, her cheek making contact with the icy and rocky ground.

He was at her side in a second. "You okay?" He squatted next to her and helped her up to her knees. "No blood that I can see."

She swept a hand to her achy cheek. "Yeah, I'm just embarrassed."

He removed a fleece glove and brushed the pad of his thumb over the tender spot on her jawline.

She pressed a hand to her chin. There'd be a nasty bruise there tomorrow for sure.

"You want to head back to the hotel?" He helped her to her feet.

She grimaced as another shot of pain spiraled down her thigh to her knee, which had been the first body part to take the brunt of the fall.

"No way. The storm might hit, and we won't be able to do this tomorrow morning."

He slipped his glove back on. "Can you walk okay, though?"

She brushed the mix of dirt and snow off her jacket and made the awkward attempt to move in front of him. She'd have to hide any wobble in her step the best she could, knowing Mountain Man here wouldn't let her continue if he sensed an injury. "I'm fine. Just make sure the urns are okay, and let's get this done."

He studied her for a moment, probably trying to do a quick assessment of the damage. "If you need me to carry you, say the word."

"Over my dead body." Her head fell at what she'd said, and she hated herself at that moment. "I, uh . . . let's go." She advanced down the trail, moving with as much ease as her body would allow without signaling to Ben she was sore.

Twenty minutes later, they reached the rock scramble Ben had been worried about. There were icy spots, for sure, but it didn't look too bad. Just a bunch of small rocks and a few boulders piled like a giant rock cake.

No biggie, she thought, lying to herself.

She inhaled a good, strong breath, but before she could even start the climb, Ben pressed a hand to her shoulder. "Give me a second. I need to assess the best route."

"Do you even remember how?"

He moved around her, catching her eyes for a fleeting moment. They looked darker, possibly a mirror of her own pain.

She carefully rested her bag by her feet and watched as he smoothed his hands over the rocks and scrambled up a couple feet.

He came back in front of her a few minutes later. "We'll need to stick to the left side because the rocks are eroded over that way." He pointed toward the stone cake.

She rubbed her chest when his back was to her. She dreaded the two-mile trek back to the car when this was over, but at least they'd be descending.

"Give me your bag. If you're crazy enough to go through with this, I need to carry that." He held his hand palm up, and she fought the urge to bite out a snarky retort.

"Fine. But don't get hurt on my account."

"I'll be fine, sweetheart. No worrying about me." His Southern accent strengthened, reminiscent of the man he once was.

"I wouldn't dream of worrying about you." She bit back her nerves and swallowed the pinches of pain in her ribs as she crouched close to the rocks, using both her hands and feet to navigate up the stones.

"It's icy. Be careful," he said.

She peeked at him out of the corner of her eye.

He was moving slowly, making sure he stayed right alongside her.

It didn't take as long as she'd thought it would to reach the top. And she was fairly proud of herself for not having tumbled down.

The ridge offered a gorgeous view of Mount Le Conte. It also took her back in time to when everything in life made sense.

"It's breathtaking." She stared off at the fir-covered mountains, the higher peaks blanketed in fresh snow. She'd been surprised the trail hadn't been overly icy, but it was early enough in the season. A few more weeks and she probably wouldn't have been able to make the hike up.

She turned around to see Ben kneeling down, unzipping one of the bags. He retrieved Maureen's urn and lifted it up to her.

She'd never been good with touchy-feely emotions. Well, she'd stopped being good at it after she lost her two best friends. Almost every one of her exes had complained she was cold and bitter, even in bed.

Ben didn't say anything; instead, he removed the lids from Nate's and Ralph's urns, and Riley did the same with Maureen's.

They walked toward the ledge, and her calves trembled from the height.

"Don't fall," he warned.

"Wasn't planning on it." She almost choked on her words as the memory of Nate falling off the cliff flashed into her mind.

She cleared her throat. "Ready?" she whispered as the wind picked up.

He held the narrow necks of the urns. They were going to pour them at the same time.

Worried a breeze would kick the ashes up and in her face, she lowered to her knees to position herself near the edge of the cliff.

"Let's do this," she murmured.

He closed his eyes, and his forehead pinched tight. A strain of emotion pulled at his face, and she felt it, too.

This was it. It was really goodbye.

CHAPTER EIGHT

"You're full of shit." Ben folded his arms and stood in the doorframe of her hotel room. "How badly are you hurting?"

"I can handle it." But as she rubbed her chest, a soft moan left her lips.

He grumbled and strode through the room, the door clanging shut behind him. "Let's get you undressed and in a hot bath. It should relax the muscles. I'll get some oils down at the spa that might help alleviate some of the pain. It'd be better than taking ibuprofen."

"I'll be the only one undressing me." She rolled her eyes and tucked her lip between her teeth as if stifling a grimace from pain.

It had killed him to watch her limp all the way back to the SUV. But he'd known there was no way in hell she'd let him help her walk, so all he could do was curse under his breath about it.

"I've seen you naked, and I'm not suggesting that. Let's get the boots, jacket, and sweater off you. I'll start the bath, and then you can do the rest. I'll run down to the shop once I know you're safely in the water."

She started to stand, as if prepared to protest, but fell back onto the bed, pressing a hand to her knee and groaned.

"Bad?" He dropped in front of her and started to unlace her boots.

She closed her eyes and nodded. At least she was finally admitting to the pain. That was an improvement.

He moved her boots out of the way and trailed a hand up her calf, which had her eyes opening, her gaze pinning his.

"What are you doing?"

"I'm going to try and help with the pain."

"How?" She rubbed the side of her leg by the kneecap.

"It'd be easier if you could remove these pants, though."

She quirked a brow, but then her mouth fell open and her eyes widened. "Wait. When did you see me naked?"

He chuckled and reached for her hand as she finally grasped what he'd said earlier. "Can you stand, so we can get these off of you? You have something on underneath, right?"

"Yeah, but you're still not answering my question."

He stood. "I'll tell you if you let me help you."

She eyed him cautiously as if she didn't trust him, and maybe she shouldn't. He couldn't even trust himself right now. Being this close to her was screwing with his brain.

He took her slight nod as a *yes*, and he leaned forward, unzipped her jacket, and peeled it off. Next, her pants. This would be the hard part. He knew how defined her legs were, and seeing her only in thermal underwear was going to give him a serious hard-on that he knew his jeans wouldn't hide.

Ben helped her to her feet so she could unzip her black ski pants. "You don't really go snowboarding, do you?" he asked with humor in his voice as she sat back down. His eyes trailed the black thermals that clung to her perfectly shaped thighs and calves.

She laughed, but then pressed a hand to her chest as if her ribs hurt. "No, of course not."

"Didn't think anyone could teach you if I couldn't," he surmised.

She mumbled something too low for him to hear, and he assumed it was a well-deserved insult. Once crouched again, his fingers skirted up her right leg, stopping at her knee.

"Easy," she whispered, and their eyes met as he applied a little pressure. "So, are you going to tell me the naked story?"

"The naked story, huh?" He grinned, and the smile on his face actually felt good. It relieved a little of the pain from what they'd gone through today.

"Yes," the word edged from her mouth.

He shifted his attention up, working on her thigh. "Well, we were seventeen, and you knew I was coming over, so you'd left the door unlocked. I came in, like always, grabbed a snack—"

"Like always," she said with a light laugh.

"And went to find you." He cleared his throat as he relived the moment from his past. He stopped massaging, but his fingertips lingered on her thigh, too damn close to her center.

His body became stiff, and he dropped his hand back to her knee. Knees were safer.

"And?" she prompted.

"And you'd left the bathroom door open in your bedroom, and I saw you through the clear glass shower, which hadn't steamed up yet." He shrugged. "Only saw your ass. No tits."

She slapped at his shoulder, and he couldn't bite back another smile. "What?" he asked casually.

"What did you do after that?"

He wondered if he should tell her the entire story—that he'd seen her from the side, touching herself, and he'd rushed from the house like a speeding bullet before he busted his own load then and there.

She'd been Nate's girl at the time, and he shouldn't have seen Nate's girl fingering herself.

"I left and came back thirty minutes later so you wouldn't know."

"You must've been early. No way I would've popped in the shower, knowing you might walk in on me."

"Mm-hm. Sure."

He applied more pressure to each side of her knee as she said, "I am so embarrassed you saw me—" She stopped talking as her head fell back and tipped up to the ceiling. "Ohhhh." It was an honest-to-God orgasmic moan, and he knew he was screwed.

It was the kind of noise he'd spent the better part of his life fantasizing about hearing from her, but he never thought it would happen, especially not from an injury-related massage.

"Oh, God, yes," she said, louder than she probably intended, and he smiled when she looked back at him.

"I'm that good, huh?" He continued to work and winked.

"How do you know how to do that?" She relaxed her shoulders and closed her eyes. Her sudden trust in him was surprising.

"I hurt my knee pretty bad in an explosion, and I had to get a lot of soft tissue work done. I learned the kind of oils to rub on it when it was hurting, as well as how to massage it to get relief."

Her mouth rounded into an O, but she didn't say anything, nor did she allow him to see her brown eyes that had flecks of golden amber in them. Eyes that had haunted him for years.

"I never thought you'd be into oils. I'm kind of known as—"

"The Hippy Doc," he finished for her.

Shit.

"Who told you I was called that?" Her eyes were definitely open now and accusatory.

He fumbled through his head with a lie of some sort to say, but he didn't know if he could stomach it at this point. "Ralph," he finally said, and he dropped his hands from her leg and stood. He turned his back and dragged two palms down his face, knowing a fight was about to ensue.

He adjusted his pants. This topic was sure to be an erection killer.

"I don't believe it. When did you talk?"

Dodging bullets and enemy fire was probably going to be a walk in the park compared to what was about to happen. Riley was going to crucify him, and maybe even get pissed at Ralph, which was the exact opposite of what he wanted to happen.

"Tell me." She was standing behind him now, pressing a hand to his back.

"Do you really want to know the truth?" He dropped his head forward, his heartbeat escalating, his body tense.

"Hell, yes."

"Then sit your ass back down."

"No," she said as he pivoted to face her, irritation swirling harsh in her irises. "Talk, damn it. And no more deals. No more massages for answers."

"What? You didn't like my hands on you?" He scowled at his choice of words. He hadn't meant to say it like that. A lungful of air left his chest, and he stepped closer to her, and the backs of her legs bumped into the bed.

She jutted her chin out and pressed a hand to his chest. "Answers."

"Even if it will hurt you?"

She looked over his shoulder for a brief moment, maybe eyeing her reflection in the mirror behind him. "Yes."

His head bowed, his chin nearly touching the top of her head. "Ralph and I have been emailing for years."

"What? No. He would've told me."

And Ralph had wanted to. Over and over again. But he had respected Ben's request to keep their communication private. "I wouldn't let him."

"Why the hell not?" She shoved at him, which had her yelping a painful cry.

"You need to take that bath, and I need to get you those oils."

"I don't need your help." She maneuvered around him and started for the door. "I don't need anything from you ever again.

We scattered their ashes, and now you and I are done." She grabbed hold of the knob and swung the door open. "Get out."

He scratched at his jaw, trying to decide what to do. Walk away? Or fight for her, like maybe he should have done a long time ago?

"Now," she hissed, and he noticed a sheen of liquid coating her beautiful eyes.

"No." The word dropped like a stone from his mouth.

"No?" A puff of air expelled from her parted lips.

"No." His long legs swallowed the short distance in three steps, and he stood before her, pressed a hand to the door, and shoved it shut.

Her jaw dropped as her eyes found his. There was something in her gaze that went beyond anger, and even beyond mourning. He recognized it because he felt it, too.

White hot lust crept beneath his now-closed eyelids as he tried to back down, as he tried to remind himself of who she was . . .

"Why are you just standing there? I want you to leave."

"I'm trying to, believe me, I am. I shouldn't be here," he said in a husky voice before opening his eyes.

"Then go."

He swallowed and brushed his knuckles over her left cheek, careful not to touch the other one, which was already starting to turn purple from the fall.

"Do you really want me to leave?" His blood was pumping and running straight down to the center of his body—making him harden with need.

Quick and shallow breaths before she whispered, "No."

And it was all he needed to hear. His mouth dropped over hers, and she went soft against him almost immediately, even moaning against his lips as he kissed her.

Warmth flooded through each limb in his body as he wrapped his hands around her hips and pulled her tight against him, forgetting that she'd gotten hurt earlier. But she didn't remind him, either. No, she kissed him back like her life depended on it.

And when his tongue parted her lips, she invited him even further into her hot mouth and fisted his hair as she pressed her pelvis against him. It was like she needed him as much as he needed her.

He didn't want to stop and think about what was happening. He had no desire to remind himself that he was tasting Riley Carpenter, and he was prepared to taste all of her if he didn't stop soon.

I'm in love with her, bro. I'm gonna ask her out. Would that fuck up our friendship?

Nate's voice, like a ghost from the past, tugged at his mind, and it was as if he were pulling a parachute ripcord of betrayal.

Christ. He forced his mouth off of hers and backed up, dragging a hand down his chest. "I shouldn't have done that" was all he could get himself to say.

"You're right." She turned from him, and his hands fisted at his sides. "Let's forget this ever happened. We were emotional about saying *goodbye* to Nate and Ralph—and that's what this was." She peered at him over her shoulder, and he quietly nodded. "A mistake," she murmured as if still trying to convince herself.

"A mistake," he repeated and reached for the doorknob. "I'm going to get you those oils, and you should get in the tub." He tried to act casual as if it hadn't happened, but how in the hell would he be able to erase the touch of her lips from his mind?

This was their third kiss, but the first real one, with her mouth parting and his tongue twining with hers. And part of him hated it would be their last.

She didn't say anything, and so he left without a word, but he pressed his back to the closed door and remained in the hall, trying to digest the moment when he'd fucked up and pulled her into his arms.

But was it really a mistake?

Riley was Nate's girl.

Will always be his.

But he wasn't sure if he'd ever be able to wrap his head around that idea.

He tapped at the door a minute later, not sure if she'd even open it.

"Yeah?" she answered.

"Can I see you?"

A few quiet seconds passed before the door creaked open.

She tugged her lip between her teeth and studied him through a space of only six or so inches.

"I know what happened between us can never happen again," he said in a low voice as his gaze moved up to her eyes.

She inhaled a breath through her nose, and he waited for her to exhale before he spoke again.

"I'd like a second chance at our last time." He searched her eyes for recognition, to see if she understood his intention. And when the door opened wide, and she allowed him in, he barreled at her with barely any restraint. Years and years of holding back had caged him, and now he was free.

But he only had a few minutes before he'd need to be once again restrained.

He curved his hands around her ass, prompting her to lift her legs up and around his hips. She held tight to his frame as he claimed her mouth, his tongue diving back in, greedy for more.

Her back hit the wall, and he held her there as he continued to kiss her with everything he had.

A groan tore from deep within his chest, and she responded by tilting her head to the side, allowing his mouth access to her neck. His erection pressed against her as he sucked at her smooth skin.

"Ben . . ." She said his name between moans. "Oh, God—"

He captured her last words with his mouth, kissing her hard, probably bruising her lips, and he knew he needed to back the hell down and soon.

There probably wouldn't be a pastor in town, or even in the entire state, who'd forgive him for lusting after his best friend's woman—especially after spreading his ashes.

He finally dragged his lips from hers, which was damn painful to do. He guided her legs down to the floor. The look in her eyes matched what he felt on the inside: regret.

"Goodnight," he whispered and looked away from her, too broken in that moment to say or do anything else.

CHAPTER NINE

ONLY A FEW ROWS SEPARATED BEN AND RILEY AS THEY WAITED AT the gate for their flight. She'd purposefully sat as far away as possible, but kept him in her line of sight. She wasn't sure why, but being able to see his face whenever she wanted gave her a strange sense of comfort.

Ben had knocked on her door later last night, but when she'd opened it, all she'd found were a basket of essential oils and his scribbled notes on how to use them. She was the holistic remedy expert and didn't need his advice. But . . . she followed his orders anyway.

When they'd met in the lobby to head to the airport, she'd said *thank you,* but not much else, since his face had been drawn so tight he'd looked like a man in the middle of a war-torn battle zone.

It had been an awkward ride to Asheville, without much in the way of conversation between them, but she'd had no clue what to say to him after what happened last night. And apparently, he hadn't either.

Ben had kissed her *twice.*

And she hadn't just let him—she'd kissed him back. Hard.

Her fingers brushed over her lips at the memory of his mouth on hers.

Daniel had never kissed her like that.

Daniel had never made her feel so much from one smoldering look, either. He'd been a logical option for her, but there'd never been much passion between them. Not for her, at least.

Last night with Ben, it had been one wild blur of a ride. And they had barely touched. She couldn't even begin to imagine what sex would be like with him. Well, actually, she'd imagined it a lot over the years and hated herself for it. But after last night, she realized her fantasies wouldn't live up to reality.

It had been nothing like the two soft and tender kisses from her youth. No, last night had been laced with so much passion she'd worried she would orgasm from the touch of his mouth on her neck alone.

His ball cap was on and pulled down low, and his thumbs were working fast on his smartphone. She grabbed her cell out of her purse, answered a few of Mandy's and Daniel's texts, then scrolled through her contacts.

She had entered Ben's number yesterday in case they got split up on the trail, but hadn't gotten around to deleting it yet. But instead of erasing it now like she should have, she sent him a message.

Riley: *Why'd you kiss me?*

Her thumb hovered above the little blue arrow. There was an intense discomfort in the pit of her stomach, but she did it—she hit *send.*

She looked up and glanced his way, and his eyes met hers. His gaze was intense. Almost too focused, and so she forced herself to look back at her screen.

Three little dots popped up a moment later. He was typing.

She closed her eyes, waiting for her phone to alert her to the text, and when it did, her stomach squeezed with anticipation.

Ben: *It should never have happened.*

Riley: *It shouldn't have happened. We both know that. But . . . how did it happen?*

The little bubbles as he typed remained like a constant tease until the text came through.

Ben: *Kiss = two mouths touch. With tongue and without. "With tongue" is also known as French kissing. But honestly, you did much better in school than me. Perhaps you could provide an adequate definition.*

Of course, he'd give her a sarcastic response.

Riley: *Okay, smart-ass. But WHY did we kiss?*

Ben: *You fell onto my mouth. Accident?*

Ben now swiped at his phone as if breezing through images on his screen without a care in the world. It annoyed the hell out of her, and she repositioned her thumbs on the phone and quickly typed.

Riley: *Sure. And the second time, when you barreled into my room?*

She waited for Mr. Baseball's response, but instead, his voice traveled through the air, hitting her a minute later—his face tense, his expression hard. And his phone was to his ear.

Before she could go see what was going on, her own phone began vibrating.

It was Mandy.

"Uh, hello?" She stood and glanced at the departure time on the gate. Five more minutes until they'd begin boarding.

"You might want to sit down for this," Mandy said softly.

"That's my mom's line. Why are you using her line?"

"Because someone else was just murdered."

* * *

"You owe me, Sheriff." He paused for a moment. "Yeah, and I remember what you said to me: 'If you ever need a favor, you can call me anytime.' Well, I'm calling in that favor." Ben stood before her with his head bowed and his thumb and middle finger gripping his temples. "I want access to the case. I want to be part of the investigation."

Riley's nerves were a tangled mess. The flight from Asheville to Atlanta had been unbearable. But now, waiting for their connecting flight, had her even more on edge.

She couldn't believe another person had been murdered. And, from what Mandy had heard, killed in the same way. Chest wound and knife to the throat.

Was Lydia Harper really gone? Mandy had caught her hooking up with Bobby just last week. And now . . .

How could both Ralph and a twenty-seven-year-old with a promising future be dead?

Was there really a serial killer in her small town? Was that what this was?

A slow roll of fear moved through her, and she tensed.

This can't be happening.

Ben made a *tsk* noise, which had her eyes flickering back up to his tall frame. "I don't give a flying fuck what you say." He dropped the phone a moment later, and she assumed he'd been hung up on.

"Guessing that didn't go well."

He tucked his cell into his jeans pocket and sat down next to her. His fingers swept up to the bruise on her cheek, his eyes narrowing as he surveyed the damage.

He dropped his hand a moment later. "Two people killed in the exact same way." His eyes darkened, anger blooming in his irises.

"I guess the police can rule out a student," she said softly. "But, do you really think the sheriff will let you in on the case?"

He leaned back. "He's a stubborn motherfu—" He stopped himself and glanced over at her. "I'll make sure I get the case files, with or without his permission. Don't worry."

But should she be worried? Ben wanted to help track down a killer, which meant it could put a target on his back. Who the hell knew the motive of the murderer? What if he or she decided to make Ben the next victim?

She couldn't lose him, too. Not when she'd just gotten him back.

Her stomach twisted at her last thought. She didn't have him. He wasn't hers to have any more. And last night only further complicated the truth she knew she had to digest.

He'd leave when this was over.

God, he'd been a major part of her life back in the day, and every fiber of her being craved for him to be a part of her life again, despite how much it had hurt when he left.

"Why does the sheriff owe you a favor?" she asked when Ben didn't say anything else.

He rubbed his face a few times as if trying to wipe away some of his tension. His jaw was stubbly, and the memory of the five-o'clock shadow, prickly against her skin last night, came to mind.

"You know Charlize, his daughter, right?"

Small towns meant you pretty much knew everyone. Charlize was three years younger than they were, so Riley had never hung out with her back in school. "Of course."

"She got into some trouble in Vegas two years ago, and I discreetly helped her out."

Her mouth rounded in understanding. Riley's mom had vaguely overheard gossip about that, but she'd never known if it were true. "Oh. Wow."

He shrugged and sat up straighter. "It was a shit move for me to bring that up."

"But if you think you can help the case . . ." She allowed her voice to trail off, not really sure what else to say.

"I'm obviously not a cop. I mostly handle private security stuff. But if we're dealing with a serial killer"—he swallowed—"I'd like to assist."

"I'm sure the sheriff will come around. If not, well, like you said, you can help out anyway." She forced her lips to curve into a smile. "Just don't get arrested or anything."

"I'll do my best not to." He smiled back.

Her eyes cruised the terminal, and she checked the boarding time.

"Is there anything else you discovered about Ralph's death you haven't told me?"

He glanced around, as if taking note of all of the people, murmured voices, and constant flight announcements sounding overhead. "Not really. The kill was clean. No weapon in sight. The room wasn't tampered with. No sign of struggle. Basically, they have nothing."

He sounded detached as if Ralph hadn't been like a second father to him. She couldn't help but wonder if being in the military had changed his outlook on death.

"Did Ralph know the murdered woman?"

She thought about the intern, Lydia Harper. Had she and Ralph ever crossed paths? She highly doubted that. Lydia wasn't from Alabama, either. She'd moved to town for her internship at the hospital.

"I don't think so."

"Hm." His mouth tightened and his brows lowered in thought as he reached for his phone again.

"Who are you calling?"

"A friend. I'm not putting much faith in the sheriff to let me in, so I need to make sure I have the new case files waiting for me when I get back home."

"Home." She whispered the word, her gaze dropping to the floor. "You said *home*. I, uh, didn't think you thought of it like that anymore."

"Always have. Always will."

CHAPTER TEN

"I DON'T KNOW WHAT TO SAY."

"What if it had been you? What if you were the doctor this killer—" Her mom pressed her fingertips to her closed lips.

Riley got off her stool, came around the kitchen island, and rubbed her mom's back. "I'm okay, though."

"I know, but this deranged maniac is on the loose, and we don't have a clue as to why the hell he's doing this." Her nostrils flared. "I don't like the idea of you going to work today."

Two of her clients had canceled, too afraid to even go outside. But they also had severe anxiety disorders, so she could understand how a potential serial killer on the loose would be even more disturbing.

"It's daylight. I'll be fine." Riley snatched a piece of buttered toast off the plate in front of her.

"Have you spoken to Daniel since you got back last night?" A dyed-blonde brow raised in question. "Lydia was his resident. I'm sure he's upset."

She took a bite of the toast and slouched back onto the stool. "He called me a few times last night, but I wasn't up for talking. I'll call him during lunch, though, and give him my condolences."

She nodded. "He's a good man. You should consider—"

"I know he is, but things are over between us."

Her mom frowned. "Okay."

Before Riley could say anything else, her phone rang.

"Who'd be calling this early?" She snatched Riley's cell off the counter and glanced at it. "Ben?" She handed her the phone. "You still haven't told me how the weekend went."

"We spread ashes. It was depressing. Nothing to say." Her voice was clipped, and she blew out an irritated breath, wondering why she'd obeyed Ben's orders to stay at her parents' house.

He'd given her two options when they'd gotten home. The second choice of him parking outside her door day and night had been out of the question.

But now that she was under what felt like the Spanish Inquisition, she wondered if having Ben outside her home wasn't such a bad idea.

She left the kitchen and went into the living room, finally answering.

"Hey, you got a second?" he asked straight away.

"Uh, yeah. I'm about to head to work."

"You weren't planning on going there alone, right?"

"I was planning on walking." She dropped down onto the leather couch. "Alone."

"Riley," he hissed. "Really?"

"It's daylight. No one is going to attack me on the streets."

"And you know this how?" A mumbled curse cracked through the phone line. "Shit, it doesn't matter right now, anyway. In about two minutes, you're going to be getting a call from the sheriff."

"What? Why?" She sat upright, her pulse skyrocketing.

"They want to question you. You were like family to Ralph."

"Oh. I was wondering when that would happen. Surprised it wasn't last week."

"Yeah, well, they were moving slow last week, focusing on his students; but it looks like this new homicide has lit a fire under their asses."

"And how do you know they're going to call?"

Silence.

"Ben . . .?"

More silence. Then, "Just be ready in ten minutes. I'm on my way."

"What? No."

The line was dead.

* * *

"WE DIDN'T GET TO CHAT AT THE WAKE, BUT OH MY, IT'S SO GOOD to see you. You certainly look different. Such a man." Her mom reached out and bear-hugged Ben, and then proceeded to squeeze his biceps.

And this was why she never brought men home. Even Daniel. Her parents had only spent a couple of evenings with him during their entire relationship.

"Mom, you can let go now."

Her mom's cheeks were bright, and any evidence of her earlier tears had vanished. "Baby girl, I've known this boy since his circumcision."

Ben coughed into a closed hand, and it was Riley's face now going crimson. "Okay, well, we need to be going."

They were standing in the foyer of her parents' house, the door still wide open, and she hoped they could make a quick exit before her mom said anything else humiliating.

Riley might have been thirty-two, but she was still very much capable of being embarrassed by her mother.

"It's been a pleasure. But like Ri said, we should go."

"'Ri,' huh?" Her mom's brows rose, and her gaze swept from Ben's sneakers, up his denim legs, and to the long-sleeved black cotton shirt. His muscles were visible beneath, even though it wasn't a clingy fabric.

"We need to go," Riley mumbled, then kissed her mom on the cheek.

"You know, Riley saw you play baseball in Los Angeles. Did she tell you that?"

Her heart nearly died at her mom's words. Why had she ever even admitted that to her?

"That was right before you blew out your shoulder and had to retire," her mom continued, making it so much worse.

Riley nudged Ben in the arm with a closed fist, urging him to leave.

Once inside his rental SUV, she strapped on her belt and focused out the window, praying Ben wouldn't mention the whole *baseball* thing.

"When did you see me?" His words sounded stuck in his throat.

She faced him as he reversed out of the driveway. They had about a five-minute ride to the sheriff's station, which was five minutes too long.

She rubbed her sore knee for a moment as she thought about what to say. When his hand moved across the gears to touch her thigh, she sucked in a sharp breath.

"Still bothering you? The oils didn't work?" There was a grim twist of his mouth as he pulled back his hand.

She gave a half-hearted shrug.

"You probably didn't follow the instructions. Maybe I should help you later?" He eyed the bruise on her cheek that she'd attempted to cover with makeup.

"Yeah, because the last time you tried helping me worked out brilliantly." She caught a lopsided smile from him out of the corner of her eye.

"I promise, no one will fall on anyone's lips this time."

"Sure . . ." She rubbed her forehead, pressure building behind her eyes.

"But let's get back to baseball." He gripped the wheel with one hand and rested his other in his lap.

A sudden warmth nestled inside her stomach at the memory of his hard-on pressed to her when she grinded against him Saturday night.

"I was at a medical conference in L.A., and a group of doctor friends I was with, mostly guys, were big baseball fans, and they wanted to catch a game."

Seeing him on the field that day had shattered her.

She had lasted twenty minutes before faking an illness. She'd spent the rest of the evening with Ben and Jerry's ice cream.

"Why didn't you approach me?"

She laughed, which had him catching her eyes for a moment. "I don't think they just let people from the stands talk to famous players." She forced her gaze back out the window because looking at his blue eyes was like looking directly at the sunlight. Painful.

"You could've tried. If I had seen you—"

"If you saw me, you would've probably up and left in the middle of the game. You know, since that's what you do. You leave."

His knuckles whitened as he held the steering wheel even tighter. "Was that the only time you saw me . . . but I didn't see you?"

"Yeah."

"Well, just so you know, I wouldn't have run," he said as they rolled into the parking lot at the station a few minutes later.

Her pulse accelerated, and her slightly trembling fingers looped around the door handle, but with Ben's hand now on her shoulder she stilled.

"Be careful in there."

"What do you mean?"

She squared her body to face him, and he heaved out a soundless breath as he pulled his arm back. "They're looking for a suspect, and you know both of the deceased. They might play hardball with you, so just use your words wisely."

A stone sank in her stomach, sending a rippling effect of reactions throughout her body. "Oh my God. I would never—"

"Of course not."

"And we were in Asheville when Lydia was killed."

"According to forensics, Lydia was killed Friday morning, which means you were still here. They just didn't discover her body until Sunday, when she didn't show up for her next shift."

She raced through the timeline in her head. "Jesus," she whisper-yelled.

"Everyone's a suspect until proven otherwise."

"Is that what you heard?"

"More like what I overheard."

Overheard? She didn't even want to know what illegal activity Ben was doing.

"Come on." Ben got out and circled the SUV and opened her door.

Her chest constricted as a new wave of emotions soared through her at the sight of his outstretched hand.

"And what about you? Are you a suspect?" She took his hand, allowing him to help her out.

"No."

"And why not?" she asked as they walked.

"I have an alibi for Ralph's murder."

"Which was?"

He reached for the police station door and opened it, stepping back to allow her entrance first. Always with the chivalry.

"I was in the middle of an argument with a pop princess."

"Care to explain?"

"Not really worth it." His lips tightened, and she knew she wouldn't be getting anything else out of him on the matter. Ben had always been like that. When he'd made his mind up about something, he was done. Well, except as children. She'd managed to tickle information out of him as a kid. She highly doubted that would still work.

"Riley?"

She pulled her attention away from Ben.

"What are you doing here?" Mandy approached her, but her eyes were on Ben.

"I assume the same as you," Riley said. "This is Ben Logan."

Mandy reached for his hand. "Hi." Her eyes continued to linger on him as if she were unsure whether she wanted to kick him in the butt for having hurt Riley years ago . . . or kiss him.

"Sorry for your loss. I heard you worked with the recent victim." Ben released his grip.

"Thanks. Our entire surgical team is here, actually. We were the last people to see her. We had an emergency surgery at four a.m., and she went home right after—" She cut herself off, tears suddenly threatening.

Riley wrapped her arms around her friend. "Hang in there."

"She was so young." Mandy hiccupped and pulled back, just as Daniel entered the room from behind a closed door.

"Daniel," Riley said under her breath.

Daniel's eyes roamed over Ben, taking him in as if sizing him up for competition. His shoulders went back, and his chin jutted forward.

Did he recognize him from her old photos? Or from the images of Ben all over Ralph's place?

"You okay, honey?" Daniel asked.

Honey. He was staking his claim.

"Shocked by all of this," Riley finally answered.

Ben reached for Daniel's hand. "I'm Ben, an old friend of Riley's."

Daniel's forehead creased as he grasped Ben's palm. He had to be wondering what the hell she was doing with Ben.

Riley shifted her attention to another doctor coming from behind the same door a second later, and her stomach churned at the sight of him: her damn one-night stand from a few weeks back.

The police officer behind the desk in the waiting area skirted her attention back and forth between Riley and the other men as if she were curious as to what might happen, too. Could she sense the tension?

Riley sure as hell could.

Mr. One-Night Stand simply nodded her way and left the station.

"Baby, did the sheriff call you for questioning, too?" Daniel asked.

Ben cleared his throat and left her side to approach the officer at the desk.

"Yeah, he did. I just don't see how Lydia's death is connected to Ralph's, but it can't be a coincidence they were both killed like this, right?"

Daniel's eyes darkened. He had to be in mourning.

And he'd been there for her at Ralph's wake, so even if she wasn't up for it, maybe she needed to do the right thing and offer emotional support to him, as well.

"If you, uh, need anything, let me know." She forced out the words and met Ben's eyes when he returned, standing alongside Daniel.

"Thank you," Daniel said. "Well, I'm late for surgery. I'll call you later." A grimace tugged at his lips. "We clearly need to talk," he added in a low voice.

All she could do was nod and watch her ex leave.

"I should go, too," Mandy said once Daniel was out of sight. "You're staying at your parents', right?"

"Yeah," she said and reached for her forearm and squeezed. "We'll talk soon, okay?"

"Of course," Mandy said before leaving.

Riley dropped into a chair. "Don't say anything."

"Say what?" Ben sat next to her and crossed his ankle over his knee, holding on to it.

A few more doctors left the station while they waited, her nerves fraying with each passing second.

"We broke up last month," she sputtered as if she needed to clear the air for some reason.

"I assume that was your doing?"

She caught a smirk out of the corner of her eye. "Why do you say that?"

"*Honey. Baby.*" A light chuckle fell from his lips. "Not to mention the death stare I got because I have a penis and was standing next to you."

Her hand landed on her chest as she fought back a laugh. "You did not just say that." She glared at him, her eyes wide, her cheeks warm from embarrassment.

Ben shrugged, his eyes almost twinkling. The man was so good at taking shitty situations and making her smile. "Just saying . . ."

"He—"

"He's too old for you," he interrupted.

She had intended to say: He knew how much Ben had hurt her, but . . . "Too old?"

"He's what? Fifty?" A dark brow raised, the nearby scar shifting with the movement. She wondered how he had gotten that one.

A scar on his face. Hand. Where else was his flesh marked by injury?

It hurt to even think about it.

"Forty-five. And I'm old enough to make my own choices. You, on the other hand, you could use a little guidance in your love life. Perhaps by dating someone other than a model, and maybe a woman who has a few numbers more interesting than her bra size."

Ben tipped his head back, and a deep rumble of laughter filled the room. "So, you've been keeping tabs on me, huh?" He rubbed his hands on his thighs. "And what do you have against models? You were never so judgmental in the past."

And she wasn't now. *What is wrong with me?* "My mother loves to irritate the hell out of me by talking about you. You're telling me Sally doesn't do the same?"

"No, my mom knows better than to talk about you." His voice was calmer this time. Deeper.

The mood suddenly shifted like wind in a storm, but then Riley caught sight of the sheriff coming into the room, and her next thoughts died on her tongue.

"Dr. Carpenter." He tipped his hat her way before changing his focus to Ben, his eyes taking on some of the hunter green from his uniform. "And why are you here?"

"Moral support." Ben stood and glared at the sheriff. "I'll wait for you here."

"That's really not necessary," she said while rising, her legs a little unsteady.

"I know," he said before the sheriff led her deeper into the station.

The place was familiar, but she hadn't been there in years.

Ben and Nate had dared her to skinny dip in Old Man Johnson's pond at midnight one summer when she had been sixteen.

Unfortunately for the guys, they had never gotten to see her jump in naked because Old Man Johnson had shown up with a hunting dog and flashlight.

The sheriff at the time had thought all three of them needed an hour in jail to learn some ridiculous lesson about trespassing.

More memories tugged at her mind, blowing through her until they nearly touched her soul. It was as if she could feel Nate, too. As if he were trying to get to her, to make her feel something—but she was sure Ben's presence was why this was really happening. Stirring up all her tightly bottled emotions. The problem was, Ben could easily break her bottle . . . and then what would happen?

She sat down in a small room that only had a desk and two metal chairs, and a harsh slap of reality hit her.

"We'll be recording this conversation." The sheriff didn't sit. Instead, he placed his hands on his hips, and someone else walked into the room. She'd never seen the man before, but she assumed it was the detective who'd been brought in to work the case.

"I'm Detective Shumsky." A pinch of the Mississippi Delta flowed through his voice.

She placed her hands on the table in front of her, not sure what the hell to do with them.

The detective sat in front of her. "You knew both victims, but we understand you were very close to Mr. Chandler," the detective started, his voice as smooth as a polished stone. "When was the last time you saw him alive?"

"It's Dr. Chandler. He had a Ph.D."

"Okay. When was the last time you saw *Dr.* Chandler?"

She glanced at the recorder on the table. "The Saturday before he died. We usually take a walk in the park."

"And did he say he was having trouble with anyone? Dating anyone that you knew of?" A fat bottom lip was all she could see beneath the gray mustache when his mouth moved, and his eyes were like silver bullets as he zoned in on her, trying to get a read on her.

"Ralph would never date. His wife, Maureen, was his soul mate, and he said he could never find another." Her lips pursed in thought. She'd always agreed with him. Once you found the one, there was no one else—which had been her problem year after year.

She blinked a few times, the harsh pain of loss moving into her throat. "Ralph was a sweet man. He'd sooner apologize for something he didn't do wrong before he'd get into an argument. So, no, he wasn't having issues with anyone." She arched her shoulders back, feeling the need to sit taller. "At least, not that he told me about."

A large hand swept over his jaw as his eyes narrowed. He was probably in his early fifties, and there was experience in his eyes, which should have made her happy, but his icy stare moved right through her skin and into her bones.

"Exactly how old were you when Nate Chandler died?"

Her heart stuttered in her chest at his words. "Nate? Why are you asking about him?"

"Please, just answer the question."

"Surely you already know the answer." Her palms pressed harder down on the table now, an attempt to ground herself.

"Three people are dead."

"Three?" Her spine stiffened. Had someone else died?

"I'm referring to Nate Chandler," he said. "Three people you knew are gone."

She took a pained breath. "I don't understand why—"

"Did you know Ralph Chandler had you in his will?"

Her heart catapulted into her throat, and she almost choked on it.

Oh, God. Her mouth grew parched, and her lips dried by the second as if in the desert heat. "Not until after he was killed."

"You spread his ashes, along with those of his wife and son. Is that correct? Just this past weekend?"

She nodded, shocked at the turn of conversation.

"And where were you when Nate fell off the mountain?"

His back-and-forth questions from the past to the present had her mind spinning. Was this a tactic? Was he trying to throw her off, to disorient her?

"I was belaying Ben Logan. Nate had chosen to climb without a rope. So, if you're suggesting I pushed my boyfriend off—"

"Whose idea was it to climb without a rope?" He leaned back in his seat and crossed his arms.

"Why are you wasting your time talking about an accidental death, when there's a killer out there?" She pushed back from the table and stood, her legs shaky, her body thrumming with unease.

"Try and calm down," the sheriff said.

Riley pinched her eyes closed for a moment. The room was closing in, the walls pushing together as a swell of fear bubbled inside her chest.

This. Is. Not. Happening.

She replayed the words over and over in her head like a broken record, willing herself to wake up and for it to be two weeks ago and for Ralph to still be alive.

When her eyes found the detective again, she sat back down, defeat washing over her.

"Answer the question." The detective clasped his hands on the table, his thick fingers threaded loosely together.

"Nate was a daredevil. He loved to free climb. I begged him not to all of the time, but it never did any good," she finally answered, a soft tone to her voice. "And I loved Ralph like a father, so if you're implying I had anything to do with either of their deaths, you're barking up the wrong tree."

"You're a brilliant woman. Top of your class. You could have worked at any hospital or with any practice in the country, from what I've been told. Why would you come back to this little town?" Shumsky asked.

"Because I was Ralph's only family. I cared about him. He didn't have anyone."

"Were you two having an affair?"

Her face pinched tight, and she tried to lasso in her anger at the question. "Absolutely not."

"And where were you on the night Ralph was killed?"

She scrambled to remember, to think of an alibi. "I was home." A thick lump moved down her throat at the realization that she'd been alone. "I would never hurt him. How could I ever stab him?"

"How'd you know how he was killed? Those details haven't been released."

Shit. "Small town. Everyone knows." She didn't want to get Ben in any trouble.

"And Lydia Harper? Where were you last Friday morning?"

She'd canceled her appointments with her patients that day, which had infuriated her least favorite, Jeremy Stanton.

"I was home packing for the trip to the mountains."

"Which was where you dumped the ashes?"

"*Dumped* isn't really the nicest of terms, but yes." She bit the inside of her cheek. Any sense of calm left within her disintegrated by the second.

"Did you have a key to Ralph's home? To his office?"

"Only his home." She pressed her clammy palms to her black skirt, rubbing them against the material.

"And were you aware of the fact that Lydia was sleeping with your ex-boyfriend, Dr. Daniel Edwards?"

Her mouth rounded for a brief moment. "Wait. What? You have your facts wrong. Lydia was hooking up with Bobby." Her fingers fused together on her lap as she filtered through the few facts she knew about Lydia.

"I know Bobby," the sheriff said straight away. "The man bled red, white, and blue for this country. Not sure if you're implying something, but—"

"Excuse me?" Riley couldn't help but cut him off. "How do you even know which Bobby I'm referring to?" She folded her arms. "There are at least twenty Bobbys within a three-mile radius of this station alone."

Silence seized hold of the room as the detective stole a look over his shoulder at the sheriff.

"Clearly, someone else mentioned his name," Riley commented.

Mandy had been in there before her. She must have brought up the fact that Bobby had been sleeping with Lydia.

"And for the record"—she began, a swift breeze of confidence soaring through her words—"Bobby may be a war hero, but that shouldn't make him immune to your investigation. You're not impartial because you've known me all of my life, and so I'd expect the same treatment for him." Her words billowed out of her mouth like smoke eating the air—hot, hard, and fast.

"What exactly do you know about the relationship between Bobby Creek and Lydia Harper?" the detective asked.

Her shoulders relaxed a little as she focused on his eyes. "Bobby was dating my friend, and she caught Lydia and Bobby together at the hospital just last week."

"So, you didn't see anything for yourself." The detective anchored his palms on the table, then began to drum his fingers. She wasn't sure if he was impatient or trying to make her nervous.

"No, I didn't witness them together myself."

"And what was your relationship with her?"

"We hung out a few times because she worked with a friend of mine at the hospital. We weren't close, though. I've never spent time with her alone or been to her place."

"Let's get back to Lydia's relationship with Dr. Edwards, then. You never answered my question. Did you know they were having an affair?"

"Daniel would never sleep with an intern. He's way too by-the-book. And there's one important detail you're missing—the man still loves me." Both the sheriff and detective remained quiet. "And *affair* implies cheating," she continued. "Are you saying this alleged relationship began while I was dating Daniel?"

There was only so much she could tolerate, and if the detective was going to imply she killed Lydia out of jealousy, that was about as absurd as accusing Daniel of cheating.

Instead of answering the question, the detective asked, "Is there anyone who can vouch for your whereabouts at the time of Ralph's or Lydia's death?"

A cramping pain developed in her pelvis, and her stomach started to burn. "No."

Were the police playing some sort of game with her? Trying to find the weak link, to see who would flounder under pressure if shaken up? They probably did this to everyone they questioned, she rationalized.

"Anything you want to add that you feel would be pertinent to the investigation?" the detective asked.

She bowed her head and gripped her temples with both hands. "No. But does this mean you're letting me go?"

"Of course. But don't leave—"

"Town," she finished for the detective. "You can check my place. You're free to go into my home. My car. I don't care. I have nothing to hide. You don't need a warrant."

"Well, thank you. That saves us some time." The detective gave a quick nod to the sheriff.

Once out in the hall, she said, "You know I didn't kill them. You know me as well as Bobby. And as for Nate, bringing him up was just low." She'd tried to remain strong through all of this, but now, tears stung her eyes.

"I don't know anything anymore, I'm afraid," he said in a grave voice.

Ben was on his feet when she saw him, and she rushed to him without a second thought, throwing her arms around him like he was the only one in the world who could comfort her.

He smoothed a hand through her hair. "You okay?" He cupped her head, holding her tight against him where she wished she could stay forever.

"No, I'm not," she murmured into his chest.

She sniffled and gained her composure a minute later, and then pulled herself free of him, away from the sense of safety he'd managed to give her at that moment.

The sheriff was still nearby, and she didn't want to say anything until they were alone.

"Remember, don't leave town," the sheriff said.

"What the hell is going on?" Ben asked as he opened the door for her to leave.

Before she could answer, her lip caught between her teeth in surprise at the man heading toward the station. "Jeremy?" She went through the exit and remained at the top of the short steps, watching him approach.

Jeremy stopped before her, his gaze meeting Ben's for a brief moment before finding her face again. "Doc."

Ben tenderly gripped her arm, encouraging her to shift closer to him.

She knew Jeremy's parole officer didn't work at the sheriff's station, so why was he there? "Are you okay?"

Jeremy's hands twitched against his thighs, and his normally slicked hair stuck out every which way. She was pretty sure he was in withdrawal. He must have found drugs somewhere last week when she wouldn't supply him with Valium, and now he'd run out.

Shit. She might not like him, but she didn't want him suffering. "We should talk," she said when he remained quiet. "Maybe you should come by today." She took a hesitant step in his direction, and Ben took one, too, right with her.

"Can't. The police need to talk to me." The slightest chatter from his teeth clicking together captured her attention as he spoke.

"About the murders?" She arched a brow. "I guess they're questioning everyone, huh?"

"We don't want to make you late, then." Ben stepped back to re-open the door for him.

"Call me if you need to talk before tomorrow." Riley waited for Jeremy to go inside before directing her attention to Ben.

"He one of your patients?"

It was probably obvious, but she said, "That's privileged information."

"Well, I don't like that guy. There's something seriously wrong with him," he said as they walked to the rental.

"You do remember what I do, right?" she asked once inside his SUV.

"Yeah, not a huge fan anymore." He got behind the wheel and

shifted to face her. "So, you want to tell me what happened in there now?"

Her hands dropped like weights into her lap. "Well, I'm pretty sure I'm one of the suspects."

"I told you they might—"

"No, it's worse than that. They act like they have evidence or something. I can't even leave town." She tried to remain calm, but anxiety clawed at her with sharpened nails. "I gave them permission to go to my apartment, even. To look around."

"Wait. What? What kind of evidence?" His face hardened with concern.

"They said my ex was sleeping with Lydia, which is crazy. And to make matters worse, they brought up Nate." She took shallow breaths, unable to find the right rhythm to breathe. "They acted like I might have been the cause of his death."

"Hell, no. I'm going back in there."

"No, please. It will only make things worse."

"They have no right to be harassing you like this." He dropped a few curse words before adding, "They better have been tough on your ex."

"Why do you say that?"

"If he was sleeping with Lydia, he sure as hell better be a suspect, too."

CHAPTER ELEVEN

"How's the tea?" Ben asked.

"It's good. Thanks." Riley sat on the couch in her office, holding the mug between her palms. Her eyes were swollen from crying, and he was so damn pissed he couldn't think straight.

He understood that the police needed to pursue every possible angle, but this was bullshit. And to bring up Nate? His blood heated, and a vein throbbed in his neck.

There was an intense heaviness in his stomach and a tension headache building in his temples. "You don't actually think Bobby Creek had anything to do with this, do you?"

"Not you, too."

"What do you mean?" he asked.

"He served, like you, and so, I assume you don't think he's capable of killing."

"What do you think we did in the military? Paint rainbows and sing 'Kumbaya'?" He arched a brow.

"Ben . . ."

"We did kill people." He cupped the back of his neck and turned away. "Murder's different, though. So no, I don't think

Bobby is the guy. But it's because I remember him from school. He was never good at getting dates, at least not back then, but he had a good heart."

"Well, maybe he's changed."

He pivoted her way, noting the darkness now hooding her eyes.

"People do change, I guess." He let the implication of his words hang in the air, because he wasn't sure which way he wanted them to blow, anyway. "What about your ex? We should talk to him, too, right?"

She looked down at the amber liquid in her cup. "The nurse said Daniel will be tied up in surgeries all day."

"Yeah, well, maybe I'll pay him a visit at the hospital, then."

Her gaze lifted. "No, that would make things worse."

"And do you think *he's* capable of murder?"

"He's a surgeon. He saves people. A murdering psychopath? No way." She took a sip of her tea. "And why would he kill Ralph? It doesn't make sense."

"And why would Bobby?"

"Good point." She lowered her cup to the table. "But I know Daniel much better than Bobby."

Her eyes were the color of brandy, the kind he and his buddies used to drink to celebrate a successful mission, and he couldn't help but get lost in the depth of them.

"There's something you're not telling me."

"Really? And how do you know?" The smallest of smiles met her lips.

"I've always been good at reading you."

"Maybe not." She hid her gaze the moment she'd spoken, and a shadow of the past dropped over the room.

"Do you remember that time you got a C on your history paper?" He sat next to her. "I think it was a piece on the Persian Gulf War. You were depressed for like a week about that grade. But you tried to hide it from me. You did your best to make me think you were fine, but I knew you. I knew you were beating yourself up about it."

"How the hell do you remember that?"

"Because I remember everything about you." He took a second to reel in his emotions. "And it's hard to forget, anyway. I'm pretty sure it was the only time you didn't get an A."

She chuckled. "True."

He reached for her hand. "The point is, it doesn't matter how hard you try, you can't hide your feelings from me."

She peered at the ceiling before her eyelids dropped closed. "You'd be surprised," she said so softly he almost didn't hear her.

The office intercom kicked on, which had her flinching and retracting her hand from his.

Riley's admin, Lonnie, whom he'd met twenty minutes ago, announced, "Your nine o'clock appointment is here."

Riley took a steady breath. "Give me five minutes."

"Okay," her admin responded.

"Why don't you cancel?" he asked as she stood, his eyes focusing on her skirt, which hugged the curves of her ass.

"I can't. I need to stay strong." She faced him but had a hand to her eyes.

The material of her skirt stopped a couple of inches above her knees, and he could see a purplish mark as a result of her fall over the weekend.

Her long legs had the perfect amount of muscle, and her silky blouse gave a hint of the fullness of her breasts beneath. He couldn't stop thinking about the feel of her body from the night at the hotel; seeing her in her bra, with her nipples poking through; the hardness of her thighs as he had massaged her legs; the way her tongue had felt inside his mouth . . .

Her looks should have been the last thing on his mind, but he'd always been a multitasker. His body wasn't ready to forget her, even if his brain was protesting for him to focus on the killer and only the killer.

He needed to protect her, and now, maybe even clear her name. He didn't need to screw her.

Screw. Wrong word. It could never just be sex. Riley wasn't like one of the women he'd dated in the past. She wasn't someone he'd fall asleep next to, hoping she'd be gone in the morning. No, she'd been the girl he wanted to fall asleep, and wake up, next to. And now, she'd become the woman he wanted to view every sunset and sunrise with.

She just didn't know.

And he could never let her know.

"You deserve time to grieve," he said.

"My patients need me." When her hand fell to her side, her brown eyes were once again coated in liquid. "You saw Jeremy. I canceled on him Friday. He needs me tomorrow, and there are others that need me today."

"I don't know." He tensed. "The idea of you alone in this office with someone like him . . ."

"It's a good thing it's not up to you." She pointed toward the door, a harsh look finding her face.

He hadn't meant to piss her off, he just wanted to keep her safe. He wanted to be there for her this time like he should have been before—he just had to fight the pull he felt toward her whenever she was within arm's length.

"Ben?" She waved a hand in front of his face, and he blinked.

"Shit." He shook his head. "Sorry."

Her features softened as she stepped closer to him. "You okay? I guess I didn't really stop to ask you that."

"Okay about what exactly?"

"Ralph's death." Her fingers skimmed along her jawline. "I was too angry at you to ever consider how sad you might be, especially since I didn't know until the other night you two had stayed in touch."

Ohh. He stood but turned his back to her. "I'm upset, of course.

But I've had men die in my arms before." Memories from war came back to his mind, coursing through him at lightning speed. His scalp prickled, his pulse quickened, and his warm skin grew hotter. "What I mean is that I've learned how to go through the stages of grief a lot faster than the norm. I didn't have much of a choice."

She pressed a hand to his shoulder, and his body tensed.

"I'm sorry."

"Don't apologize." He shifted his hand to his chest and up to reach her fingers. "I made it out. And I carry the names of those who didn't inside of me. And I'll carry Ralph with me, too."

She was quiet for a moment before he heard a soft sniffle, and he pivoted around to face her. "What's wrong?"

"That's just a lot to carry." Her voice cracked as a tear slid down her cheek.

He gathered a breath and palmed her face, finding her eyes, trying to stitch up his emotions before they, too, leaked out. "I'm strong enough to handle it."

He just wasn't sure if he was strong enough to resist her.

* * *

"I'm friends with Bobby's mom. You don't think he's the killer, do you? I saw that movie once where the guy came back from Iraq—"

"Mom." Ben held up a hand. "Really?"

She shrugged.

"Who told you about Bobby, anyway?"

"Small town. Clearly, you've forgotten that," she noted.

Yeah, he'd forgotten how fast news traveled here, which also meant the neighbors knew Riley had been questioned.

Just great. "You happen to have the suspect list for me? It'd save me the trouble of obtaining it myself."

"Funny."

Ben stretched back in his chair and stared at the tuna sandwich. He didn't have an appetite right now, but he knew his mom would lose her mind if he left without eating.

"Well, I for one am glad your friends are coming here to help out. I was wondering if they could stay here?" She tapped her fingers on the counter as if restless. "I've already started putting your bedroom back together."

"They're definitely not staying here."

"I'd like time with them. They're the cutest couple." Her cheeks flushed. "You know your father gets jealous whenever I'm around Aiden. That accent . . . There's a reason why he won't take me to Ireland like I've always wanted." She sat in the chair across from him and jerked her chin up, motioning for him to eat. "He thinks I'd leave him for some hot Irish hunk." She smiled. "Maybe I would."

"Sure." He rolled his eyes and grabbed half of the sandwich. "Anyway, they'll be arriving tomorrow morning, and I already booked them a room at the hotel." He swallowed a few bites of food. "Please, don't decorate my old room. You know I'm not moving back home."

"And why not? Vegas is so . . . Vegas."

He laughed. "What's that supposed to mean?"

She smoothed her hands over her blouse before they fell into her lap, and she shrugged. "Women. Booze. Gambling."

"And what's wrong with that?"

"What you need is to go to church. When was the last time you went?"

"Mom," he grumbled and scratched the back of his head. "Can we just focus on the situation at hand? What are you doing to keep yourself safe?"

"Your father's not letting me out of his sight. He even called out of work for the week. He has his gun ready for anyone who even tries to come through the door."

His dad had about the same moves as Chuck Norris or one of the other action heroes from the '80s or '90s. "Yeah, well, hopefully, we'll get this wrapped up in a week, but if not, I'll fly someone in to watch you."

"What about Peter? He's cute."

Ben laughed again. "First of all, I fired Peter—didn't you hear about the scandal?" He shook his head. "And secondly, why do you care what your bodyguard looks like?"

"It'd be nice to have something good to look at if I'm stuck in the house all day," she said, far too casually for his liking.

"Mom? You realize there's a possible serial killer on the loose, right? Two people are dead. One was your friend."

She stiffened, her mouth went tight, and her eyes became dull, almost lifeless, in a flash. "I can't think about it. I just—" Her sentence died as she began to cry.

"Shit." He moved quickly to his mom's chair and knelt at her side. "I'm sorry. I know we all have our own way of dealing with things, and so you've been distracting yourself by focusing on me. I get it." He held her hand.

"I can't accept this is real," she said, her voice breaking. "I'd rather just think of this as you finally visiting home." Her bottom lip trembled, and it gutted him that he'd not only devastated Riley with his absence—but his own mother.

He swiped at her tears, her mascara smudging beneath her eyes.

"I understand. And I'm sorry." He rose to his feet a few moments later and helped his mom to stand. "We'll have dinner with Ava and Aiden tomorrow or Wednesday, okay? I'm sure they'd love to see you."

"I'm so thankful they could fly out here to help out on such short notice."

"Me too. Aiden left his father in charge of the bar, and Ava was already on vacation from work. But you know how we roll," he said with a smile in his eyes. "When one is in trouble, we move heaven and earth to help out."

"I'm so glad you have friends like them."

Ben was, too.

But there was one friend he missed more than any others. And now that he had her back in his life, how the hell would he ever let go?

CHAPTER TWELVE

"I'LL BE FINE. DON'T WORRY ABOUT ME."

"Mandy . . ." Riley shook her head as if Mandy could see her through the phone. "I'm just asking you to be careful and watch your back. Don't be alone with Bobby, okay?"

"And who's watching yours? Maybe you should stay with Daniel instead of your parents until the killer is caught. He may be a doctor, but he's also tough."

She thought about telling her how Ben was protecting her, but she didn't want a lecture from her friend. Mandy would worry too much about her, and she'd rather Mandy focus on keeping herself safe right now.

"I'll be okay, but I do need to talk to Daniel. Is he still in surgery?"

"Last time I checked, yeah."

"Maybe you could stay at the hospital tonight instead of going home. I hate the idea of you being alone." Riley doubted Bobby was dangerous, but if there was even the slightest chance he could be the killer, she couldn't lose her best friend.

"Probably will, anyway. I have a late shift."

"Okay. Well, if you see anything suspicious, tell the sheriff, okay?"

"Yes, Detective Carpenter."

"This is serious."

"Girl, I know. But I'm trying to keep my sanity together so I can operate and not accidentally kill anyone. I'll process all of this and grieve after the killer is behind bars."

"Okay." Riley said goodbye a minute later and tossed the phone on the passenger seat as she drove.

When her last appointment ended early, she left the office and drove around town, circling it like a lost traveler.

Her wheels slowed as she neared the old high school baseball field.

What she hadn't expected was to see Ben standing on the pitcher's mound, kicking up dirt behind him.

She was pretty sure it was him and not a mirage, and when she pulled into a parking spot and saw his rental SUV, she knew he was real.

He tugged on the brim of his hat, squared his shoulders, then wound back his arm and threw toward home plate, even though he was alone.

His free hand immediately darted to his shoulder, and although he was quite a distance away, she could have sworn she saw him grimace. The man was in pain, but he must not have cared because a moment later he reached down for another ball. But as he stood, he shifted her direction.

She was caught.

Shit.

He shook his head, clearly pissed at seeing her. He gathered a couple balls off the field and headed her way.

She leaned against her truck and waited for him, practically holding her breath as he strode her way like a vision from the past.

She could see the sixteen-year-old Ben again, the boy who didn't have a care in the world.

"What are you doing here?" His voice was rough, but the sound tickled her skin in a strange way, sending a flow of heat down into her abdomen.

He opened the door to the back seat of his rental and tossed the bag and glove inside.

"I was going to ask you the same thing." She shoved off the truck and waited for him to face her again.

Ben closed the door, pressed both palms to the side of the SUV, and dropped his head. "Thought I'd throw a few for old time's sake before I came and picked you up." There was pain in his voice as if his words had been dragged through the muck.

Her heart squeezed in her chest, and she stood behind him, tenderly pressing her hand to his injured shoulder. "Still hurt?"

"Nah, I'm okay." He pivoted to face her, so she retracted her arm.

"You were never a good liar." She gulped because the look in his eyes had turned dark, almost grim.

He lifted his hat and swiped a hand through his dark locks. "Is this your truck?" With his cap back on, he sidestepped her and approached the vehicle.

She crossed her arms and watched him circle it. He smoothed a hand over the hood as if it were a horse. "Yeah, why?"

"Figured you'd be driving some flashy Mercedes or something." He smiled, and his white teeth blinked in the sunlight.

"You know how much I love the bed of a truck."

She'd surprised herself when buying the truck last year, trading in her Mercedes—good call on Ben's part—for the Ford. She had worried the purchase would be a painful reminder of her past, but she considered it to be part of her own personal therapeutic journey to move on. To move forward in life.

It hadn't worked, though.

She rarely drove it, and mostly walked everywhere. She'd told herself the town was small and walking was good exercise, but in her heart, she knew the truth. The past still had a claim on her soul, and it wouldn't let go.

"Good choice. Great engine."

"I know." She smiled, but it was an uncomfortable smile. She was nervous. And it had nothing to do with the shit day she'd had and everything to do with the man standing in front of her like a ghost from her past. Baseball hat and all.

"I dropped you off at work. How'd you get your truck?" He crossed his arms.

"My parents brought it to my office. I had wanted to pay Daniel a visit, and I didn't want to bug you. I figured you'd be busy. I was planning on letting you know I wouldn't need a ride home."

"Mm. And did you speak with your ex?"

She glanced at her watch. "No, he's still in surgery, but I left him a half a dozen messages to call me as soon as he gets out."

He nodded. "Good. I want a word with him, too."

"He won't talk to you," she quickly said. "But he'll talk to me."

"I don't want you alone with him in case—"

"He's not a killer." She turned her back and opened her truck door.

Ben positioned himself in the passenger seat next to her when she started the engine. "What are you doing?"

He shot her a lopsided smile. "Either you're riding with me, or I'm riding with you."

"You're frustrating."

"I know." He strapped on his belt. "But it looks like we have some time to kill before your ex gets out of work, so—"

"If we spend time together, that doesn't mean we're okay." Her cheeks warmed, and she hated herself for allowing years of conflicting emotions to gather like a storm inside of her so damn fast, especially at a time like this.

He took off his hat and rested it in his lap. His forehead was slightly sweaty, and his dark hair out of place . . . but he looked sexy, like always.

"Where to, then?" he asked as his blue eyes met hers.

"How about Swayze Park?" she suggested, regretting her words the moment they left her mouth.

He cleared his throat, scratched his chin, and looked away from her. His large, muscled chest lifted with a deep breath.

Was she asking for trouble?

"You want to go to a park with a killer out there?"

She knew his reservations about the park had nothing to do with the killer, and everything to do with their past.

Swayze Park was where they used to hang out.

So, why in the world had she suggested such a thing?

"It won't be dark for a few hours."

"Fine, but we should grab some food," he said. "I barely ate today, and I gotta maintain this body, you know." He flashed her a wickedly sexy grin. "This town manage to get a drive-through in the years I've been gone?"

She smiled. "A couple. But I'm not much of a fast-food eater, and you shouldn't be, either. You know the crap they put in that stuff? If you eat that garbage, I don't know how you stay in such good shape."

"So you noticed, huh?" He jokingly flexed his bicep, and she chuckled.

She couldn't believe the man had her laughing right now.

"Well, what do you suggest, then?" he asked.

She thought about going back to her apartment and packing some sandwiches. Would that create a more romantic vibe, though?

"Okay. I'll eat processed meat"—she held up an index finger—"just this one time."

"Thank you for your sacrifice, ma'am."

* * *

"Admit it. It's better than kale, isn't it?" His eyes crinkled at the edges as he smiled.

"Never." She chewed on her fry, and she hated that he was right. The food was damn good.

They were sitting on a blanket in the back of her truck, her long legs stretched out in front of her. And it was as if the rest of the world didn't exist.

"I'm bringing in help," he said after polishing off the rest of his burger.

"What kind of help?" She cleaned her hands with a napkin and tossed it in one of the grease-soaked brown bags.

"Aiden's a friend of mine. He's flying in tomorrow, and he's bringing his fiancée, Ava. I actually need her more than him."

"Oh, really? And why is that?"

He pushed the trash off to the side and scooted closer to her. He was sitting opposite of her, and his fingers wrapped around her slim ankle. She'd already kicked off her heels, but she had her legs crossed to try and keep Ben from getting a view up her skirt.

He edged closer, on his knees now, and slid his large hand up her calf muscle.

She bit back a groan at the gentle caress of this thumbs rubbing circles on each side of the tender area by her knee. "Ava used to work for the government as a biochemist, but it's her computer skills I'm interested in."

He kept his eyes on her leg, focused on the massage, so she stared down at his long, dark lashes before her eyes swept up to his scar.

"Is she the one who helped you get the case files?"

He nodded.

"What was it like?" she asked in a soft voice. "Being in the military, I mean. How are you handling being out? I've worked with soldiers who have PTSD."

He stopped touching her and lifted his hands for a second, and her pulse made a panicky climb. She wanted his hands back on her.

"Uh." He kept his gaze downcast. "I'm fine. The military was good for me. It helped tame me."

She chuckled. "I highly doubt anything could tame you."

He gifted her with his blue eyes, and her heart sang at the contact. "Well, I met a lot of great people, and they've become close friends."

"Like Aiden?" She hated there was a throb of jealousy inside of her. She had once been his best friend, and he'd replaced her.

"Yeah. There's a group of us who got out of the Marines about the same time. Some of us have struggled with civilian life more than others."

"Have you ever seen a therapist?" she spat out without thinking through her question first. "It could be helpful." She didn't mean to prod, but she couldn't help but worry about him. "I spend a couple of weeks a year in the D.C. area working with veterans. It's what I'm most passionate about."

His mouth twisted for the briefest of moments. "I've talked to someone a couple of times, but not regularly. I don't know. I'm fine. One of my buddies, Michael, still struggles with PTSD, a lot more than the rest of us. The guy is so damn smart. Never able to turn his brain off, and it's hard for him to stop thinking about what happened overseas."

"Do you always do that?"

He looked up again and slid his hand further up her thigh. "Do what?"

"Deflection. Instead of talking about yourself, you quickly switched to your friend."

"My friends matter to me," he said, his voice gruffer this time. She wondered if there was a hidden meaning, too—like he was referring to her. But maybe she was reaching.

"You really do carry the weight of everyone on your shoulders, don't you?"

He didn't answer. He shifted on top of her and straddled her lower legs, and she instinctively pressed a hand to the hem of her skirt, her knuckles brushing against his crotch in the process.

"What are you doing?" she asked when his hand settled on her leg.

"I'm trying to help you, but my shoulder is sore. Bending over to massage you from the side is—"

"I knew you were lying about your shoulder." Her brows darted together with concern, and she reached out for him, but he shook his head.

"I'm good. I should've known better than to throw a ball. I can scale a building and throw a mean left hook, but pitching is off-limits."

His thumbs stroked her leg. He kept the weight of his body off of her, but she worried his knees would start to hurt from kneeling on the bed of the truck. The plaid blanket beneath them wasn't exactly thick.

"You don't need to do this."

"I want to."

"I know it was your dream to play professionally," she said after a minute. "It was a tough break about your arm."

He gave her a too-quick smile. It was one of his fake ones. She remembered seeing it when he'd congratulated her and Nate on becoming a couple.

"Hey, I played for two years. Dream fulfilled." He lifted his shoulders. "Besides, in hindsight, my years as a Marine were more meaningful than baseball. I should've stayed in the service."

"Can you go back?" She wasn't sure if that was how things worked, though.

"I have my business now, but . . ." He stopped massaging her, and she stifled a groan, wishing his hands were back on her, and it had nothing to do with the slight pain in her leg, and everything to do with the wetness at her center.

"But?"

"A couple of my friends have formed an international spec ops group." He shifted and sat alongside her.

She crossed her ankles again and tugged at her skirt, pulling the material as far down as possible. "Spec ops?"

He tipped his chin in the direction of the setting sun that blazed like a ball of fire about to explode above the trees. "Rescue missions, government assists with taking down terrorists, and such."

Her mouth rounded in surprise. "And are you thinking of joining them? What about your business?"

"I miss the chase, the action. Vegas isn't all that exciting anymore. I miss making a difference. Plus, it'd be nice to work with my friends again." He sighed. "I'm probably just talking."

"Well, it sounds dangerous, but you were never very good at staying inside the box. I always liked that about you."

"Really? I thought it was my rugged good looks and six-pack."

She chuckled and elbowed him in the side. "Well, obviously."

A knuckled fist brushed over her cheek, catching her off guard, and she glanced his way, but he settled his hand back in his lap.

"Well, I, um, would love to meet Aiden and Ava when they arrive. I'd like to thank them for their help," she said when a few awkward minutes had passed between them.

"Of course." He looked at her out of the corner of his eye as she twisted to the side to better face him.

His eyes shifted to the hem of her skirt, and he slowly dragged his attention up and back to her face.

Warmth spread through every limb in her body. "What are you thinking about?" she asked, noting his shoulders tense.

"Just going through the facts about the investigation in my head."

Sure. At the moment, the case was the last thing on her mind, and she'd bet his, too. "And?"

"Well, uh, can you think of any reason why the police would be questioning that patient of yours? What was his name again?"

The heat quickly dispersed from her body. "His name is Jeremy, and I assume the sheriff asked to speak to him because of his record."

"His record? We talking batting averages or time served?"

"I guess I can tell you this since it's public knowledge. He got out of prison not too long ago."

"What was he in for?"

"Attempted murder. He stabbed some guy in the chest and threatened to slit his . . ."

Ben straightened, his shoulder blades pinching back.

"Shit. You think . . .?" Riley knew Jeremy was dangerous; she could feel it in her bones, but why would he target Ralph and Lydia? Had she missed something during their sessions?

"I'll have Ava look into him, but for now, you need to keep your distance." Ben stood and jumped out of the truck bed.

"I have an appointment with him in the morning. I can't miss it. It'd be unethical for me to bail on my responsibilities, especially if he's in crisis."

"No," he said as she slipped back on her heels. "A *hell no*, just so we're clear." He helped her out of the truck. "You're not going to be alone with that son of a bitch."

"Innocent until proven guilty." But what if Ben was right? She saw the way Jeremy looked earlier. He was coming undone at the seams. What if he snapped and killed her in her office tomorrow? "I have a panic button beneath my desk. If I get scared, I could press it," she added.

"And why do you have that?"

"A patient tried to strangle me, and so I had it installed."

He cursed, let go of her, and spun away. "Jesus, Ri."

"What?" She circled him.

"I'm thinking maybe we ought to also take a look at your patient files." His forehead tightened, his expression wry. "You think any of your clients are capable of murder?"

Her thoughts raced as patient faces appeared in her mind. "I-I don't know. But I doubt any of them know Ralph. Lydia—no idea, but not Ralph."

"The murders could be random. It's possible." He closed the space between them and palmed her face.

She sighed in frustration. "I can't talk about patients with you, or the police for that matter. Well, not without a warrant. I'd be violating the oath I took as a doctor."

"And what if I broke into your office without your knowledge? Or had someone hack your files? You'd be in the clear."

"Ben!" She pushed his hand away from her face and stabbed a finger at his hard chest. "You could go to jail. Plus, these are my patients. I'm not comfortable with that." She stood firm. "The answer is *no*."

"Sweetheart, there's no one that will be taking me down. I'll do whatever I have to do to clear your name and keep you safe—with or without your permission. I owe you that much."

"You don't owe me anything." *Maybe an explanation, but . . .*

He stepped so close, it forced her hand to flatten against his chest, and she tipped her chin to find his eyes. His heart pounded beneath her palm, matching hers.

"I won't let you access my files, but I'll give you the names of anyone I think might be capable of murder."

His jaw tightened. "Fine. Get me the names as soon as possible. We'll talk to your ex tonight, and we'll have Ava run a background check on him, too. Probably have her look into Jeremy and Bobby, also."

She nodded, unable to speak. Unable to digest that this was really happening.

A murderer was wreaking havoc on her town.

And Mr. Baseball was back in her life.

CHAPTER THIRTEEN

RILEY WASN'T SURE HOW THIS WAS GOING TO PLAY OUT. DANIEL had agreed to meet her at her apartment at 10 p.m., but she hadn't mentioned Ben would be with her.

Now that she and Ben were parked outside her building, she was worried they were making the wrong move. "I should do this alone."

"Fuck no," Ben said without hesitation.

"We were together for fifteen months. He wanted to start a family with me. He'd never hurt me. He still loves me."

Ben scratched at the black stubble on his jaw. "I don't care if he promised you the world. I don't trust him."

"And why not?"

He scoffed. "The guy rubs me the wrong way. Trust me when I say something is off about him."

"This is so typical of you. You never approved of any guys who asked me out. Well, not until Nate, at least."

"Because no one had ever been good enough for you. All those guys ever wanted to do was steal your virginity. You think I was about to let that happen? Hell, no." He glowered at her.

"They weren't all bad." She was stalling. She didn't want to go up there and accuse her ex of murder. How does one even start a conversation like that? She knew in her heart he was innocent, but still, they had to talk.

"Oh, come on. Every guy with a pulse wanted to fu—"

"Not everyone, apparently," she murmured, and her words had Ben looking out the front window.

"You made the right decision by saving yourself for Nate." His gravelly voice stirred something deep inside of her, shaking loose the pain that had bound to her insides like a permanent fixture.

Did Ben think she'd slept with Nate? Was it possible that he believed that? That Nate had let him believe that?

No . . .

But she needed to focus right now on her conversation with Daniel. She was already too sidetracked by Ben's presence.

"You can come in, but let me take the lead."

"Of course," he said and had the nerve to wink at her before getting out of the truck. "Is he here yet?"

She pointed to Daniel's black Lexus in the parking lot. "He still hasn't given back my key, so I assume he's already inside."

Ben circled the truck, his chiseled jaw locked tight. She already knew what he was thinking; he didn't have to say it.

"I'll get the key back from him soon. Happy?"

"Not good enough. I'll be installing new locks and a security camera tomorrow."

She crossed her arms. "That won't be necessary. I'm staying at my folks' place, remember?"

"And after . . .?"

She grumbled but there was no point in arguing right now. "Let's just get this over with."

Out in front of her apartment, she twisted the knob and found it unlocked.

Daniel was in the living room, and he stood as soon as he saw her. "I've been worried about you." He started her way, but when Ben came in next, he stopped mid-step. "Logan."

What was it with men calling each other by their last name? Was it meant to intimidate? She'd never understand the male psyche, even with all of her years of education and training.

Ben didn't say anything; instead, he gave a curt nod and shut the door.

"We need to talk," she said.

"That's why I'm here," Daniel shot back.

Riley glanced at Ben. "Uh, would you mind getting us some wine?" She was trying to put some space between the two men, even if for a minute.

"Sure." He went into the kitchen, which was open to the living room, so she wouldn't exactly have privacy, but she figured it'd buy her a little time to try and relax Daniel while Ben searched her drawers for a corkscrew.

"What's he doing here?" Daniel mouthed, his eyes narrowing Ben's way.

She motioned for him to sit back down. "Can we just talk about what the police said to you?"

Daniel's eyes lingered in the direction of the kitchen, focusing on Ben.

"Daniel, please, sit."

"He shouldn't be here. You hate him," he said in a low voice before finally taking a seat, and she joined him on the couch.

"I, um—we have something more important to talk about." She steeled her nerves and rushed out, "Were you sleeping with Lydia?"

His face remained impassive. "The police asked me the same thing, and I'll tell you what I told them: we weren't sleeping together. She was obsessed with me. She had a crush on me that went beyond normal." His voice remained even, despite the insanity of his words. "It had become so bad I recently asked she switch teams. I provided the paperwork to the sheriff to prove it. Hell, she even tried sleeping with half the staff, thinking it'd make me jealous."

Bobby . . .? Her eyes thinned as she processed the news. Was it possible Lydia used Bobby like that? "Why didn't you ever tell me any of this?"

Daniel scooted closer and rested his hand on her thigh. "I didn't want to worry you."

Before she could say anything, Ben appeared before them with two wine glasses. "Drink?" he asked Daniel through barely parted lips, a hard expression on his face.

Daniel lifted his eyes to meet Ben's. "I've actually got to go back to the hospital. I got paged just when I got here." He looked over at Riley. "I'll drop you off at your parents' on my way."

"I don't need a lift." Riley took the glass from Ben instead.

Daniel stood and reached into his pocket for his car keys.

Her lips tucked inward, her mind scrambling to make sense of everything.

Daniel's brows stitched together. "I don't want to leave you here alone. And honestly, I'd rather you stay with me instead of your parents. I can protect you."

She hated that two men were now trying to dictate her safety. "I'll be fine. And Ben is here, so I'm not alone."

Daniel eyed Ben, a sharp look of distrust etched in the faint lines of his face.

"Just go," she said. "We'll talk tomorrow."

Daniel hesitated, but when he finally left, Ben said in a flat voice, "I really don't like him."

"He feels the same about you."

"Sure." He shook his head, swirled the wine around in his glass, and gulped down the last drops. "I also don't trust him."

She frowned. The day had been long and exhausting, and all she wanted to do was to curl up in her own bed.

"What are you thinking?" Tension tugged at each of his words as he spoke, a reflection of the dark look set in his eyes.

With his glass on the table now, he shoved his sleeves to his elbows, and a tattoo on the inside of his forearm drew her eyes. It was the first time she'd seen it since he'd been home, and she couldn't help but wonder if the ink had something to do with her.

He stepped in and wrapped a large hand around her waist. The gesture was too intimate, and yet, it was what her body craved. Any touch by him was like a little drop of heaven misting over her, making her feel whole again. Complete.

"I'm just so confused," she said softly, her back arching and her breasts nearly brushing up against his chest.

"Confused about the killer?"

She should lie and say *yes*, but instead, she wanted to tell him the truth. "I'm confused as to why all I can think about, or want, is you. It doesn't make sense, especially at a time like this, but—"

Ben's mouth captured her words, and he parted her lips with his tongue. She wilted against him and circled her arms around his neck, allowing him to deepen the kiss. To take her away from this place. Away from the tragedy surrounding them.

He moved her backward, and she fell onto the couch. And in a moment, he was on top of her, cradling her face, kissing every inch of the tender skin until finding her lips again. His hand tucked between the two of them, tugging her blouse free from the skirt, and she gasped when his fingers shoved her bra up and he palmed her breast. An intense ache gathered between her thighs.

He trailed kisses along her jawline and to the shell of her ear, sending a quiver down her spine.

When he pushed upright and stared down at her, she gripped his forearms, the veins even more prominent as he held up the weight of his body. Her focus swept to his tattoo, and her stomach tightened.

That tattoo was of three triangles. One was larger and shaded, but they all intersected.

"When did you get that?"

His blue eyes became almost black as a darkness veiled them. "I was in London on leave. Got drunk." He cleared his throat, but his voice was raw when he said, "I, uh, we should probably get going."

He stood and turned his back to her, his hands landing on his hips as he bowed his head.

She rose, unsteady in her heels, and began tucking her blouse back into her skirt, as if that would wash away the sins of their few stolen kisses.

But who was she kidding? It had been so much more than that.

"The triangles, they represent us, right? Me, you, and Nate."

He kept his back to her, but she could hear a deep expelled sigh. "Yeah."

She touched his back, but the man didn't even move. Not even a flinch. It was like he was made of stone.

"I need to take you home." The sudden deep timbre of his voice was bone chilling.

Nate.

He couldn't do this—whatever *this* was—because of Nate.

Hell, she shouldn't kiss him for the same reason. Right?

And she saw the answer in his eyes when he slowly faced her. Remorse cut through him. "The better man died on the cliff. The *wrong* man. Nate loved you so fucking much." His voice broke, hollowing out her heart.

Her emotions throttled her, holding so tight she'd suffocate from the pressure.

He edged closer. "And all I can ever be is a lousy goddamn replacement."

CHAPTER FOURTEEN

Four, maybe five whiskeys later, Ben ordered another double shot of the top shelf brand at the local bar on Main Street.

After dropping Riley off at her parents' house he'd been in the mood to get drunk.

If she hadn't brought up the tattoo, if she hadn't reminded him of Nate . . . they'd probably be tangled beneath the sheets right now.

Had he been stupid for ending things earlier? Or an asshole for ever kissing her?

The back-and-forth tug of war between what was right and wrong made him dizzy.

"Ben Logan, I heard you were back in town, but I didn't believe it."

He blinked a few times, trying to focus on the woman now sidled up next to him.

It was Charlize, the sheriff's daughter. She must have moved back home, which made sense, considering the trouble she'd gotten into in Vegas.

"I'll be sticking around until the killer is caught, whether your pops likes it or not."

She swiveled on her stool, tapping her long nails on the bar counter, rife with scratches from decades of use. "Yeah, I'm sure he hates you being here."

The incessant nail drumming continued until he eased a hand over hers for the briefest of seconds. "What is it you want?" His foul mood leaked into his speech, tension roping around each of his words.

"I want to know why you slammed the door in my face after we hooked up two years ago." An obvious bitterness crowded the lines in her forehead.

"That was a mistake." He'd woken up with her naked in bed and had immediately kicked her out. Maybe he'd been an ass, but he didn't even remember sleeping with her. Too much tequila.

"It doesn't have to be."

"There won't ever be another time. Sorry to disappoint." His hand fell to his lap, and he stole a glance over his shoulder at the few people still hanging out in the place. "You shouldn't be out at night with a damn killer on the loose." Before he could say more, his attention swept to two men arguing in a dimly lit section of the pub.

One man was silhouetted by the soft glow of the lamp hanging above a pool table, but the other man he recognized.

Daniel?

"Eh, excuse me." He tossed enough bills on the counter to cover his drinks and stood. "Been great catching up. Have a friend take you home. It's not safe out there."

Ben strode through the room and in Daniel's direction as a guy shoved Riley's ex up against the wall.

"What's going on?" Ben asked from behind.

The stranger turned, and a pair of dark green eyes met Ben's face. "Bobby Creek?"

Bobby's brows furrowed, and he let go of Daniel. "Logan?" He faced Ben and extended a hand. "Been awhile, man. How are you?"

Daniel stepped up alongside them, which had Bobby tightening his grip on Ben's hand.

"Maybe we should all talk outside?" Ben suggested as he caught the twitch in Daniel's jaw and the bunched hands at his sides.

Ben wasn't sure what the hell was going on between the two guys, but he had to assume it was related to the murder investigation.

Thankfully, Ben didn't need to strong arm anyone to follow him. Once in the parking lot, Ben focused on Daniel. "I thought you were supposed to be at the hospital."

Daniel fingered the collar of his shirt, tugging it from his neck. "I was," he said with a pinched expression. "I followed this son of a bitch here."

"Say more bullshit like that. Please." Bobby pivoted to face Daniel, who now leaned against a red Volvo far too casually, considering that a very jacked former soldier was standing before him. "Give me a reason to knock your teeth in."

"Because hitting me won't put a larger target on your back," Daniel seethed.

"Sure, so you can run back to the sheriff and make up more lies, you cocksucker. I know it was you who told him about me and Lydia. But did you tell him about the two of you? How you treated her?"

Ben quickly moved between the men and extended his arms, trying to prevent blood from spilling. Well, more like trying to keep Bobby out of jail, because he wouldn't mind so much if Daniel had the shit knocked out of him.

"You guys need to back off. Passing blame around won't help us find the killer," Ben said as calmly as possible.

"Unless we're looking at him." Daniel tipped his chin in Bobby's direction, the veins in his neck popping at the base.

"I'd never hurt Lydia. But you . . ." Bobby moved forward, but Ben's hand landed on his chest, holding him back.

"This isn't the time or the place." Ben angled his head toward the bar. "There're people inside, and it'll look pretty shitty for all of us if they catch us out here fighting."

, A bit of iciness dropped from Bobby's gaze. "We'll talk later." He staggered back a few steps in his black boots, reminiscent of his military days. "I didn't kill anyone." He briefly met Ben's eyes and then headed for his pickup truck.

"Jesus." Daniel rubbed a hand down his face. "That prick was the last person to see Lydia alive. He's the guy."

Ben leaned against the side of his SUV and flicked his wrist toward the few bar patrons staring out the windows, motioning for them to look away.

A breeze tapped at his skin, clearing some of the alcohol-infused fogginess from his mind.

"You slept with her, too, though. Didn't you? And what was he talking about? How'd you treat Lydia?"

Daniel came closer, smelling like disinfectant and death. "He's a goddamn liar. The man hates me because he loved Lydia as much as she loved me."

"And who do you love?"

"Riley." He rolled his dark eyes. "I wasn't sleeping with an intern, for Christ's sake. But you . . ." He stabbed a finger in the air and cocked his head. "You broke Riley's heart. And I'd appreciate it if you'd back the fuck off and get out of town."

"What the hell does this have to do with me?" Ben pushed away from his rental. "Who do you think you are?" He fought the urge to capture the man's wrist and drop him to the ground in one quick move. Alcohol or not, his reflexes were lightning-fast.

"I'm the man who has been trying to pick up the pieces. I'm the only person she's formed a real relationship with since Nate died. She's been broken for a long time. And it's your goddamn fault, so I won't have you coming here and destroying her all over again."

"And you're not together anymore."

"That's temporary, and I won't let you screw things up for me."
Daniel's hands tightened at his sides, his knuckles whitening. "I'm
the man she's been fucking, and based on the way you were
looking at her earlier tonight, you're just the man who wished he
was fu—"

Ben's hand connected with his jaw before he realized
he'd swung.

Daniel stumbled back, and Ben closed the short gap between
them and fisted the fabric of his shirt. He whirled his hand back
and kept his knuckles hovering before the guy's face.

Daniel jutted out his chin as if daring Ben to punch again.

Anger blurred Ben's eyesight, and his arms started to shake. He
wanted to kill the bastard. He wanted to ram his fist so far down
his throat he'd cough blood.

"When you're gone, I'll be back in her bed, and you'll be back
in her memories where you belong."

Ben blinked a few times, trying to find his control. But all of
the years he'd spent missing Riley suffocated any sense of
reasoning.

"Do it. Hit me. Let her feel bad for me and hate you even
more," Daniel whisper-yelled.

"I want her to be happy," Ben said in an even tone. "That's all
I've ever wanted." He slowly released his shirt and lowered his
hand to his side. "But it won't be with you."

Daniel rubbed his jaw. "You're wrong about that."

CHAPTER FIFTEEN

"You look like shit." Riley folded her arms and eyed him. If she was angry at him for the way he ended things last night, she didn't show it. Her gaze was soft and relaxed.

He pressed a hand inside the doorframe, his Ray-Bans lowered, meeting Riley's eyes. "Thanks," he grumbled.

"Have too much to drink last night?" She lifted a brow.

Something like that. "I want to be at your office for your appointment."

"My admin will be there with me. I won't be alone." Her almond-shaped eyes tightened.

"And last I saw, she didn't resemble a former UFC fighter, or appear to be packing heat. So, I think I'll be coming along."

"And what about your friends at the airport?"

Ben shifted his focus to her bottomless brown eyes. He could get lost staring at her. He used to lose focus whenever they did homework together.

She'd be reading from a textbook or discussing how to solve chemical equations, and his mind would wander—he'd explore her heart-shaped face, from the freckles that dusted over her nose and beneath her eyes, to the slight dimple in her right cheek that appeared when she smiled.

He'd always imagined what it'd be like to press his mouth to the soft crook of her neck and breathe in her intoxicating smell.

Whenever she'd caught him losing focus, she'd make a funny fish face at him, which had had him laughing his ass off.

"I had to adjust my plans when I learned you'd be alone with a potential serial killer." He pressed his sunglasses back in place. "My parents are picking Ava and Aiden up as we speak."

She glanced over her shoulder at the sudden sound of clicking heels. "Let's go before my mom comes."

Once in the car, he started up the engine, backed out of the driveway and began the short trip to her office.

He lazily draped his arm over the steering wheel as he drove. "I had a run-in with both Bobby and Daniel last night. They were arguing, and I stepped in." He lowered the country tunes in the car, a song by Florida George Line playing on the radio.

"Jesus. Did anyone get hurt?"

He arched his shoulders back, a tight band of pressure traveling up his spine and into his neck. Thinking about that asshole sleeping with Riley had him wanting to knock Daniel in the face again.

"Maybe a little. I wouldn't worry about that, though."

"And what should I be worried about?"

"I have a bad feeling about your ex." He could understand Daniel murdering Lydia to prevent Riley from finding out about an affair—crazier shit had happened. But Ralph . . .? "Why'd you say you and Daniel broke up again?"

She pushed back into the leather seat and cast her attention out the side window. "Are we really talking about him and not Bobby, right now? Or even Jeremy for that matter?"

"Yes," he said quickly.

Her shoulders sloped down. "Daniel gave me an ultimatum: move to Cleveland with him or it was over. I'm Ralph's only family, and so I can't . . . I mean, I *couldn't* leave him."

"Ralph was why you said *no*? Did you tell Daniel that?"

Was it possible? Was Daniel sick enough to take out any obstacles that would prevent him from being with Riley?

"I might have mentioned that, but honestly, I just wasn't ready to take our relationship to the next level regardless."

"And when you said *no* to moving, what happened?"

"He apologized for the demand and turned down the job offer he'd received . . . but it was too late for me. I knew we weren't destined to be together, and so I insisted we go our separate ways."

"How has he acted since the breakup?"

"I still don't understand what you're getting at."

He parked in front of her little brick office building. A row of southern magnolia trees lined the property, capturing the spirit of the region. The trees were taller than her office, and the dry limbs with rust-colored undersides stretched out, begging for spring, so the flowers could blossom.

Ben had a vivid memory of Riley sitting beneath a magnolia at Swayze Park when she was sixteen. He'd found her resting against the tree trunk, with her knees pressed to her chest. She'd been reading one of her mom's romance novels. Her cheeks had bloomed red when he'd snatched it from her and read a few of the more colorful lines.

When death had tried to steal him in the war, he used to drag up memories like that; he'd hang on to them to stay sane. Riley had kept him alive during those eight years. He only wished he'd had the nerve to reach out to her when he'd left the military to become a ballplayer.

Then again, he'd had his reasons, hadn't he?

"Ben?" She reached over and removed his sunglasses.

This wasn't going to work, was it? He could try and push her away all he wanted, but his walls were paper thin around her.

How had he had such resolve to hold back as a teenager? How was it that in his thirties he'd become less powerful in fighting his feelings?

143

Fourteen years should have deteriorated his desire for her, not increased it.

"I think Daniel has a motive. If he saw Ralph as hindering the progression of your relationship, maybe he killed him."

She clutched his Ray-Bans in her lap now, chewing on her lip in thought.

"Maybe he really was having sex with Lydia, even while you were together. Bobby said Daniel didn't treat her well."

"And you believe everything he says?" She sighed. "Band of brothers, huh?"

"Ri, this isn't about me."

"You sure about that?" She handed Ben his glasses back, and he tightened them in his hand, nearly breaking them.

"Just think about it, okay? What if Lydia threatened to tell you about the affair, and so he decided to kill her, too?"

"This is a stretch. He's the first man to get me to open up since . . ."

Daniel's words from last night flew back into his mind, and his skin crawled at the thought of him ever going near Riley again.

His hand settled on her thigh atop her red dress slacks. "We'll figure this out. I'll protect you."

"Yeah?" She leveled him with her gaze. "And who will protect me from you?"

* * *

"AND YOU CALLED HIS CELL AND HOUSE?"

Riley pressed her palms to her admin's desk. It was quarter past nine, and Jeremy was still a no-show.

"His cell is going to voicemail, and there's no answer on the house line," Lonnie said and shrugged.

Riley slowly turned around and faced Ben. "What do you think this means? Jeremy never misses an appointment."

"Maybe he got spooked after the police questioned him yesterday."

"We should check his house. Some of my patients canceled, so I'm free until lunch." She turned her back to him once again. "Transfer my calls to my cell. And, Lonnie, be safe. Lock the front door, okay?"

Lonnie nodded. She was probably in her mid-fifties, and she seemed vaguely familiar to him, even before he'd met her yesterday. Maybe she'd been a mother to someone he'd gone to school with. The way she was eyeing him made him think she didn't like him, though. It was the general vibe he'd been getting from most people in town since he'd returned.

"You'll be staying with your parents while I go to his place," he said once they were outside.

"No way. He's my patient." She halted outside the door and crossed her arms.

"And I don't know this guy. I'm not willing to put you in danger."

"It's not up to you. I'll go with or without you." She held firm, and his stomach twisted at the idea of taking Riley along with him to interrogate someone. Because that's what this would be—an interrogation. And aside from him hating the idea of Riley being caught in the crossfires if anything went south, he also knew himself.

He knew what he was like when questioning a suspect. He could go dark. He slipped into a different persona, and it'd probably scare the hell out of her. He'd learned to do it as a Marine, and he'd kept his training with him while running his security firm.

"Then we let my friends look into him first. I need to have my bases covered. I need to know what kind of situation I'm walking into." *And I need a sidearm.*

"And what if we don't have time to wait?" She edged closer to him.

"You're not going to back down, are you?" He lifted a brow, pissed at her stubbornness, but also slightly turned on by her determination and confidence.

She shook her head, and he tipped his chin skyward. "Fine. But give me the details about him on the way, and if I sense trouble— we're out of there, got it?"

"Deal."

They strapped into his SUV a minute later, and she rubbed her hands up and down her thighs as if a sudden nervousness had set in.

Was he making a mistake? Was he letting his feelings for her cloud his judgment?

"Jeremy lives with his grandfather, Franklin Stanton."

Shit . . . "Are you kidding?" This wasn't what he needed right now. *Please tell me Beth is—*

"Pretty sure you also dated his granddaughter, Beth," she cut off his thoughts. "Took her virginity, right?"

He scrubbed a palm over his prickly beard. Had Nate told her that? He'd never mentioned his sex life to Riley back then, and frankly, he'd gone out with a lot of girls to try and erase thoughts of Riley from his mind.

It had never worked, though.

And after all these years, it looked like it still hadn't worked.

"Um." He coughed into a closed fist. "I don't remember her having a brother." He decided to ignore the whole virginity subject.

He didn't need Riley to give him the address anymore, either, so he pulled out of the parking lot.

Everyone knew where Franklin Stanton lived. It was the only house in town that resembled a castle.

"Beth and Jeremy are cousins," she answered.

"He didn't grow up here, right? I don't remember him."

"Moved here a couple of years ago and got into trouble right after."

"Who was it that he tried to kill?"

"I can't remember who. I only remember why, since we have to talk about it in our sessions."

"And is that something you're not allowed to discuss because he's your patient?" He raised a brow. "I need to know what we're walking into—remember?" He slowed the car a little, prepared to change directions if needed.

"No, it's public knowledge from the trial. Some guy harassed his girlfriend at the bar, and he lost his mind."

"Anger issues, huh?" He glanced at her out of the corner of his eye. "What else do I need to know?"

"I really can't say—I'd get in trouble."

"This is me we're talking about. I need to know, or I stop driving."

"He's, uh, got a drug problem. Well, I think so, at least. He hasn't admitted it, but he's got all of the signs."

Great. "So we could be showing up to this guy's house while he's high and holding a gun." He pulled off to the side of the road and faced her. "I can't do this. I can't bring you with me."

She looked out the passenger window, her body tense. "Whoever killed Ralph and Lydia—they did it in private and with a knife. If it's Jeremy"—she faced him—"he won't try and kill me at his own house and with you there." Her shoulders lifted slightly as her gaze skated down his chest. "Besides, I'm pretty sure you can take him if need be."

If it were anyone else, he'd have said *no* and turned around.

"Damn it," he said through gritted teeth and pulled back out onto the road.

"Beth lives with Jeremy, by the way," she noted as they rolled up to a large black gate a few minutes later.

He cursed under his breath at the thought of seeing Beth.

Riley had the story wrong about her. He hadn't taken her virginity. No, she had taken his. And he had regretted it right after.

He'd even thrown up. A sick feeling of guilt had twisted his insides as if he'd betrayed the one woman he'd actually cared about.

The window scrolled down, and he reached out to press the intercom. "Ben Logan here to see Jeremy Stanton."

CHAPTER SIXTEEN

"HE LEFT TOWN YESTERDAY AFTERNOON." BETH DROPPED BACK onto the massive leather sectional in the entertainment room. "He was worried the police were going to try and pin the murders on him."

"Yeah, pretty sure skipping out on your parole officer won't buy you any love, either," Ben responded.

Riley's lips twitched as she eyed Beth. She'd never liked her back in high school, and watching her wet her lips and pull on the strands of her bleached-blonde locks as she gaped at Ben had Riley hating her even more.

When Nate had casually mentioned that Ben had slept with Beth, she'd become so sick that she'd had to leave school. She'd told her mom she had a stomachache and spent the next two days in her bedroom, avoiding both Ben's and Nate's calls. It wasn't until Ben had shown up at her house, demanding to see that she was still alive, that she had come out of her room.

Ben had looked different to her, too—like somehow having sex had turned him from a boy to a man.

It had hurt her. Hell, it had nearly killed her.

And every time Nate had mentioned Ben's latest sleeping

partner, she'd had to act like the news didn't poke holes in her heart or deflate her lungs of oxygen.

"Does the sheriff know Jeremy left town?" Ben stood firm with crossed arms, his eyes constantly cutting left and right—scoping out the room as if on a battlefield.

It made her feel safe, though.

"Of course not," Beth sputtered and slipped her fingers beneath the tiny strap of her tank top, as if trying to be a tease. It was obvious she wasn't wearing a bra. Her surgically enhanced breasts were jutting through the material as if ready to launch into space.

"Where'd he go?" Riley sat next to Beth.

Beth puckered her lips. "Jesus, I don't know. We barely talk. The guy is crazy. He keeps to his wing of the house, and I stick to mine. He's only good when he's high."

Before Ben said anything, he reached into his jeans pocket. "Give me a sec." He pressed the phone to his ear. He must have had it on vibrate since she hadn't heard it ring.

Ben strode across the room and stood in the interior of the doorway to the room, keeping his eyes on her the entire time.

"So, you guys ever screw?" Beth whispered.

Riley coughed. "What?"

"Oh, come on. No one in school ever understood how the three of you were all just friends. We had bets on who you'd fuck first." She sighed. "No one saw the whole *you and Nate* thing coming. Everyone's money was on you and Ben."

Riley's eyes widened, and her stomach dropped in surprise. Was this woman serious? "I . . . I don't understand." She made eye contact with Ben, wondering if he could hear the conversation.

"Oh, come on. Nate was a good-looking guy, but Ben is in his own league." She rolled her tongue over her teeth. "He dating anyone now? I'd love to see if he got better with age." Her mouth teased into a broad grin. "I'm betting he did."

Riley's stomach spasmed as she focused back on the Playmate. "I, uh—"

"We have to go," Ben cut her off, suddenly on approach.

"What is it?" she asked, noting the look of worry in his eyes.

"There's been another murder." A deep, weighted sigh followed.

Riley stood, but couldn't get herself to speak—to ask who died.

"Our town is trending on Twitter." He held his phone out so she could see. "The murderer has been dubbed the *doctor killer*. Plus, someone leaked to the press that the weapon used was a surgeon's scalpel."

A doctor killing doctors? Or a doctor setting up a doctor?

Lydia had been a doctor and Ralph . . . well, he had a Ph.D., which had technically made him a doctor.

Please don't say Mandy died. Fear flowed down her spine, making her limbs numb. She clutched her stomach. "Who was killed?"

His gaze flicked over to Beth. "Can we have a minute?"

"Uh, sure." Her face grew serious for the first time since they'd seen her, and she finally left the room.

Riley's stomach rolled, and her throat started to close up. "Which doctor?"

"Patrick Phelps. You know him?"

Her mouth opened, but she couldn't speak.

"Riley?" He gripped her shoulders. "What is it?"

Her eyes fell shut as she whispered, "My one-night stand."

"Your what?"

An emptiness filled the pit of her stomach. "My mistake from a few weeks ago."

* * *

AIDEN WAS TALL, MUSCULAR, AND VERY ATTRACTIVE. AND ON A normal day, she'd probably swoon at his Irish brogue.

But today wasn't a normal day.

Today, she'd learned that someone else connected to her had died.

Ava and Aiden, whom Riley had instantly liked, had been working for the past three hours on the case. She and Ben had been with them in their hotel room for most of that time, and her nerves were unraveling by the minute. She was thankful to have them, but it was all a bit surreal.

Riley was used to being the problem-solver. Well, for the last five years that she'd been in practice, at least.

She had canceled her afternoon appointments and sent Lonnie home for her own safety. But how long could she stay hidden in this small room?

"He was in Charlotte last night at the time of death." Ava shifted the computer around and pointed to the screen. "Jeremy checked into a hotel around eleven p.m., and I have visual confirmation of him in the lobby. He's not our guy."

"So Jeremy's crazy, but not our killer," Ben said.

"Not unless he's got a body double," Ava replied.

Her stomach wrenched. "I don't have an alibi. My parents were asleep, and I could have easily snuck out without notice."

No one said anything, and it had her wondering what everyone was thinking. Did anyone in the room actually think she was guilty?

"Daniel was at the bar last night with Bobby, and Ben can confirm that," Riley said while eyeing Ben as he made coffee.

"The time of death is a ballpark number. They can't narrow it down to the exact minute, which means it's possible Daniel or Bobby could have done it." Aiden's words should have comforted her, but they didn't. "Or it's someone else. We just don't know."

"Before we can rule out either of those guys we need to find out where they were prior to the murder," Ben said.

"It's also clear the killer knew the victims. No sign of forced entry or struggle. The victims probably felt comfortable with the murderer," Ava noted.

Ben faced the room holding a steaming cup of coffee. He offered it to Riley, but she declined. She didn't need anything else to make her jittery. "You still think it was Daniel?" she asked.

"Well, did your ex know that you slept with Patrick?" Ava glanced at her fiancé for a brief moment before her attention skirted back to Riley.

"I certainly didn't tell him, but people talk in this town. I was drunk when I left with him, and plenty of people probably saw me stumble out of the bar and get into his car." She pressed the heel of her palm to her forehead, regretful of her first ever one-night stand. "Not my finest moment in life."

Ben lowered the rim of the cup from his mouth and went over to the window. He shifted the drapes back and stole a quick glimpse outside.

"What we know right now is that three people who had a personal connection to you are dead." Ava began tapping at her keys again. "Someone is either setting you up, or you're—"

"The final target," Riley finished, feeling like her lungs were collapsing. "I don't understand who would want me dead."

"I think the best place to start is with a list of the patients who've threatened you before," Ben said. "We have to exhaust all possible leads."

"And if the killer is actually trying to set me up . . . why choose me? It doesn't make any damn sense." There was a dull pain working its way behind her eyes.

Aiden's brows drew together. "Well, it's always possible the killer murdered other people to cast suspicion away from himself. By having multiple deaths, it hides the true victim and confuses the motives. You could have been a convenient target for him."

"Convenient," Riley hissed and clutched her stomach.

"If that's the case, the killer gave himself a backup plan, though," Aiden said. "Daniel looks guilty, too, especially if he was jealous of your, uh, date with Patrick."

"I don't know if that makes me feel better or worse," Riley said in a daze.

"But Daniel had an alibi for Lydia's murder. He was at the hospital at the time of her death," Ava said. "As long as he checks out for one of the deaths, the police will probably shift their focus to suspects who don't have a solid alibi."

"Didn't you say a time of death is an estimate? It's possible Daniel snuck out of the hospital, walked to Lydia's, and came back before anyone noticed," Ben noted.

Ava nodded. "True. We also still have Bobby to consider; although, we need to look into any connections he may have had with Ralph and Patrick."

"But right now, I'm the only one without an alibi for each murder," Riley whispered, growing faint.

Ben set his coffee on the nightstand and stood before Riley. He wrapped a hand around her forearm and held her eyes.

Riley's lips pursed in thought, but before she could say anything, Ava cursed. "Looks like the sheriff is on his way to your apartment."

"Shit. I forgot I gave him permission. My face is going to end up on the news. I'll be named *the doctor killer*, won't I?" Riley muttered under her breath, remembering she'd powered off her phone when they'd arrived at the hotel, per Ben's request. He'd been concerned the sheriff would call her in for questioning again, and he didn't want her leaving until they could talk through everything.

From what she saw on TV earlier, her little town had made it to national news, and the media was already circling the hospital and precinct like vultures.

And she'd be in the spotlight next.

"I can't do this." She shirked her arm free of Ben's grasp and darted for the door.

There weren't any suites at the hotel, and staying in such a tight space with three other people had her gulping for air.

Once outside, she stood beneath the faded red overhang and peered down the walkway, checking for any approaching guests. Thankful she was alone, she clasped the black railing and sucked in such a deep breath she became lightheaded.

"Ri."

"This is too much." Her voice collapsed from weakness.

"I know, but we need to stay strong. We have to figure this out together."

That's what she had wanted when Nate had died—for them to hold each other up, to get through the toughest of times together.

"I shouldn't have blamed you for Nate's death," she rushed out without thinking. But maybe she had to get this off her chest.

Riley spun around to face him, and Ben edged back a step.

"Let's not do this now. We need to focus." His blue irises deepened in color, taking on some of the darkness from the clouds that hung low in the sky, threatening a downpour.

"We need to. I'm either going to end up behind bars or become the next victim."

Ben lurched toward her and cupped her face with his rough palms. "Don't say that. Don't even think that."

She tipped her chin to meet his eyes again. "No one knows when it's their time to go. And I don't know how long I'll have you here, so let me speak." She sniffled. "Please."

"Riley," he whispered. "I can't do this now."

She seized hold of his wrists and tugged at them, but he wouldn't let go. He was too strong . . . and yet, a sheen coated his eyes as if, he too, might break down. "I'll go back into that room, and I'll try to be objective about all of this. But first I need this conversation to happen."

He closed his eyes. "There's nothing you need to say to me. But I—"

"Did you read my emails?" She needed to know. "Did you at least read my words when I asked you to forgive me?"

He released his hold on her and pinched the bridge of his nose for a quick moment. "I only read them once they stopped coming."

"I don't understand."

He glanced over his shoulder as if checking to make sure they were alone. "I'd stare at the subject line when your messages came in. I'd try and get myself to click them open, but I never could. A few months after the emails stopped coming—a few months after I'd taken my first bullet . . . I read them. I read them all."

"*First* bullet?" Her body tensed, and so she locked her hands at her sides, her fingertips biting into her palms as she tried to handle the conversation that she had so desperately wanted. "Why didn't you write me back?"

"I did. I wrote probably a hundred emails."

Her lips parted, and her heart shriveled in her chest.

He shook his head lightly. "I never sent them."

"What?" She took shallow breaths, and her fingernails dug even deeper into her palms.

"I was afraid that, if I reached out to you, I'd only end up hurting you more."

"Hurt me how?" Her mind was all blank spaces. She couldn't think. She couldn't comprehend what he was trying to say.

"Men were dying all around me. I knew what Nate's death had done to you, and I was worried that if we became close again—and I died—that it would . . ." He dropped his words in the air, leaving them for her to absorb.

"That wasn't fair for you to make a decision about my life like that." She turned away, too distraught to look at him. "I was upset when you left, but I had thought it was, in part, my fault. I yelled at you for kissing me the night before he died, as if that had caused his death. And then I blamed you for allowing him to free climb. I . . . I should never have done that, and I hated myself for it. I hated myself for so long. But when you never answered me . . . I started hating you."

Ben stood alongside her and gripped the railing. She focused on his scarred hand and thought about his wounds—about what he'd gone through over the years while she'd been busy being so damn angry at him.

"That wasn't the only reason I didn't respond. It wasn't the reason why I never sought you out when I came home and started playing ball . . ." He let his voice trail off as if the words were too heavy to say.

She'd played this moment out in her head so many times over the years, but she'd never anticipated it'd go down like this. She'd never thought that when they saw each other again they'd kiss and that she'd be so desperate to forgive him. Hell, forgive herself.

"Nate wasn't a better man, by the way. You were both good men. Amazing men," she said softly, hoping to calm her rapidly beating heart. "I was lucky enough to have two phenomenal men care about me, but—"

"Guys. We need to talk." Aiden's words stole her own, and a sharp throb pulsed inside her chest.

Ben reached for her elbow. "Come on." He guided her back into the room as if he were afraid she wouldn't come on her own— and he'd never leave her alone outside.

"What is it?" Ben circled the desk and stood behind Ava's computer.

Ava swiveled in her chair to find Ben's eyes. "I created a code this morning that would enable me to virtually check the browsing history on Jeremy's, Bobby's, and Daniel's computers. I wanted to see if there was any suspicious activity. My program would flag anything out of the norm, and I'd get an alert."

Riley sat on the bed and tried to focus, but her mind continued to reel from her conversation with Ben.

Too many questions littered her mind, mostly focusing on what would have happened if Ben had sent his messages. Where would they be now?

"And you found something?" Ben rested a hand on the back of Ava's chair as he narrowed his eyes in the direction of the computer screen.

"Bobby was researching different drugs that could knock someone unconscious but go unnoticed on a blood test. He deleted his browser history and the cookies on his computer, but nothing is ever truly gone from cyberspace," Ava said.

"You think it's him, then?" Riley stood and looked at Ben, and she noticed a tremble of disappointment lurk in his eyes. He didn't want it to be Bobby. "You think the police know about this?"

"The FBI will probably be called in soon, especially since the town is turning into a media circus. So, if they don't already have someone with the adequate computer skills needed, they will soon," Ava said.

"FBI?" Riley wasn't sure if she felt more hopeful or intimidated by the three letters.

"Do we still have any FBI pals left? Or did we burn all our bridges?" Ben asked Aiden, his voice throatier than normal.

Aiden gave him a quick shake of the head. "With Jake gone, I'd say we shouldn't risk contacting anyone in the agency."

"Jake?" Riley sorted through the names Ben had mentioned to her, but she couldn't remember if that name had been one.

"Former Fed. He was in the Marines with us," Ben answered before looking back to Aiden.

"We can't give them what we have, or we could end up in trouble for interfering with the investigation." Aiden tucked his hands into his back pockets.

"And the last thing you need is to draw any more government attention," Ben said brusquely.

Riley had no clue what he was talking about. She was in the dark, and she hated it.

Aiden winked at her. "Long story. No worries, love. We've got your back. A friend of Ben's is a friend of mine."

"So what do we do now?" she asked.

"We clear your name and keep you safe." Aiden glanced at Ben and said, "And then we find the arsehole who killed these people and put him in the ground."

CHAPTER SEVENTEEN

RILEY ENDED HER CALL WITH MANDY AND BREATHED A SIGH OF relief.

She didn't like the idea of Mandy living alone with the "doctor killer" on the loose, especially if it were Bobby. She'd finally managed to convince her to stay with someone else, and preferably with a strong male, or a guy with a sidearm tucked beneath his bed.

Fortunately, Mandy had someone in mind, and she'd promised to room with him for the time being.

Now that she could relax without that worry on her mind, she fell back onto Ben's bed and closed her eyes. She was alone in Ben's hotel room, which was a few doors down from where Aiden and Ava continued to work.

"I think I'm in the wrong profession."

"What do you mean?" Ben turned on the coffee machine, clearly in need of the liquid fuel to keep him going. That, or he was still nursing his hangover from last night. She had a sneaking suspicion she had something to do with why he got drunk.

"This whole mess has proven I'm incapable of rational thought. I'm a hypocrite to offer my patients advice and provide therapy when I can't keep myself from falling apart."

"Don't most psychiatrists actually become shrinks because they need therapy themselves?"

She sat up and glared at him. "That's such a stereotype." But he was right. Well, at least about her.

"We should probably turn your phone on soon. I'm assuming if the sheriff doesn't hear from you, he'll be banging on my door looking for you." He sipped his black coffee and stood before the bed. "That, or your mom will show up."

"Not sure which would be worse."

His attention flicked to the floor, and his brows knitted. "Did you ever get your key back from Daniel last night?"

"Uh, no. You said you were going to change the locks, and so . . ."

No, she couldn't believe it. There was no way Daniel could be the killer. She couldn't possibly have been sleeping with a killer without ever noticing the signs—could she? She was trained to read people.

Besides, Bobby was the one who had the odd browsing history, not Daniel. Of course, Daniel would never need to research which drugs would go unnoticed in the bloodstream.

"Maybe we need to get to your place." He stood and held his palm out to her as if worried her knees would buckle. "Daniel could've planted evidence."

"But the police are already there. It's too late. Plus, I know Daniel has nothing to do with this."

"And I'm not taking any chances when it comes to your life."

She finally took his hand, and the warmth of his touch sent a soothing feeling down her spine.

They stopped by Aiden's room to let them know where they were headed, and then they went to the parking lot. Most of the media vans had left, and he was pretty sure where they'd gone.

"A dozen messages," she said after turning on her cell.

"Don't even bother listening to them. We'll talk to the detective and sheriff when we get to your place."

"And what if they slap cuffs on me?" she asked, her heart pounding so loud it echoed in her ears.

"I won't let that happen," he said through clenched teeth, and then he pulled out of the parking lot.

She wanted to believe him; she truly did. But there was a psychopath out there, and it looked like she was somehow wrapped up in the middle of a murdering spree.

Ben was strong, but was he powerful enough to protect her from the eye of the storm?

* * *

THE APARTMENT COMPLEX LOOKED LIKE AN ACTIVE CRIME SCENE. There were police vehicles and a half a dozen white media vans. How'd the press find out so quickly that her place was being searched?

Then again . . . small town. If even one squad car had been outside the building, it would have drawn attention.

"I'd suggest you stay in the car, but I don't want you out of my sight." Ben unbuckled and reached for her hand. "If the reporters already know your name or anything about you, they're going to come at you swinging hard. It could get rough."

"I can handle it," she lied, knowing she was about to break as if she were a weak dam.

"I have your back." He tipped up her chin, commanding her eyes to meet his.

"Okay," she softly said. "Thank you."

It took her a few minutes, but she forced herself out of the SUV. Ben looped his arm around hers in a protective manner, and they started in the direction of the pack of reporters.

Ben was putting a target on his own head right now, just by being with her. By holding on to her arm like this, it would surely give off the vibe that she was important to him. And she wasn't sure what that would mean to the killer, whoever the hell that might be.

She stopped when they reached the heels of the media frenzy. "You sure you want to do this with me?"

He faced her and brushed his knuckles over her cheek. "I've never been more certain about anything in my life." He looked stoic at that moment. "What I mean is that I should have been by your side a long time ago. Regardless of my fears of what might happen between us in the future, I promise it won't stop me from helping you right now."

She digested the meaning of his words and forced a nod. "Let's do this."

Her legs shook like they had the one time she'd actually tried to climb with Ben and Nate. Her heart had thrashed wildly in her chest, and her calf muscles had trembled when she'd stood on the little ledge on the cliff in the mountains. She'd known Ben wouldn't let her fall, but her fear of heights had killed her momentum, and she couldn't ever make it further up the mountain that day. Or any day after that.

And that's how she was feeling right now. She trusted Ben, even if her heart was scared to. But she wasn't sure if she could really push forward and do this. Could she face an inquisition?

And when a reporter slung the very first question at her, it had her rocking back on her heels and snapping her eyes closed.

"Dr. Carpenter, are you a suspect or a potential victim?" someone shouted.

But when the second one came, it stilled her heart: "Did you really push your boyfriend, Ralph Chandler's son, off the mountain? Is it true?"

"Back off," Ben gritted out, and the rough texture of his voice had her eyes opening.

"Are you Ben Logan? The friend to Nate Chandler? The other benefactor in Ralph Chandler's will? Did you two push Nate off that mountain together? Are you also a suspect, Mr.

Logan?" the third reporter hollered, shoving a microphone in Ben's face.

He remained impassive as long as they were attacking him. But anytime the questions were directed toward Riley, his face darkened and the vein in his neck visibly throbbed.

He continued to urge Riley through the group, and they made their way to the first police officer standing near the staircase. "This is Riley's place," he informed the man.

The officer's brows darted together, but he radioed the sheriff.

"Send them up," the sheriff responded.

Ben nodded at the officer and guided her up the stairs. "You'll be okay." He pressed a hand to the small of her back as they walked to her apartment.

"Been trying to get a hold of you all morning." The sheriff tipped up his cowboy hat and crossed his arms, blocking her doorway.

"I had my phone off. I came as soon as I turned it on." She stole a quick look behind him, catching sight of two uniformed officers rummaging through her things.

"Do you have a warrant? If not, we'll kindly ask you to leave. Riley has changed her mind about the search," Ben said.

The sheriff tucked his hand inside his jacket and snatched a folded piece of paper. "Thought you might say that."

Ben opened the letter, looked it over, and handed it back. "That was fast. Almost like you've already made up your mind about the case."

"Well, since Riley here was sleeping with Patrick, it does raise some concerns, wouldn't you say?"

She stepped closer to the sheriff, and Ben wrapped a hand over her shoulder. "You have some nerve," she said.

"Where are you getting your facts? This all sounds fairly speculative to me." Ben rubbed the side of her arm, an attempt to calm her, and the gesture didn't go unnoticed by the sheriff. His eyes rested on Ben's hand for a moment.

"Small town, son. Maybe if you had stuck around, you would remember a thing or two."

Ben stood alongside Riley now. "And if I hadn't been in Vegas, who would have saved your daughter from getting killed by the loan shark she took too much money from?"

"Watch your tongue." The sheriff's eyes darkened.

"And you should consider doing the same."

Riley shifted her attention back and forth between the two men as they stared at each other in an apparent blinking contest. She knew Ben, though. He'd win. She could feel it in her bones.

Maybe she'd be okay because she had him on her side now.

"You should know that Daniel Edwards also has a key to Riley's place, and he was here last night without her presence." Ben backed up a step, allowing the sheriff to process the information. "Maybe you ought to think about motives for a minute and ask yourself why the hell an upstanding citizen like Riley would snap and murder people."

"Everyone is an upstanding citizen . . . until they're not," the sheriff said dryly.

The homicide detective who had questioned her the other day was approaching. "We're good to go," he said and caught Riley's eyes. "We'll need to ask you a few questions about Patrick Phelps. We can escort you to the station, or you can meet us there."

They weren't arresting her. Not now, at least. Surely, if they'd found something at her place, they'd cuff her.

Relief washed over her as she digested the news.

Daniel hadn't tried to frame her for murder.

"I'll bring her," Ben said when Riley didn't speak.

After they fought their way back through the crowd, which also included her neighbors glaring at her as if she were a killer—Ben grasped the steering wheel tightly without starting the engine.

"Something is bothering me about all of this."

She almost smiled. "Well, I would hope so."

He dropped his head back, staring up at the ceiling. "I just think we're missing something, and I can't stand that feeling."

"Oh."

"I was interrogating the right-hand man of one of the leaders of an al Qaeda terrorist cell about nine years ago. It was supposed to be an easy in-and-out mission. Capture and question, so we could go after the main guy . . ." His voice trailed off as his eyes closed.

She wasn't sure where he was going with this, but she remained quiet, waiting for him to continue. It was hard for her to imagine Ben with a gun in hand, taking down terrorists. Kiteboarding, skydiving, and mountain biking—yes. But killing bad guys, not so much. Of course, his skills would come in handy in her current situation.

"Anyway, this guy was dirty. Like, really fucking dirty. He'd trade secrets to anyone if it meant further lining his pockets. But in our case, when we questioned him, something had felt off. He gave us information too easily, even for such a rat bastard."

"What happened?"

He slowly rolled his head to the side and opened his eyes. He reached beneath his shirt for the chain and pulled it out, mindlessly running his thumb over one of the two silver dog tags. She assumed he still wore them as his way to stay connected to the service—to those he'd lost.

His chest lifted as he took a deep breath. "I reported to my superiors I was worried we were being set up, that something was off."

"And did they listen?"

His Adam's apple moved as he swallowed. "No, they said the intel was clean when they checked it. But the SEAL team sent in . . . they were killed after parachuting into the compound. The motherfuckers had been waiting for them."

She shifted to better face him and reached for his hand. "I'm so sorry."

"The thing is, I'm getting the same feeling now."

"You really don't think it's Daniel, do you?" Her pulse escalated, and he squeezed her hand.

"I don't know, but we'll figure it out. We don't have a choice, right? We won't let what happened in the Middle East happen here. We'll find justice for Ralph—for everyone who was killed." He raised their clasped palms to his lips and brushed a kiss over her hand. "I really messed up, didn't I? I should have emailed you back. I shouldn't have hidden from you like a damn coward for half my life."

"You never needed to be a replacement for Nate, you know. I didn't need a replacement." She edged closer to him, her lips hovering near his mouth. "I just needed you."

He kissed her—and the kiss freed something inside of her.

It wasn't the time or place for this, but here they were, with reporters accusing her of murder, and her tongue was inside of his mouth, and her heart had never felt so full.

She wanted to be closer. She wanted to stay in the moment for as long as possible until the harsh and cruel world disappeared.

She climbed over and awkwardly straddled him. Her back pressed to the wheel, and it dug into her spine.

"Riley." He held her face in his palms, his eyes smoldering. "We can't—"

She pressed a finger to his lips, trying to silence him, but his brows tightened and his lips curved at the edges.

"I was going to say we can't do this here. There are too many reporters and police nearby. So, unless you want a picture of you grinding on me all over the internet . . ."

Her cheeks warmed, and she immediately scooted off his lap. God, how could she have been so careless?

"You're right." She smoothed her hands over her blouse.

"But later, if you'd like to pick this back up, I'd be happy to oblige." He smiled, and the weight of the world almost fell off her shoulders.

She almost forgot they were about to head to the police station where she'd be questioned in regard to a man's murder—a man she'd hooked up with, even if she barely remembered the one-night fling.

"And you're sure kissing me is what you really want?" she asked with a slightly shaky voice, worried he'd pull away again like he had last night.

"Well, I have a bit more in mind than that." He shot her his signature lopsided grin before pulling out of the parking lot. "But yeah, being with you is all I've ever wanted."

His last words became trapped in her mind, rotating round and round as she tried to make sense of them.

He'd always wanted her?

Until the quick kiss, before Nate died, he'd never shown the slightest bit of interest in her. Well, not sexually, at least.

But, had she been wrong all those years?

Was it really possible that Ben had always had feelings for her? Was he that good at keeping secrets?

No, she told herself. It wasn't possible.

It couldn't be true because that would mean she made an even bigger mistake than she thought possible all those years ago.

CHAPTER EIGHTEEN

She hadn't been at the station long because she didn't have much else to share. She barely knew Patrick Phelps, aside from the one drunken night. And when they'd begun asking her whether he'd also been sleeping with Lydia, her eyes had glazed over . . . she had no damn clue.

The sheriff had quickly let her go. They didn't seem to have anything to hold her on, other than speculation, which was good news, at least.

Ben didn't want to provide the sheriff with what they'd discovered about Bobby and his browsing history yet. He was worried the police would become a hindrance to his own investigation; and although she wished she could trust the officers to handle the case, she trusted Ben more. Well, with this, at least. Trusting him with her heart was something she was still deciding upon.

Afterward, Ben and Riley filled Ava and Aiden in on what had happened at Riley's apartment, and then they headed for her office.

"That's it." Riley looked up from the list of names she'd written down, and Ben came before her desk and lifted the notepad.

"Two names? You've spent an hour on your computer, and that's all you're giving me."

She shrugged. "They're no longer my patients, but the others . . . I can't get into their mental health. I can't betray my patients, nor do I want to lose my medical license."

"But you're okay with losing your life," he bit back.

She braced the arms of her leather chair as her gaze shot to the window. Darkness draped over the town, and rain pelted against the building. It felt ominous. Like something evil was to come. Another strike by the killer.

And was there really someone out there, potentially watching her? Waiting for her to be alone?

Ben flicked the pad with his index finger. "And what did these two people do to you?"

"The first name on the list, well, he strangled me. And the second person developed an infatuation with me and sent creepy letters." Chills rushed over her skin as she remembered the haunting photos she'd received of herself from her previous patient. Love letters that had become twisted and sick. She could have had him arrested, but he needed psychological help and not a prison sentence. So, she'd filed a restraining order and sent him to a male psychiatrist.

"Shit. I don't like this at all. Even if these guys are innocent, I'm not comfortable with them living within a hundred miles of you."

Her gaze traveled the room and met his blue irises. "You can't protect me forever."

His expression turned hard. "You sure there's no one else you want to tell me about?"

"We ruled out Jeremy, so no, I don't think so."

His cell began ringing before he could say anything. "It's my mom. One sec." He set the notepad back on the desk, went over to the couch in front of the window, and sat. "What's up?" He leaned forward, resting his elbows on his knees, keeping the phone to his ear.

She pulled her keys out of her purse and unlocked her bottom drawer.

"I don't know if dinner is going to happen," he told her.

She retrieved a large white envelope, locked her drawer, and set it in front of her.

"Yeah, I know I promised you dinner, but—" He glanced at Riley and sat all the way upright. "Okay. Yeah, I'll ask her." He paused while, she assumed, his mom talked. "Okay, see you at six tomorrow."

When he was off the phone, she said, "Guessing she roped you into dinner."

He chuckled lightly and strode back in front of her desk. "Yeah, and she'd like you to come. She knows I won't let you out of my sight, so it'd be a deal-breaker for dinner if you don't show."

"Hm." She rolled her tongue over her teeth in thought. "She still make a good lasagna?"

"Damn good. And cooking is kind of her way to avoid the craziness going on."

"Well, in that case, yes."

His attention dropped to the envelope. "What's that?"

"The letters from my patient in case you wanted to see them."

"I'll probably kill the guy if I read them." His jaw tightened as he looked at her again. "Maybe I'll let Ava have a look."

"Probably a better idea."

She powered down her computer while Ben phoned Ava and supplied her with the two patient names.

"Really? Yeah, okay." Ben glanced at Riley. "I'll tell her." He ended the call a moment later.

"What was that about?"

"Bobby was a student of Ralph's last year. He was taking night classes at the college, but he dropped out a couple of months ago."

"So, he does have a connection to Ralph." Surprise had her cheeks warming.

"Looks that way." Irritation covered his face. "He got a C in Ralph's psych class, but there aren't any reports of threats from him to Ralph, or anything like that."

They both sat down on the couch near the window, and she focused on the sound of the tap-tap-tap of the rain, trying not to get caught up in the way Ben's hand felt now that it was positioned on her thigh.

"You okay? Thinking about Ralph? The killer?"

"I should be thinking about that," she answered.

"But you're not?" He found her eyes, and he gently squeezed her leg. Not too tight, but enough for her to feel a pulse of heat settle between her thighs.

She swallowed. "No, instead I'm thinking about you. I haven't really been able to stop thinking about you since the moment I saw you last week."

His brows lowered, and a tight band of tension swept through the room. She'd swear if she reached out, she would actually feel the air on her fingertips.

Ben dropped his gaze to her chest. Her palm met her collarbone, and she found the top button of her blouse undone. He was staring down at the hint of cleavage there, and she slipped her hand lower, so her fingers dipped beneath the lace of her bra.

But it was *his* hands she wanted on her.

"This whole love-hate thing is confusing," she said in a rush, her throat almost hoarse. She wished she could numb her chest, where pain flared with new life.

When his hand left her thigh, she flinched, hating that she'd vocalized her thoughts.

"You never finished telling me the other reason why you didn't want to come home. The reason why you didn't want to see me again."

His eyes fell shut, and he remained quiet as he slowly dragged his scarred hand from his jaw down his throat.

She took a panicked breath. She needed him to help her get rid of the noise in her head—to silence the world around them.

"I don't know if I can." Emotion sliced through his words, and he opened his eyes.

"Please, I need you to."

He stood and kept his back to her. "I, uh, was in love with you." His hands settled on his hips and he dropped his head forward.

Her chest caved at the weight of his words, but she approached him anyway and rested a trembling hand on the hard edges of his back.

"I wanted you for a long time, but I didn't want to ruin our friendship, and I didn't think you felt the same, and so I tried to keep it from you." His back lifted with a deep breath. "I dated half the girls in high school to try and get you out of my head—because I knew Nate loved you. I never told Nate how I felt. I thought he was the better choice for you, and so I stepped back."

"Better choice?" she murmured in disbelief. "Who were you to decide that?" She dropped her hand, and he faced her.

His stunning blue eyes met hers, but it was as brief as the space between heartbeats.

"You should've said something," she said, her voice breaking.

"What difference would it have made?" His eyes cut back to hers.

Her pulse elevated as she said through clenched teeth, "You would've found out I loved you too, damn it!" She spun away from him, unable to look him in the eyes.

"No." He gripped her arm, but she jerked free of his touch and stepped away. "No, I don't believe that. Why would you say *yes* to Nate when he asked you out, then?"

She looked up at the ceiling, tears burning her sight.

Guilt had tugged at her heart for so long, and now she was about to say the truth out loud for the first time in her life.

But she needed to face him to do it. And maybe Nate would be able to hear her apology from heaven.

"I was pissed that you never asked." She pivoted around, and he was the one backing up now, his palms in the air as if he couldn't understand her statement. "All I'd ever wanted was for you to be the one to ask. And so, when he did, I said *yes* out of spite. I regretted it the moment the word left my mouth, but then I was too scared to take it back. I was afraid Nate would hate me, and you were always with some new girl, and I—"

"Are you goddamn kidding me?" His voice rattled through his gritted teeth. "How could you sleep with him? How could you use Nate like that just because you were angry at me?"

"I never . . . We never had sex. I couldn't bring myself to do it. Every day I told myself I'd end things with him, but I did love him —just not like that—not the way I loved you." She looked up at the ceiling as if it might collapse on them.

"Riley."

She forced her eyes back on him, scared of what she'd see. "I had planned on finally breaking up with Nate. When you kissed me that day, I knew in my heart I couldn't keep living the lie. Even if you and I could never be together, it wasn't fair to Nate. But then he—"

He fisted his hands in the air before him as if trying to reel in his anger. "And you blamed me. I spent my life thinking you'd hate me if you knew that I wanted you. You were Nate's girl. How could I be his best friend but lust after you, especially after his death? I didn't come home because I was afraid I wouldn't be able to stop myself from telling you how much I loved you."

She hadn't realized she was crying until now.

"I can't want you. Don't you get it? It's fucking wrong to want to screw you. It'd be betraying him, betraying his memory."

"'Screw' me?"

He cursed under his breath. "That's not what I meant."

"Why'd you kiss me earlier?"

He stabbed at the air in her direction. "Because I was right not to come back. I was right about what would happen if I was around you. I can't resist you, damn it."

She stepped closer. "And how'd you know I'd want to kiss you back? All of these years, if you thought I didn't feel the same for you, what made you think I'd—"

He smashed his mouth to hers and gripped her elbows, holding her against him. It was a punishing kiss. Hard and almost bruising.

Tears kept falling down her face, and then his lips lifted, and he kissed at the drops of liquid splattering her cheeks.

And then he grabbed hold of her wrists and lifted them, slinging her arms around his neck. He kissed her again, his tongue caressing hers.

He yanked at her blouse, freeing it from her pants, and his warm hand skirted up her back, and she fisted his hair, yearning to be as close to him as possible.

He stopped kissing her a minute later, and his eyes narrowed. "I can't take you here. I can't let this happen on the floor of your office. I've wanted this too long."

"I can't wait."

"I want you on a bed." He palmed her face. "We both messed up in the past. We made mistakes." His hand slid around to the back of her head, threading through her hair as he held her firmly in place. "But if we're really going to do this . . . I want it to be perfect for you."

Her lips curved. "If it's with you, it will be."

CHAPTER NINETEEN

Up against the door. The wall. On the floor. Now the bed.

Ben had kissed her all over his hotel room the moment they got inside. And now that she was finally on the bed, he was going to make this last for as long as possible.

There was a thickness in his throat, though, as the guilt of what he was about to do gnawed at him.

But Riley never slept with Nate like he'd always assumed, and he wasn't sure if that made it okay now—probably not—but nothing in the world would stop him. He'd move heaven and hell to be with her.

His core tightened as he yanked off his shirt.

Her gaze dipped to the curves of his body, and her tongue teased between her lips as she eyed him.

After his pants dropped, she didn't seem to notice the jagged scars near his ribs or the bullet wounds dotting the skin on his left hip.

"I always wondered if you were a boxer or brief kind of man. In my fantasies over the years, I'd alternate between the two," she said with a smile in her eyes as she removed her shoes and pants.

Her matching red panties were see-through, and he could tell she was smooth beneath. His heart beat wildly, and a guttural noise moved from his chest and left his lips as she tortured him by slowly unbuttoning her blouse.

He couldn't wait any longer to touch her. To take her.

Anxious, he unclasped her lace bra, and when he freed her breasts, he took in the sight of her while removing his boxers.

He gently forced her onto her back and climbed on top. She dragged her focus down between his thighs, and she bit her lip.

Holding his weight with one hand, he dropped his lips over hers, shoving his tongue deeper into her mouth with a fierce primal need, as if an animal inside of him were in charge and he was running on instinct.

"Oh, God," she cried against his lips a minute later when his fingertip brushed over her center, and he could feel her wetness soaking the lace.

He scooted down the bed and hooked his finger under her panties, caressing her tender spot.

She arched back and gripped the comforter. He grabbed hold of her hips and lowered his mouth. His teeth grazed over her pelvic bone and he finally ripped the panties off, his tongue darting over her flesh.

"Ben." She ground out his name and braced his shoulders. "Not yet. I'm not ready. Please," she begged, but her words only had him pushing her further to the edge, unable to stop himself.

He'd waited too damn long.

And a few minutes later, she changed her tune. "Oh, God. Don't stop."

He swept a hand up, cupped her breast, and squeezed.

She tensed and orgasmed soon after.

He nipped at the inside of her thigh and trailed kisses up her body. Once he settled back on top of her, he pressed his mouth to the crook of her neck and inhaled her sweet scent.

His body tensed when she reached down and banded a hand

around his shaft. His forehead rested against hers, and he closed his eyes at the touch he'd spent a lifetime longing for.

She wasn't pumping or moving at all—just holding him . . . and damn if he wasn't going to lose his mind.

"I want to feel you in me," she whispered, and he lifted his head to find her eyes. Her beautiful browns were glossy as if emotion were choking her.

"I don't have protection. I wasn't thinking."

She wet her lips and cupped his face with her other hand. "I don't care." Her eyes narrowed. "I'm on birth control is, um, what I meant. And I trust you."

Could he have unprotected sex? It'd be the first time in his life.

But this was Riley.

Riley Carpenter, the woman of his damn dreams.

She arched her hips, pressing his hardness against her. "I need this. I need you."

He pressed both palms alongside her and positioned his tip at her center. She guided him in, and then he thrust hard. He went in as deep as possible. Maybe even more so.

"Fuuuck," he yelled as he slammed back into her for a second time.

Skin to skin, their bodies grew sweaty as they moved, as they rocked together in a rhythm that could only be described as perfect —like they were made for each other, and only for each other.

He kissed at the new tears on her cheeks, knowing they weren't from sadness because he felt the same way.

The weight of the guilt started to shed, and in its place was something else. Something he couldn't quite grasp or understand. Not now, at least.

And once she'd come again, only then did he allow himself to lose control and spill inside of her.

"Don't get off me. Not yet," she said softly, and he brushed the hair from her face.

"I don't want to crush you."

Her hand curved around the arm that was holding most of his weight. "I'm pretty sure you're strong enough to hold yourself up a little longer." Her lips teased into a smile.

"Did this really happen?" He brushed his thumb over her pink, slightly swollen lips.

"Sounds like something I should be asking."

"What? A guy can't get emotional?"

She chuckled lightly. "Mm. Is that what you are?"

"Would it be an insult to my manhood if I say *yes*?"

She arched up to press a quick kiss to his lips. "I'm pretty sure nothing could question that." Her cheeks became even rosier.

"Maybe we should go at this again, just so you know I'm really a tough guy," he said, purposefully deepening his voice.

"I think you're absolutely right. How about awkward shower sex?"

"Hon, nothing would be awkward about it with me." He lowered himself so her beautiful breasts smashed against his chest, and he shifted his mouth to her ear. "And it's been something I've thought about ever since the day I saw you touching yourself in the shower."

"Ben! You said—"

"Maybe you could do it again. I'd love to watch you . . . before joining you." He met her eyes again and smiled.

"You're dirty, aren't you?" She lifted a brow.

He released a breath. "Mm. You have no idea. Not sure if you want to find out."

Her lips pursed in thought as she smoothed her hand over the cut of his muscular arms. "I really do," she said in a husky voice.

* * *

"BENJAMIN LOGAN!" SHE THREW HER CHOPSTICK AT HIM, AND HE raised his palms in the air, grinning.

"What?" He smirked.

"You did not just say that to me." She laughed as he tossed her utensil back at her.

"You asked me what I found the sexiest about you, and I answered honestly."

"But you're supposed to say something romantic, like my personality."

"*Personality* is a romantic answer?" He popped another sushi roll in his mouth and fought back a laugh at the cute way her nose crinkled.

Eating sushi in bed naked . . . with Riley.

Dreams really do come true.

Of course, he'd never thought it would happen, and he wished to hell it wasn't a serial killer that had finally brought them together.

He shoved the thoughts of Ralph's death and the killer back into the dark corner of his mind and focused on the beautiful woman sitting casually on the bed, her back to the headboard, her full, round breasts on display.

"By the way, that thing you did with your tongue in the shower —and um . . ." She allowed her words to trail off.

He shifted his food out of the way and moved closer to her. "Felt good, right?" He shoved her take-out to the side, reached for her wrist, and yanked her forward. He fell back, and she landed on top of him.

"I never knew how incredible it could be, in fact." She shifted upright so her ass was pressing right against his erection, and she began to wiggle her hips. "I thought you were hungry, so why are we back in this position?"

"Well, you started talking about sex. What did you expect to happen?" He gently pulled on the strands of her long blonde hair. The silk locks were smooth between his fingers.

"You're the best I've ever been with. Like, hands down, the best," she said.

He cleared his throat, and his muscles tightened in his core. "Ri

—as far as I'm concerned right now . . . I'm your only. I don't want to think about you ever being with anyone else."

She playfully slapped at his chest, but he caught her wrist and brushed his lips against her palm, then purposely tickled her hand by rubbing it against his five-day-old beard. He really needed to shave again.

"But, sweetheart, if you keep grinding your ass against my co—"

She was the one kissing away his words this time.

And he let her.

He'd let her do whatever the hell she wanted.

He owed her a lifetime of pleasure.

He still couldn't wrap his head around the fact that they'd both been in love as teens and too scared to admit it.

Nate came back to mind, and he instinctively shifted his face, breaking their kiss.

"What's wrong?"

He couldn't bring himself to tell her what he'd been thinking. He knew deep in his heart that Nate would want both Riley and him to be happy, even if that meant they were happy together.

He hadn't accepted that until tonight, though. He'd been living in fear of his feelings for so long, he'd stopped thinking clearly.

But on that cliff last weekend, when he should have said goodbye—he hadn't. His mind had gone blank. He'd been strangled by emotions that had wrapped around his throat, cutting off oxygen to his brain.

Ben had to go back.

He had to truly let go and move on.

He had to make peace with the past.

"I just wish it didn't take fourteen years for this to happen," he finally answered her.

"You're here now."

He could see the emotion on her face, the tears threatening

again. He didn't want to see her sad right now. They would have plenty to deal with when the storm cleared and the sun came up. For now, he just wanted her happy. "How about I do that thing with my tongue again?"

CHAPTER TWENTY

"YOU SLEPT WITH HER?" AIDEN ELBOWED BEN BEFORE RESTING his arms on the railing of the balcony outside of the hotel room. "She's why you never came back to Alabama. You were afraid this would happen."

"And I was right." Ben cupped the back of his neck. He hadn't told him he'd had sex with Riley, but Ava and Aiden had seen the evidence all over Riley's shy face. Plus, Riley had been partially dressed in Ben's clothes.

"Dude, she was your best friend's girlfriend. Isn't there some kind of bro code or something where you're not supposed to do that?" He shook his head. "I mean, in Dublin, a man could die for that."

"I'm about to knock you in the face."

"I'm just giving you a hard time. Easy." Aiden stood straight and crossed his arms over his chest.

"It's complicated, anyway," Ben said.

"Usually is. But, uh, you okay? Was this a one-time thing, or . . .?"

It was more of an all-night thing. They'd only slept an hour that morning before heading to Aiden's room. They had fourteen years to make up for, and as far as Ben was concerned, he had only gotten started.

"I don't think so." He thought about telling Aiden about Riley's confession to him, but he didn't want him getting the wrong idea about her. She'd been young, and she'd made the wrong decision by dating Nate. And Ben had been an idiot for running off when Nate had died. They'd both made mistakes, and it was time to correct them. But first, they needed to catch a killer.

"Well, you feel like chatting about your feelings or something?" Aiden creased his brow as if hoping to hell Ben would say *no*.

"I'm good, man."

"Thank fuck." He tilted his head to the closed hotel door. "Let's go inside then. Now that we got that heart-to-heart out of the way, we can get down to business."

Ben rolled his eyes, but said, "I missed you."

"Jesus, mate. You really did get soft, didn't you?"

Ben punched him in the arm. "I can still throw down with you in the ring. Any day and time."

"Ha. You still think you can take me, do ya?" He opened the door and glanced at Ben over his shoulder.

"You know it."

Ava was sitting next to Riley, and it was obvious Ava had offered to talk to her, as well. But Ben was pretty sure she wouldn't say anything to Ava since they were basically strangers.

Riley fiddled with the hem of the gray shirt. His tee hung to her mid-thighs, and it was matched with her red dress pants from yesterday. It was all he'd had to offer her though since she had requested a clean top to wear.

"Well." Ava tied her long dark hair up into a high ponytail and sat back behind the desk. "The patient names you gave us checked out. The guy who sent those letters was actually committed two months ago. And the other guy lives in Atlanta with his mom."

"I didn't think it was them." Riley sighed.

"From what we can tell, there are no red flags in your ex's record, either. Not even so much as a parking ticket, actually," Ava said.

"So, are we going under the assumption it's Bobby or someone we haven't identified?" Ben asked, dropping into the swivel chair on the other side of the desk.

"Bobby's background is pretty clean. I even chatted with his commanding officer in the military, and he said he was a stand-up guy," Aiden said.

"But . . . based on his connection to Lydia and Ralph, it's not looking so good for him," Ava added since it was also probably clear to her Aiden didn't like the idea of pinning the murders on Bobby as much as Ben.

"You know, I didn't mention this yesterday, but the detective asked me if Lydia was also sleeping with Patrick," Riley said as she stood.

"Daniel said Lydia was sleeping around to try and make him jealous," Ben reminded her. Not that he truly believed anything her ex said.

"Why kill Ralph first, though?" Aiden asked. "Unless all of the kills were premeditated and purposeful. Ralph and Patrick were distractions and Lydia was the true target?"

"Bobby can't have Lydia so no one will?" Ben lifted his shoulders, doubting the possibility.

"Maybe Bobby hated that Lydia loved Daniel, so he's either trying to frame him for the murders . . . or kill him next," Riley said, her eyes widening as she processed the thought. "We need to warn him."

Ben hated the asshole, but did he want him dead? Maybe a little. "I don't think he'll try and kill Daniel. If it truly is Bobby, murdering Daniel would tie back to him too easily. It'd be a stupid move."

"Maybe we should go to the police with this?" Riley's shoulders sagged. "But we can't, can we? It'd get you guys in trouble. Hacking the police station is pretty damn illegal, last time I checked."

"We'll handle this. I promise. I won't let anyone else die," Ben said as his phone began to vibrate in his pocket.

It was his mom. He didn't feel like discussing whether she wanted to serve Merlot or a Cab at dinner, but he answered anyway. "Yeah?"

"Are you okay? Are you watching the news?" she rushed out.

Ben spun around and looked at the TV. He pointed to it, motioning for Aiden to turn it on.

"There's been another murder," his mom said when the screen flickered on, showing a castle-like home he recognized.

"Call you back." He ended the call and focused on the TV.

"I'm going back online to see what the police have," Ava announced.

The reporter appeared onscreen a moment later, one of the same people who'd crammed questions down their throats yesterday. "Elizabeth Stanton was found dead in her home this morning by her grandfather. Unofficial reports suggest that a partial print was recovered at the scene. The police have yet to confirm or deny this information, but we'll keep you up-to-date." The reporter's green eyes narrowed. "It looks like the killer is no longer focusing on doctors. The sheriff has advised everyone to keep a lookout for anyone or anything suspicious. We're going to scroll a number across the screen; call if you have any information for the police."

Aiden turned off the TV and faced Ben. "Well, this is a goddamn plot twist."

Ben's hands went to his hips, and he bowed his head in thought. "Jesus, we were at her house yesterday."

"Do you know her aside from that?" Aiden asked.

"We dated in high school," Ben answered.

Aiden heaved out a deep breath. "And did you touch anything in the house while you were there?"

"Is it my print they found?" Riley asked. "Is this it? Are they going to lock me up?"

"You get into their records yet?" Ben looked to Ava, and she nodded. "Time of death?"

"Roughly five a.m.," she answered.

"You were with me. You have an alibi," Ben said with relief.

"And the sheriff will never believe you." Her eyes began to well.

Ben's face tightened. "He'll have to."

CHAPTER TWENTY-ONE

THE BUZZ OF FLUORESCENT LIGHTS DREW BEN'S EYES AS HE followed the sheriff into the room. He was thankful it was him being questioned, instead of Riley.

The walls were gunmetal gray, and based on the lack of cameras or any technology—excluding the recorder on the table that looked like it belonged in the nineties, when a Radio Shack still existed—he doubted the room had ever been used prior to the killing spree.

Of course, he didn't want his home town dealing with crimes, but he couldn't help but worry about the station's lack of experience.

Ben took a seat and held out his hands, palms up. "Just you and me, huh? Where's that special detective you brought in?"

The sheriff's broad body occupied the other chair, and he swiped his large mug of a hand over his bald head.

"You find something funny?" The mottled skin on the sheriff's forehead pinched tight.

"Why? Do I look amused?" He casually leaned back in his chair and clasped his hands in his lap.

"You look like a damn cocky bastard is what." Stubby fingers scratched at an already pock-marked cheek.

"You mean I look confident. I have alibis for all the murders, and so you're wasting your goddamn time right now." Irritation sprung into his tone, even though he tried to remain as cool as possible.

Leaving Riley to come to the station had him about a hundred shades of pissed off right now.

"Your print was found on the buzzer outside Elizabeth Stanton's home. And based on our sources, you two dated back in school."

And here we go. He glanced heavenward and tucked his tongue inside his cheek, fighting back the desire to curse.

Sources? Yeah, sure. Source. Singular. Your daughter.

Now he knew why the sheriff looked like he wanted to stab a dagger in his heart. He was damn certain Charlize told him about what happened in Vegas.

Maybe he'd been a dick to Charlize, but this wasn't the time or place to drag bruised egos into the middle of things.

"Guess that favor you owe me fell through the cracks," Ben mumbled when silence competed with his thoughts. He wanted to get out of there and back to Riley, and so, he probably needed to bite the bullet and get this over with as fast as possible.

"What were you doing at the Stanton residence?"

He raised his chin and cupped the back of his neck with both hands. "I was following a lead. I had concerns about her cousin, but when we spoke to Beth, she said he'd taken off to Charlotte." Ben tipped his head toward the door. "Looks like you knew that since Jeremy's out there in cuffs." He assumed Jeremy had been arrested for taking off, violating his parole.

"Yeah, well, I told you to back off the case."

"I must've misunderstood."

"You watch yourself. I'll arrest you for obstruction of justice."

There was a knock at the door, which saved Ben from flinging the sarcastic response that edged onto the tip of his tongue.

"Come in," the sheriff hollered and shifted in his seat once the door opened.

The detective didn't enter the room. "He can go," he said and closed the door.

"Give me a minute." The sheriff stood and left which had Ben rising to his feet, rocking back on his heels.

He'd been in rooms like this one before, and it hadn't bothered him in the past. Hell, he'd been holed up in a cave in Afghanistan for thirty-six hours one time while the Taliban had searched for him. It hadn't exactly been the highlight of his life, but he'd gotten away with only a bullet in his hip. And so, he considered any day alive to be a good day.

But right now—a thickness started to grow in his throat, making it hard to swallow. His breathing quickened, and the urge to claw at the walls, to climb up and punch a hole in the ceiling to break free, had him bearing his knuckles down on the table and hanging his head low.

He needed to get to Riley. Worry hollowed out his gut, and every bone in his body was telling him something was wrong.

She's with Aiden, he reminded himself. *She's okay.*

The door crept open a moment later. "I guess you're good to go," the sheriff said as if he wanted to choke on his own words.

Ben didn't care to ask any other questions or say anything.

He tore out of the station, darted out into the downpour, and rushed for the SUV.

And when he arrived at the hotel parking lot, still crowded with media vans, he noticed one other car.

Daniel's.

Motherfucker.

Once upstairs, Ben abandoned all sense of self-control at the sight of Daniel in front of the hotel room, arguing with Aiden.

If Daniel wanted someone to fight he was game.

"Get out of my way, or I'll move you," Daniel said to Aiden.

Aiden continued to stand with crossed arms, blocking the entrance to the hotel room.

"What the hell are you doing here?" Ben rasped.

"I'm taking Riley out of here," Daniel said over his shoulder. "Did you assholes not hear about the murder yesterday? I'm going to keep her safe, not you. She won't even return my calls because you probably took her damn phone." He slowly turned toward Ben. Anger stained his cheeks; the skin was tinged red all the way to the tips of his ears.

"She's not yours to protect." Bitter bile rose in Ben's throat at the thought of Daniel going anywhere near Riley ever again.

"We've been through this before." Daniel poked a finger at Ben's chest. "You'll be going, and I'm staying. So back the fuck off and let me in the damn room. I'll handle things from now on."

Ben's hands disappeared into his pockets, and he gripped his car keys in his palm, fisting them to control his desire to pop the guy in the face.

Aiden edged behind Daniel, prepared to grab the man if needed.

"Let me talk to Riley." Daniel blew out his cheeks.

"Go, before your pretty-boy face requires plastic surgery." Ben's tone evened out. "If you think I'm afraid of a little prison time—I'm not."

"And if you think I'm afraid of a fight you're mistaken." Anger crept back into his brandy-colored eyes, and Daniel rolled his shoulders as if loosening up to prepare himself.

The door behind Aiden flung open a split second later. "Guys, the sheriff is making an arrest," Ava rushed out.

Riley hovered behind Ava. She'd been about three seconds away from witnessing a fight had Ava not opened the door.

"Go," Ben ordered over his shoulder as he headed into the hotel room, following Aiden.

"Let him in. He can hear what happened." Riley stared at Ben with downturned lips, a silent plea for him to back down.

And for her, he would, even if he didn't like it.

"The police issued a warrant for the arrest of Bobby," Ava said once they all stood inside the hotel room.

Ben had to replay Ava's words in his head, too focused on Daniel inside the room to think about much else. "Don't move an inch." He extended his arm in front of Daniel when Riley sat on the bed. If the guy thought he'd sit next to her, he was out of his damn mind.

Aiden crossed the room to stand behind Ava once she retook her seat at the desk, and Ben remained a shield between the bed and the ex-boyfriend.

"How do you know that?" Daniel asked.

"Don't worry about that." Aiden kept his focus on the screen.

"Guess that's why the sheriff let me go—they were going to make an arrest," Ben said.

"Bobby's print was a match," Ava said. "And when they searched his car, they found a ten-inch scalpel. Maybe he got it from the hospital. No traces of blood on it, but clearly, they were confident enough to hold him on charges."

Daniel's tense jaw relaxed, and he pressed his back against the wall near the door.

Ben swept his attention from Daniel to Riley, trying to survey her mood and see how she was holding up.

"You should go now." Aiden shifted his focus to Daniel. "And that's not a request."

Riley swallowed, but she kept her eyes cast down on the cheap, worn carpet.

"Not without her. Nothing changes." Daniel pushed off the wall.

"The killer is caught. You don't need to worry about me anymore." Riley's whispered words blew across Ben's heated skin, and a slow curl of worry wrapped around his spine.

Did she really believe the killer was Bobby? Of course, he had no intention of voicing his doubts with Daniel in the room.

"I can't leave you here. I don't trust them." A line etched between Daniel's brows as his pupils constricted.

"I'm okay." She stood, trying to maintain her confidence, but Ben noticed the slight falter in her step as she passed him and advanced toward Daniel.

He wanted to reach for her wrist as she passed, to stop her from going to him. But he didn't control her, and if she needed to stand her own ground, he wouldn't try to stop her.

Daniel angled his head and focused on Riley. "Please, come with me."

"No, but I'll call you." She reached for his arm, and the simple gesture had Ben's core clenching. "I promise."

"I'm worried about you." A gruffness littered his words like trash distastefully chucked out the window of a speeding car.

Ben didn't believe Daniel. Not for one second. The only person Daniel was worried about was himself. His lies were as vivid as the sun casting a glow over the Vegas desert while it lowered from the sky.

How could Riley not see that? All Ben could see was a killer when he looked into the man's eyes.

"I can take care of myself. Just go. Let's see what happens with the police, and I'll be in touch." Riley's voice remained steady as she spoke.

"I'm calling you later. If you don't answer, I'll worry and come back." Daniel lifted his chin and met Ben's eyes again. "If you hurt her, I'll kill you."

Ben ignored Daniel's words, anxious for him to get the hell out of there.

"Sorry, but Daniel's still a friend," Riley said once he was gone and rubbed her swollen eyes.

"What are you thinking?" Aiden asked Ben.

Ben waited for Riley to sit back on the bed before he spoke. He didn't want her knees buckling from the weight of the words that he'd deliver. "This feels like either a setup or shitty police work."

"What?" Riley's eyes dampened.

"The killer didn't leave evidence at any of the other crime scenes," Aiden said. "And now, the police find the murder weapon in his car? And a print at Beth's house?"

Ben sat next to Riley and brushed his knuckles over her cheek.

"The killer has us all looking one way as a distraction," Ben said, wishing he were wrong. "There's no way in hell Bobby killed Beth yesterday," Ben added. "And no, this isn't me defending him because he was military."

Riley's sweeping eyelashes lifted, and she focused on Ben. "Why can't we let this be over?"

Ben held her hand, interlocking their fingers together. "You're a smart woman. You know as well as we do that this arrest doesn't make sense."

"And there's also something you guys need to hear." Ava's words hijacked Ben's thoughts, and he shifted on the bed without dropping hold of Riley's hand. "When you were at the station, I found something that might support the theory that Bobby isn't the guy."

"What'd you find?" Ben's heartbeat accelerated.

"Remember when I hacked into Bobby's computer? Well, something was bothering me about it, and so I went back in today." Ava tapped at her keyboard. "When I looked this time, I found fragments of code that shouldn't be there," she explained. "Someone else hacked Bobby's computer before I did. I missed it the first time. I'm sorry."

Riley pulled her hand free from Ben's and stood. "I don't want to hear this."

Ben hung his head, his stomach swelling with guilt. He didn't want to put her through the ringer, but if Bobby wasn't the guy, he couldn't let an innocent man go to jail—or have a murderer on the loose.

"I'm sorry, sweetie, but you need to hear it," Ava said calmly, and when Ben looked back up, she was now standing before Riley.

"What if you were never the fall guy?" Aiden interjected. "What if it was always Bobby, and you're the person the killer really wants?" Aiden voiced Ben's own thoughts.

Riley's jaw tightened and her eyes closed. "No."

Denial. He understood why she was clinging to the false hope of Bobby being the murderer. She'd lost a father figure and friends, and grief had settled hard inside of her, materializing into a fear so strong that it was roping her into this false reality—which was probably right where the killer wanted her.

"Can we have a minute?" Ben looked at Aiden and then to Ava.

Aiden nodded, and once his friends were outside, he grabbed a bottle of water. Instead of drinking it, he held it between his palms and bowed his head.

"Whatever you're going to say, you should know I'm prepared to disagree with you."

He muddled through his thoughts and found her beautiful brown eyes. "Well, I wouldn't expect anything different from you. You always loved to argue with me, if I remember."

"Ben. This isn't the Middle East. This isn't a case of misdirection."

"I know it's not Iraq or Afghanistan. We're not dealing with a terrorist, but we are dealing with a psychopath, and I strongly believe he's still out there."

"And my heart is telling me that it's over. And if you care about me, if you love—" She stopped talking as her eyes brimmed with liquid.

In one swift movement, he pulled her into a crushing embrace, unable to stop himself.

He'd hold her forever. He'd keep her safe, and he wouldn't let go. Well, not until the real killer was found.

And then, he'd either arrest the bastard himself or bury the motherfucker.

CHAPTER TWENTY-TWO

BEN ROLLED TO HIS SIDE AND CHECKED THE TEXT THAT HAD come in.

"Is it important?" Riley asked.

When he dropped to his back, there was a darkness in his eyes, changing the opaque blue orbs that had devoured her with a single stare only a moment prior.

"What's wrong?" She stiffened and started to sit up, but he tugged at her wrist and shook his head. "It's not still about the case, is it?"

Three days had passed since Bobby's arrest.

Three days of continuous messages from her ex had also rolled in. One thing both Daniel and Ben had in common seemed to be an obsession to continue to worry about her safety, despite the killer being locked up.

Ava and Aiden were still in town, and even though Ben hadn't revisited his theories about Bobby being the fall guy, Riley knew their continued presence meant he hadn't given up on the idea.

Riley had decided to take time off work to grieve. She wouldn't be in the right state of mind to help others if she felt broken herself.

"It was a message from my friend Jake."

"The one in London?"

He nodded, but something seemed off now.

"Is he okay?"

"Ugh, yeah. Just checking in."

She lifted her chin to look at him, noticing the lie that colored his irises a darker shade now. "What aren't you telling me?"

"Nothing. But, we should get out of this room at some point."

Deflection. Her hand swept to the wounds on his hip bone and her stomach squeezed.

Ben had opened up to her yesterday about some of his time overseas, as well as his injuries. Of course, she'd prodded, but she was pretty sure it had been almost cathartic for him to get the memories off his chest.

He pulled her on top of him a moment later. Affection glowed in his eyes, and it pulled at the strings of her heart.

"I've enjoyed distracting you with my hot body and all, but you probably need to breathe in some fresh air." He pressed a tender kiss to her mouth.

She chuckled and pushed off his chest to better assess him. His cerulean blues were still marked with worry, even if he was trying to hide it with a joke.

"I will if you tell me what Jake really said."

He heaved out a sigh and closed his eyes.

She shifted to try and grab his phone, but he beat her to it, swiping it off the nightstand.

"Come on. Your eyes were shut." She rolled off of him and stood.

"Great reflexes. What can I say?" He sat up.

She grabbed her bra off the floor and fumbled with the clasp as she tried to put it back on. "Damn it. You asked Jake for help, didn't you?"

The sheet was casually draped over Ben's lap, but the hard

edges of his Vegas-bronzed muscles remained on display as he watched her. "Ri . . ."

She gave up on her bra and tossed it. "Don't 'Ri' me. You haven't given up, have you?"

"Do you blame me? How can I, when lives are on the line?"

She opened her arms wide. "It's over. If you're looking for an excuse to stick around because being with me is not enough—"

He rushed to his feet and braced her elbows, the sheet falling to the ground. "I'd give anything to be here only for you."

"Then be here for me. Please." Emotion thickened in her throat, and she swallowed, trying to dampen her dry mouth.

Hesitation passed over his face before his gaze dropped to her naked body.

"Be here for me," she said again, her words whispering across his closed mouth.

She needed him to take away the pain.

To crush it.

To bludgeon it until there was nothing but peace left inside of her.

Ben kept hold of her eyes as he shifted his hands beneath her bottom and guided her up and into his arms.

She wrapped her legs around his hip bones, and she peppered him with quick kisses until she gave him all the control, hoping he'd somehow manage to heal the heart he'd once broken.

* * *

"THANKS FOR LETTING ME INVITE MANDY," SHE WHISPERED INTO Ben's ear at the table.

After their semi-argument that morning, he'd suggested they head to his moms for dinner that night to have a break from the small hotel room.

He reached under the tablecloth and squeezed her hand. "Of course."

"Your accent is swoon-worthy." Mandy focused her attention on Aiden. "How do you get anything done with him around?" she asked Ava.

"Mandy . . ." Riley laughed, knowing she was referring to Aiden and Ava's sex life; with Ben's parents at the table, Riley's face warmed with embarrassment.

"His accent did win me over." A shy smile met Ava's lips.

"Yeah, right." Aiden nudged her in the side.

"Did you know Ben once imitated an Irish accent in high school?" Riley took a bite of the lasagna and peeked at him out of the corner of her eye, expecting to see a touch of red crawl up his neck, too.

"Now that's something I'd like to hear." Aiden leaned back in his chair and eyed Ben, a mischievous smile on his face.

"Not on your life, man," Ben said.

"Oh, come on." Riley took a quick gulp of her wine. "He was attempting a Scottish accent when we were reading Macbeth in tenth grade, but it always came out like a mix of Irish and Australian."

He pinched her thigh beneath the table, and she stifled a gasp with her hand.

"Ohhh, please let us hear it," Mandy insisted. She was sitting on the other side of Riley, so she had to crane her neck around her to try and get a look at Ben.

"Anyone need a refill?" Riley hopped up from the table, knowing Ben was going to shoot daggers her way in a minute. He hated acting, and he hated being put on the spot. He was an adventurous guy, but the man had stage fright, and it had always amused her.

She left the dining room and went into the kitchen, hoping he'd follow her and pin her to the counter. The idea of someone catching them making out turned her on; it made her feel like a teenager again. She'd missed the chance at stolen kisses with him in their youth.

Ben had slept next to her every night since Bobby had been locked up, and they'd made love every night, too . . . but he'd been a little distant, and she was worried it was because he was, in fact, going to leave town when this was all over.

But she truly believed it was over. The only reason she wasn't going to argue about it was because she wasn't ready for him to go.

So, if he wanted to stick around and chase false leads, she'd let him. She wasn't prepared to have whatever conversation would come before he left.

This wasn't a fling.

This wasn't some one-time, week-long love affair.

But what the hell was it?

Mandy came into the kitchen. "You slept with him. How could you not tell me?" She sat up on the kitchen island and glared at her.

"I, uh." Riley bit her lip and peered at the closed door leading to the dining room. "It just happened."

"You hate him." Mandy angled her head, her eyes thinning as if worried.

"It's complicated. I think we'd need another bottle of wine, and for it to be only us when I explain it." She snatched the already open Merlot.

"And I need to hear it. What about tomorrow? Can you spare an hour of your time for me?"

"I'm not sure if Ben will let me out of his sight, and I can't tell you with him around." She considered the options, but she knew Ben was hell-bent on keeping her safe.

"The killer's in jail. It's over, sweetie."

"Ben's not so sure." She couldn't believe she was saying the words out loud.

"That's crazy. He just wants an excuse to stick around and steal my best friend from me." She puckered her lips, making a sour face. "I miss you. You always made time for me when you were with Daniel, but Ben's back for a week, and it's like the world has disappeared."

Riley lowered the bottle back to the counter. "Shit, I'm sorry. It's not all my doing, though. I told you he's worried about me."

"And maybe he's screwing with your head." She squeezed her forearm.

"I've waited for what feels like an eternity to have my best friend back, and I'm not ready to let him go again." The truth was a hard pill for her to swallow. "What if he doesn't stay?"

"I'm your best friend now. You don't need one that hot, anyway. Clearly, it didn't work out for you the first time." She smiled. "Sexy guys and gorgeous women cannot be friends. It's against nature or something."

Riley chuckled, and her friend managed to shift her mood quickly, as always. She had missed spending time with her. Maybe she could manage an hour tomorrow, but she'd have to think of a way to convince Ben.

"Are you back at your place now that Bobby's in jail?" Riley deflected.

"Mm-hm."

"And was this guy you were bunking with of the so-called hot variety?" Riley smiled.

Mandy swiped a hand through the air. "Not my type."

She lifted the wine again. "Well, maybe we can meet tomorrow. You still have a key to my place, right?" Speaking of which, she needed to get her key back from Daniel. Of course, she was sure Ben still had every intention of changing her locks, anyway. He'd already phoned ten different security companies, but he'd found each of their safety protocols inadequate.

"I do." She smiled, and they headed back into the dining room to rejoin the group.

A few minutes later, and with a somber look, Ben's mom lifted her wine glass. "Let us remember those who lost their lives, and promise we'll always keep them in our hearts."

Tremors shot down Riley's arm as she tried to hold her wine steady in the air.

Ben reached for her hand, offering her the strength she needed to remain at the table without sobbing.

She raised her glass even higher and squeezed her eyes tight, praying for it to be over. And at the very least, she prayed that Ralph was at peace, and with his wife and son.

CHAPTER TWENTY-THREE

"ARE YOU OUT OF YOUR MIND?" BEN FOLDED HIS ARMS OVER HIS naked chest, standing before her wearing only his dog tags and a towel. It was wrapped loosely below his sexy V, and she couldn't help but stare at the little trail of hair beneath his belly button.

"If you're going to yell at me, could you at least put some clothes on first? It's distracting."

She turned away, grabbed her silk scarf off the bed, and draped it loosely around her neck. "Where are my keys?" She scanned the room.

"You're not going anywhere."

"It's daylight. And Bobby's in prison. No one is going to come after me."

"You're a doctor. You graduated top of your class with a four point oh, and dozens of hospitals begged you to work with them. How can you be this naïve?"

"Did you look into me?" She closed the gap between them and poked at his still-wet chest.

"You were a suspect, so Ava checked you out. Can't be too careful."

She blew out a flustered breath. "You'd better be joking."

"Mm. I wouldn't joke about a murder investigation," he said in a low voice, and she wasn't sure if he was serious or not.

He flattened her palm against his chest and covered her hand with his, stepping in even closer. A quiver of excitement blew down her spine. She always got excited when they were this close because she knew what it meant: he'd make love to her.

She screwed her eyes tight and tried to maintain control of her body. He was going to try and use sex to stop her from doing what she wanted, and maybe she did need to remind herself that she was a brilliant doctor. She'd become a lust-filled teen, losing all rational thought, ever since the man had stormed back into her life. And she had a half a dozen hickeys on her neck to prove it, among other places. The man had a weakness for her inner thighs, and she couldn't exactly complain.

He closed a hand around her hip, tugging her so close that she could feel his hard-on beneath the towel.

"It won't work. Not this time. You can't distract me with sex."

"Oh, I can't?" He lifted a brow and squeezed her ass as if the denim wasn't separating his palm from her skin. "I thought that's what you wanted. You asked me to distract you from this hellish world and make you forget everything."

Okay, so she'd said that multiple times in one variation or another over the last few days, but . . .

"I miss my friend. I need a little girl time. Plus, I'd like to catch her up on what's been going on in my life."

"Like me?" He squeezed again, harder this time, and she bit her lip at the promise of what his touch could bring—what he could give her. The man was a mountain in his own right, and she could climb him forever.

"Maybe." She purred the word and slipped her hand between them and beneath the towel. She could play dirty, too. She held on to him tight, applying the amount of pressure he liked.

The towel fell at their feet, and he inhaled a sharp breath but didn't lose sight of her eyes. "You could talk to Ava. You've become close over the last few days."

"I need out of this place. I need some fresh air." She pumped him harder and peeked around him to glance at his reflection. He was standing before the mirror, and his hard ass cheeks flexed tight —the man had a body like no other.

"There's only one way you're going." He removed her hand from his length. "And that's with me."

"I can't gossip when you're around."

He shrugged and grabbed his towel. "Then wait until it's safe."

She balled her hands at her sides. "It *is* safe. You've been keeping quiet about whatever you and Aiden have been doing on that computer of Ava's . . . but I'm betting you're coming up empty."

He casually wrapped his towel around his hips again and looked at her with heavy-lidded eyes. "I'm not talking about this with you right now. You've made up your mind, and so have I. We're at a crossroads."

"No." She swiveled around, her hair whipping against his body in the process. "You're a stubborn ass, but I'm an independent woman who can make her own choices. And I'm going to meet my best friend."

"Riley."

How could he make his voice so damn commanding with only one word?

"Listen, I went through people like a serial online dater after you left." Her shoulders collapsed with the weight of her words. "I could never find another you. Another Nate." She slowly turned to face him, and he sank down on the bed. "But Mandy moved here this year, and we instantly clicked. We have everything in common. Do you know how rare that is?"

"I'm sorry, I—"

She silenced him with her hand in the air. "I don't know what's going to happen when you're gone, but she's the only friend I have right now, and so if you leave me . . . I'm gonna need a shoulder to cry on, and I'll need her."

He clasped his hands in his lap and stared down at the floor. "I think it's pretty damn clear what I want."

"Not to me." She shook her head lightly. "But I don't want to talk about it right now, anyway. I'm meeting up with Mandy, and you can drive me if that'd make you feel better, but it's my decision, and you're not invited inside."

He scratched at his jaw. "A public place. Lots of people around. I'll be in the parking lot in the car."

She knew she wasn't going to win, but she hated giving in. But on the off chance that Ben was right, and that Bobby wasn't the killer—she'd let him keep her safe. Because she did have a brain.

"Let me shave and get dressed, and we can go."

She fought the smile that tugged at her lips. "I've kind of grown attached to the stubble. I wouldn't mind it tickling the inside of my thighs again later."

His gaze fell to her denim-clad legs. "You've got enough markings there from my love bites. I don't want to scratch you up with this scruff." He rubbed his jaw.

"'Love bites'?" She chuckled. "I think you just knocked your manhood down a peg. I was wrong before when I said it wasn't possible."

He smiled and was on his feet so fast she barely had a chance to realize what he was doing.

He roped his hands around her waist, lifted her like she was a feather, and tossed her on the bed.

She took a deep breath and stared at him.

"You're going to be late." He dropped the towel.

* * *

"Harder." Ben's throaty voice shot through her as she shifted up and down on top of him, riding him. "Give me everything you have."

Her nipples pebbled, and her stomach tightened as her pelvic bone met his with each movement. She grabbed hold of his wrists and forced his hands to her breasts, begging for his touch as she took all of him. She wanted their bodies as close as humanly possible.

Her body began to tremble only a few minutes later, and then he flipped her over to her stomach.

He shifted her hair off to the side and smoothed a hand down her back. "You're going to want to grab on to something," he said gruffly.

She was on all fours, and he thrust inside of her. Her spine curved back, and she cried out, loud enough for the neighboring guests to hear.

He held on to her hips, and her breasts bounced as he continued to hit her already sensitive spot. And when he came, he bent forward and kissed her shoulder blade.

"Mm." She collapsed onto the bed and dug her fingers into the rumpled comforter.

He trailed kisses down to the small of her back and grabbed her butt. "This ass. It really is—"

"The sexiest thing about me. I remember." She chuckled and rolled to her side to look at him.

"Honestly, it's your smile," he said a moment later, staring at her mouth.

"That would've been my answer about you." She sighed. "You're such a heartthrob. You know that, right? All the girls were head over heels for you back in school."

"Yeah, well," he said while facing her on his side now, lacing their fingers together, "unfortunately for them, they could never measure up to the one person I truly wanted."

She drummed her fingertips on his chest with her free hand. "Well, you have me. So, what are you going to do with me?"

He pressed a firm kiss to her mouth and pulled back only enough to growl, "Make you a hell of a lot later than you already are."

CHAPTER TWENTY-FOUR

"You don't have anywhere else they can sit?" Ben scanned the crowded restaurant, counting over thirty people.

The hostess held up her palms. "Do you see any empty tables?"

"The booth is perfect," Riley said.

"It's fine, Ben." Mandy stepped around him to follow the hostess.

"Wait." He captured Riley's arm before she could leave him.

"It's safe in here." Her eyes dropped down to his hand. "Plenty of people."

"If Daniel shows up, text me." He released his hold of her, even though it was the last thing in the world he wanted to do.

"You'll be parked out front. You'd see him before I would."

"And there's the employee exit out back. I can't cover both doors." He'd scoped the place out when they'd arrived, realizing he'd probably need to phone Aiden for additional support.

"You still think it's Daniel, don't you?"

"You don't care what I think. Remember?"

"I do care, but Bobby's the one in jail."

He lightly tugged at her elbow, encouraging her to move closer to the entrance so no one could overhear them. The soft music wasn't loud enough to mask their conversation. "I get that you want it to be him so this will all be over, but how do you not see what I do?"

Concern, or maybe a hint of anger, stung her eyes. "Are you jealous? Is that what this is?"

"Of course I hate that he got to be with you, but that was my own damn fault for not being here," he answered in all honesty. "But this has nothing to do with my feelings."

She edged closer. "Are you sure about that?" And with that, she turned and walked away.

And he let her go . . . because what if she was right?

What if his hate for the son of a bitch had clouded his judgment, and he only wished it was Daniel so he could shove a Glock in the guy's mouth and pull the trigger without remorse?

Christ. What is wrong with— His thoughts were cut off by the vibration of his phone in his pocket.

It was Jake on the line. He'd called his Marine buddy the other day when he and Ava decided they'd need additional reinforcements.

He hadn't wanted to bring more of his friends into this, but there'd been no choice.

"Hey, man." He left the restaurant and got back behind the wheel of his SUV. He'd been waiting for this call since Jake had texted him earlier in the day.

"I have Alexa on the line," Jake said straightaway. "I'm also connecting Aiden and Ava. Give me a sec."

Ben's chest tightened, his nerves stretching so tight they'd snap at any moment.

"Hey," Alexa said. "I think we finally found something."

Relief poured through him as he waited for her to continue.

"So, using facial recognition software, I was able to get three hits on your man Daniel Edwards. In addition to the man Daniel claims to be currently, there were also two Americans who had approximately an eighty-percent match to his face. If Daniel had plastic surgery at all, it would account for those stats. He could truly be Daniel Edwards, or he could have previously been one of these other men."

"Could you text me the images of these guys and their names?"

"They should be coming in now," she said. "I also went ahead and looked into the backgrounds of the other men. One of them is dead."

Ben tapped open the text and impatiently waited for the images to load. "So, you think that could be our guy then?"

His gut rarely failed him. And so maybe his judgment hadn't been off, jealous or not.

"It's possible. He was also a surgeon," Alexa replied.

"How'd he die?" Ben asked, his curiosity piqued.

"Boating accident with his sister in the Pacific. Bodies never recovered." Alexa's soft English accent floated through the phone.

Ben swiped through the pictures and stopped on the third. The nose and chin were a little different—but the eyes . . . they were the eyes of a killer. They were Daniel's eyes. "The guy who died, is he the second image you sent? Calvin Grey?"

"Yeah," Alexa said.

Ben zoomed in, his stomach becoming shaky. "It's him. I'm almost sure of it."

"You really think so?" Aiden asked.

Ben nodded as if his friends could see him. "Yeah. What else do you know about him?"

"Well, he and his sister were raised by a single dad. The man had a heart attack when Calvin was twenty-four, even though he didn't have any prior medical or heart conditions. The ME reported concerns that it was a drug-induced heart attack, and he suspected foul play. But nothing ever came to light. After the death, Calvin's sixteen-year-old sister, Natalie, moved with him to L.A."

"Where were they from originally?" Ben asked.

"A tiny town in South Dakota," she said. "Calvin's father had been arrested multiple times due to child abuse when Calvin was a teen."

"Maybe Calvin killed him because of it," Ben suggested.

"Calvin had an alibi at the time of death."

"Of course he did," Ben grumbled. "Anything else?"

"Actually, yes. I'm texting you a link to an article in the *L.A. Times*. You'll want to have a look at it."

"The campus serial killer." Ben read the headline of the article. He vaguely remembered hearing about it, but he'd been in boot camp at the time. He checked the date. It was almost fourteen years ago.

He should have called Alexa sooner, damn it. He appreciated the hell out of Ava, but he'd been stubborn in not wanting to be a burden on Jake and Alexa. And where had that gotten him? Lives might have been saved.

It'd always been dangerous to mix emotions when on an op in the Marines, but it'd been impossible to do the same this time.

He gripped his phone tighter as guilt weaved tight around his organs and squeezed.

"There were four seemingly unrelated murders on the college campus," Ava said. "And I checked out the case file on the murders—it's still considered an open case. Guess whose name was one of the suspects."

"Calvin." Emotion pushed into Ben's chest, and anger clawed at him, creating fresh wounds.

"Yup. His sister had been a graduate student at that campus, and she'd been dating one of the victims. He'd been the first of the four killed. The murders stopped, and the police never found the killer, but I'm betting it's because a week after the fourth victim died—"

"The boating accident happened," Ben finished for her. "How fucking convenient. Why stage his sister's death, too, though?"

How long had Daniel been getting away with murder?

"Natalie was about to complete her master's in computer

science, and she was writing her thesis on cyber warfare. She was an expert in hacking," Alexa explained.

"Oh, shit." Ava joined the conversation. "Maybe she's the one who hacked Bobby's computer to frame him! She could have easily helped create the new identities for herself and her brother."

"Are we talking about two goddamn killers?" Ben's nostrils flared as he stared at his phone in disbelief. "You got a picture of the sister?"

"Yeah, give me a sec," she said.

"Thank you for your help. All of you," Ben said in a gravelly tone as he waited for the next image to download.

The image was pixelated at first, and he cursed the cell service in his small town as he waited.

"You get it?" Alexa asked.

He narrowed his eyes, disbelief flooding him.

His gaze flickered out the front window for a moment before he dropped his phone and barreled out of the SUV and toward the restaurant.

The corner booth was empty.

He didn't see Riley.

He didn't see Mandy.

And never in his life had he felt so sick.

CHAPTER TWENTY-FIVE

Riley blinked a few times, trying to adjust her vision. It was too dark to see anything, but it was cool and damp as if she were in a basement.

"Hello? Talk to me. Where am I?" Riley forced out the words, noticing a slowness to her speech. Whatever drug she'd been injected with had weakened somewhat, but it was still swirling around her system.

She tried to move, but something tight rubbed against her wrists as she shook her arms. And when she attempted to lift her head, a rough texture rubbed against her throat, pinning her down.

Her legs were free, but she didn't know how that'd help her from getting off whatever she was attached to.

A sudden glow filled the room, casting shadows overhead.

And then the light blinked out, and darkness devoured the space once more.

"Hello," she cried out, scrambling to recall what exactly had happened before she woke in the dark.

Vague memories of a knife—no, a scalpel . . . in the restaurant bathroom, pressing to her jugular, came to mind.

No, it can't be.

She fought at the restraints and tried to scream, but it came out more like a broken sob.

"He loves you. I don't understand it, but he does," a voice bellowed from somewhere to her right.

Riley stiffened at the sound of Mandy's calm voice.

Her chest tightened, the weight of an anxiety attack coming on. She hadn't had one since Nate died and Ben left, but she remembered how it felt with unmistakable clarity.

It was as if she were being buried alive and there wasn't enough oxygen.

"I don't understand." Riley closed her eyes and tried to slow her breathing before she fainted. She had to keep it together.

Ben had been right about Bobby, and she hadn't listened to him. Why the hell hadn't she listened to him?

Mandy pressed something beneath Riley's ear. *The scalpel. And not the one planted in Bobby's car.*

"Why are you doing this?"

"You don't deserve him. He couldn't see that, but I'll help him understand." Her voice was different. The normal sweetness to her tone had been replaced by something grim and dark. Something utterly disturbing.

But then, recognition struck her. "Are you talking about Daniel?"

The blade nicked Riley's skin, causing a slight burn. The muscles in her legs tightened with the anticipation of more pain to come.

"I tried to make things right for the two of you."

With the scalpel at the side of her neck now, where the collarbone met her throat, she couldn't fight, or she could cause more damage to the jugular.

She focused on thoughts of Ben, on the man she had loved with all of her heart for her entire life, despite her attempts to clear him from her mind over the years.

They needed more time together. This couldn't be it.

I'm not ready to die.

Fear tried to envelop her, to pull her into a foggy haze—but she had to resist. She had to remember her training. "We're friends."

"And how do you think that came into being?" Mandy chuckled lightly, the sound ricocheting off the walls and barreling right into Riley's heart.

"Daniel had never been in a real relationship before you. He doesn't normally trust women, and then you came along, and you screwed with his head. You made him weak."

Her words practically obliterated her control, but she had to hang on.

"I moved to this small hick town to make sure you didn't hurt him. You were so easy to fool, too. I had hoped for a little bit of a challenge since you're a shrink, but God, you failed. You failed miserably."

Riley sucked in a tender breath.

"You chose Ralph over Daniel. That was your first mistake."

"You killed Ralph because I wouldn't move with Daniel?"

Mandy was a surgeon. The woman knew how to use a scalpel, and she could probably hack her up while keeping her alive long enough for this sick, twisted ride.

"I was doing Daniel a favor. Get rid of Ralph, and you two could be happy." Her voice was calm. She spoke as if her words were logical. As if she truly believed she was in the right.

A sociopath.

She went through the characteristic checklist: *shallow emotions, can't empathize with others, a self-made reality, always five steps ahead, charming, liars . . .*

Textbook definitions whirled around in her head, but now that she was at the mercy of a killer, it was hard to come to terms with the truth. It was hard to negotiate with someone who was capable of such manipulation—because in Mandy's world she was doing what was right.

She'd fooled Riley into believing they were friends. It'd all been an act. Their friendship one giant manufactured lie.

And for what?

Riley's stomach folded in on itself. She continued to fight the bile as it rose in her throat. "Does Daniel know?" He couldn't possibly know, could he?

Mandy remained silent, and so Riley asked, "Did you choose to frame Bobby because you found out he was cheating on you?"

"Do you honestly think I cared about him? Or that my tears over patient losses were genuine?" A soft hiss left her lips. "Bobby was a convenient choice. I told you what you needed to hear to help me. I knew you'd blabber to the police about him."

"Yeah? And what'd Lydia do to deserve to die?" Riley wouldn't be able to get her to back down. No, Mandy would never give up, but she could at least buy herself some time by keeping her talking until Ben got there.

He'll come.

He has to come.

Mandy must've moved positions because the scalpel now rested on Riley's abdomen. It didn't poke her skin, and so she tried to relax her stomach.

"Daniel has certain needs you couldn't always keep up with. And so, he had sex with a few of his interns. It's human nature for men to fuck around."

"You're right." She allowed her voice to break as if she were truly regretful. "Daniel deserved more." Maybe it wasn't much of a lie because Riley never did love him.

"So you admit it?" The blade lifted.

She expelled a slow breath. "Daniel's an amazing man. A world-class surgeon. I should have been better to him." She tried to keep her voice from wavering, to sound believable.

"So you would've forgiven the affair? If you had found out that Daniel was fucking a twenty-seven-year-old intern, you would have taken him back?"

Riley swallowed the lump in her throat, the pressure gathering behind her lids. "I would have forgiven him, yes."

"You're lying," she said sharply. "I don't believe you."

"I promise."

"Do you really think I give a damn about your promise?"

The scalpel dug deep into her core, but it didn't perforate the flesh. It was a tease of what was to come, as the cold metal began to slowly scratch.

Chills raked over her body, and she tensed with each slow circling of the tip around her belly button.

"You lost your chance at being with him. I thought I could forgive you for sleeping with Patrick because you said you were drunk and it was a mistake. And that asshole doctor probably did take advantage of you." She whispered quick curses under her breath. "But Ben . . ."

"Ben." She repeated his name like a soft echo, not sure where the conversation was going to go. Mandy had clearly made up her mind about Riley long before taking her.

"You still love Ben."

Mandy could never understand love. How could she? Whatever she felt for Daniel was—

"You ran right into Ben's arms. You screwed him." The blade shifted back up her body and met her throat once again. Mandy's breath touched her ear, and Riley's fingertips curled inward as she prepared herself for death.

Some people say that when they think they're about to die, a montage of memories plays through their mind.

But not for Riley.

No, all that flashed through her mind were scenes of the future —of what she so desperately wanted.

To be a wife.

A mother.

"Please." She cried out the word in her last attempt to somehow change Mandy's mind. "You don't have to do this."

"I really do. But I'm not done yet."

"Don't hurt anyone else. You have me. I'm who you hate," Riley rushed out, knowing her pleas wouldn't impact Mandy, but the desire to live had taken over.

"I can't let Ben live. The man won't give up on trying to find your killer."

"No!" She tried to jerk up, but the abrasive material around her throat wouldn't allow for much movement.

"You're so willing to fight for Ben, but you wouldn't do the same for Daniel." Mandy's palm landed on Riley's chest, and she pushed down, an attempt to still her. "It's over, sweetheart. I'm going to comfort Ben as he mourns you, and then I'll have sex with him. I'll slit his throat as he comes."

Tears streaked her face as she continued to resist, forgetting the scalpel at her throat.

But the sudden light in the room had Riley freezing.

She could see Mandy's face now, her lips twisted in surprise.

"Back away from her!" a familiar voice roared through the room. But from Riley's vantage point, she couldn't see anyone other than Mandy.

Mandy kept the blade in position but looked over her shoulder at the intruder. "I can't do that."

"You don't have a choice," the deep voice rumbled through the room.

"She needs to die," Mandy said firmly. "This has to happen."

"Don't make me shoot. I'll do it. I will." A touch of fear, of sadness, slipped through his words.

"No, you won't," Mandy said calmly and looked back at Riley.

But the sound of a bullet whistled through the room not even a second later.

The scalpel clattered to the floor, along with a heavy thud.

Mandy . . .

Riley flinched and allowed her gaze to fall to the ground, to see if Mandy was still alive. But all she could see was her open palm.

"Is she dead?" Riley asked in a whisper.

Daniel crouched next to Riley. He was probably checking Mandy's pulse, but all she could see was his back.

"She's gone." He slowly rose and faced her, his skin blanched and colorless.

Oh, God. Daniel had killed for her.

His focus snapped to her throat as he tucked the gun in the back of his pants. "Shit, you're bleeding. Let me get your hands free first. She must have a key on her." He knelt alongside Mandy's body, and a minute later, he had the cuffs off and the rope removed.

His shirt came off next, and he held it to the wound at her neck. "You okay?"

"I'm a bit faint, but it could be from the drugs she gave me, too."

"We need to get you bandaged. Keep the shirt tight on the wound."

"How'd you know she had me?" Riley asked as he helped her off what she realized was a gurney from an ambulance.

"I got an anonymous note in my locker at work, saying that you needed to die, and it was being done in my honor."

His eyes flashed to the floor as they walked past Mandy. She was face up. Her eyelids were closed, but blood continued to ooze from the bullet wound in her chest.

Her nerves bundled tight and she quickly forced her gaze away.

"Mandy's one of the few interns I work with who has such neat writing, and so I made a guess it was her."

"You should have called the police. You could've gotten hurt," she said, as he slowly guided her up a set of unfinished stairs.

"I didn't want to take the chance that the police wouldn't get to you in time." He spoke in a low voice once they reached the upstairs. "I was also worried they wouldn't believe me since they think Bobby's the killer. I mean, I thought the same way until I got the note today."

"I don't know how to thank—" She cut herself off upon realizing where she was. "I don't understand," she murmured. "Why would Mandy bring me here? Did she know you owned this place? Has she been here before?"

In the fifteen months that Riley had dated Daniel, she had only visited his farmhouse once. He had mentioned it in passing to her one afternoon earlier that year, and she had insisted upon taking the hour drive outside of town to see it.

He'd bought it as an investment when he first moved to Alabama but never had time to do anything with it. Well, that's what he'd said, at least.

Gnarled roots and overgrown fields had surrounded the white dilapidated home. It'd have been the perfect setting for a horror movie, she had joked upon seeing it.

And now . . .

"I guess I mentioned it." He lifted his shoulders before slowly dragging a palm down his face. "Luckily I had a gun in the safe upstairs."

"She's clearly obsessed with you." *Like Lydia was . . .* "But how'd you know she'd bring me here?"

His gaze flickered to the shirt she held tight to her neck. "Let me get you patched up," he said instead.

She wanted to press for more information, but she was too disoriented. "Why don't we wait here for the police? I don't think we should leave," she said after he applied a patch and some tape to the wound.

"And I don't want to stay here." He nudged her in the back, directing her toward the back door, off the side of the kitchen.

"I need to call Ben." She turned around.

"Why do we need to call him?"

"I have to tell him I'm okay. He'll be looking for me."

A sudden darkness blanketed his eyes. She'd never seen this look on him before, such a noticeable anger. "The son of a bitch stepped all over your heart fourteen years ago."

"He's my friend. And so, I—"

He lowered his forehead. "No." A mirthless, haunting laugh moved through the air, taking her by surprise. "I just killed someone for you. And all you can think about is *him*?"

He slammed her against the wall, and a rush of terror crawled up her spine. Her breath hitched as panic catapulted into her throat, nearly suffocating her.

"Do you know how much I love you?" He cocked his head and mounted his hands over her shoulders, pressing them to the faded flower wallpaper. "Do you know how much I've sacrificed for you?" His nostrils flared, and he dropped his forehead to touch hers. "Sweetheart, you and I belong together. Mandy died so we could be together."

She shifted her head to the right to try and push him, but it was a futile attempt against his cage of a body.

"Mandy was a murderer. She didn't make a sacrifice." Defiant tears gathered in her eyes.

"Do you love Ben?"

Yes. "Let me go. Please."

"Answer the goddamn question," he growled, his minty breath on her face.

Who the hell took the time to eat a mint on their way to rescuing someone?

"Was Mandy telling me the truth? Did you screw him?"

A lick of fear curled up her spine, putting her on high alert.

"No, I love you." Her mind raced, competing with the drugs and the lightheadedness. "I still care about you . . . I promise."

He pulled back and found her eyes, searching for the truth.

"I've missed you," she tried to say as calmly as possible.

"Prove it to me."

She needed to get to his gun. "After the hospital, once this has all blown over"—she wrapped a hand around his waist—"we can be together."

He snatched her wrist before she could reach the weapon and spun her around so fast that she smashed face-first into the wall.

"You disappoint me," he snarled and shoved her harder, the barrel of the gun now at her temple. "This is all your fault." A bitterness trampled his voice. "I killed her for you, but maybe she was right—you're not worth it."

I'm going to die.

"She's all I've ever had, but I chose you. I fucking chose you, don't you get that? Don't you see how special you are to me?" A sharp sadness weaved through his words. A killer who was grieving. It was beyond fucked up.

She thought she had known him. How could she have been so wrong? How could she have not seen the signs given her profession?

He lowered the gun and edged back. "Maybe we can run away together." His attention lifted to the ceiling as if in thought, as if he were working through a puzzle in his head. "You can learn to love me."

"I do love you. I don't need to learn." Her stomach protested, but she reached for his face, palming his cheek.

"I'll dispose of Mandy's body," he said a moment later. "And then we leave. We never come back." He nodded, his eyes blank and devoid of emotion.

Her eyes stung, and the fear of death whispered across her skin and made her body even shakier.

His gaze softened a little as he lowered the gun. "I need to patch you up better if we're going to be on the road."

"Yeah, okay." She had to stay alive long enough for Ben to find her. He had to find her . . .

He forced her into a bathroom, where he grabbed some supplies, and then he pushed her in the direction of the kitchen table.

"This is going to hurt." He eyed her neck, and she shrank back in the little neon-green vinyl chair.

She squeezed her lids tight, not wanting to watch him work, and settled her hands on the Formica table.

Ten minutes later, he stood from his crouched position. "You should be good, but you'll have a scar."

"Thank you." She finally opened her eyes, but found him pointing the gun at her with one hand, while extending a hand to her with the other.

Her fingers trembled as she reached out, but then her gaze snapped over his shoulder and to the hall leading to the front door. She could have sworn she caught a glimpse of someone.

She tried to mask her surprise, but it was too late.

Daniel yanked her up and spun her around so her back was to his chest.

He used her as a shield and pressed the gun to the side of her head.

Ben. She met his blue eyes, and he gave her the slightest of nods as if he were trying to let her know it'd be okay.

He had a gun drawn as he entered the kitchen, and his eyes dropped to the white gauze at her throat. The muscles in his neck strained before he focused on Daniel.

"That's far enough," Daniel instructed.

Ben stopped walking. "No one has to get hurt."

He was a Marine, she reminded herself. He'd taken down terrorists. He could take down her ex.

"Mandy's dead. I had to kill her," Daniel seethed. "So, someone's already been hurt."

Riley had to figure a way to diffuse the situation before Daniel shot her, but fear overcrowded her mind.

"Yeah? And when did you figure out Mandy was killing people? Before or after you started accusing Bobby?" Ben's eyes narrowed. "I'm betting after. You would've done a better job at making sure the trail didn't lead to you."

Daniel tightened his hold, but he didn't say anything. She

couldn't begin to imagine what was going through his head right now.

"It must have been difficult for you—killing your sister like that," Ben said calmly.

Sister? Panic caught in her throat, and she looked down at the floor, putting everything together.

Daniel remained silent.

"Was it you who killed your dad, or did Natalie do it?" Ben continued.

"So you know," Daniel finally said, a dark undertone reverberating through his speech. "And who else knows the truth?"

"You trying to decide if you need to fake your death again and take on a new identity? Your sis was the one with the computer skills. You sure you can do it without her?"

"This wasn't supposed to happen again." Daniel's voice was lower this time, almost apologetic sounding.

Maybe if he was torn, or capable of feeling guilt, she could talk to him—convince him to drop the gun.

"Natalie should've stayed away. I asked her not to come to Alabama. She applied for the damn internship, anyway," Daniel said, his grip on her slightly loosening.

"Bodies do tend to pile up whenever she's around. It must be hard to live a normal life when your sister is a psychopath." Ben's words contradicted the calmness of his tone.

"No," Riley mouthed to him, worried she was two seconds away from dying, but Ben wasn't looking at her.

Ben may have been a soldier, but he clearly had no idea how to talk to a mentally unstable person. He was taunting him.

"Tell me, do you help her get away with the murders, or do you kill, too?" Ben's eyes tightened to thin slits.

"I don't need to tell you anything," Daniel replied, his voice flat and lifeless.

"Let me help you," Riley spoke up. "You don't have to be a killer."

"Don't psychobabble me, baby. I went to enough shrinks as a kid—I don't need another one in my ear." His fingertips dug into her flesh, and the feel of the twitch of his cock hardening from behind had her nauseated.

Did the bastard get off on her fear? Shit, had she made things worse?

"Talk to me then," Ben said, lifting his chin. "Brag to me about how you've gotten away with murder for decades. When did you realize that your sister was as fucked up as you?"

Ben quickly looked at Riley, and she witnessed confidence in his eyes.

"Was it your idea for her to go to med school when she began her new life?" Ben asked. "Didn't you think that'd be risky for someone like her to have power to control whether someone lived or died on a regular basis?"

"You have it backward," Daniel said, but once again eased up on the grasp he had around her waist. "It was my way of helping her control her urges. You see, having such control over life or death is therapeutic. It helped keep her calm."

"Guess you'd know. That's why you became a doc, right? The killer gene run in the family?" Ben arched a brow. "Did you ever get tired of cleaning up her messes, though? For getting blamed for the murders she committed?" Ben's eyes followed Daniel's hand as it skated up Riley's stomach. "You're the smarter one, right? The more in-control one. Did you give her the idea of the campus serial killer to cover up for the murder of her boyfriend?"

Riley's mind spun as she replayed Ben's words.

Ben shrugged lightly. "Doesn't really matter, though, does it?"

"You're right. It doesn't matter," Daniel said in an eerily steady voice. "I'll be taking Riley with me, and you can spend your days looking over your shoulder—wondering when I'll be coming for you."

A quick smile met Ben's lips, one that Riley recognized.

He had a plan.

"You really think so?" Ben asked.

"Yeah, I do—"

A scream, like that of a dying animal, pierced the room as Daniel's body hit the floor.

Blood was everywhere.

A stickiness touched her skin, and she blinked, disoriented.

"Riley." Ben gathered her in his arms a second later.

"You shot him," she said in a daze. "And, oh my God, you didn't miss."

Ben pulled back and held her face as if worried she'd look back at Daniel and faint.

"I didn't take the shot."

"What?" She lifted her eyes to find Aiden standing there, tucking a gun into the back of his jeans.

"Ben was the distraction. I had to get into position to get a clean shot," Aiden explained. "He was buying us time."

Ben gently gripped her forearms, but he peered back at Aiden. "You should leave. The police will be here soon."

"Leave?" she murmured, confused.

Aiden gave her a curt nod. "Glad you're okay." And then as fast as he had appeared—he left.

"The police are coming?" She touched her wound. It was still tender, but that didn't matter so much anymore, did it?

She was in a house with two dead people: one she'd shared her secrets with, and the other she'd had sex with. How would she ever recover from that?

But she was alive.

She had to try and focus on that.

No more people would die.

"We had a fifteen-minute head start on the sheriff." He eyed her wound. "Are you okay?"

"I don't know," she said softly. "I, uh, still don't understand this all."

"It's a little complicated."

"You were right about everything, though. You never gave up."

"I'm sorry it took me so long to get to you. This house is listed under one of his other names."

Other names? She didn't know what to say. She had so much on her mind, but—

"Aiden can catch you up. A lot happened while you scared the shit out of me by vanishing." He palmed her face again, and she noticed liquid in his eyes. "I was terrified I was going to lose you. I'm so damn thankful that didn't happen." His voice cracked as a tear rolled down his cheek.

She collapsed against him. "Thank you." He tipped her chin up. "Why'd Aiden have to go in such a rush?"

He shoved his hands through her hair and held her eyes. "Because I'll be going to jail tonight, and I didn't want him along for the ride."

CHAPTER TWENTY-SIX

"Don't! Please," Riley yelled, as an officer held onto her forearm, preventing her from reaching for Ben.

The sheriff nudged Ben in the back, directing him into the squad car, but he didn't get in.

It took three people to hold Ben back from getting to Riley. One burly guy clung to his midsection from behind, while the other men wrapped their arms around Ben's biceps, digging their heels into the ground to use their weight to keep him from launching forward.

Ben continued to struggle but glanced at the sheriff over his shoulder. "Let her go, and I'll get in the car."

The sheriff huffed, but he finally nodded in the direction of the men holding Riley.

The moment she was free, she tore toward him.

Her arms looped around his neck, and he pressed his cheek to hers. "It'll be okay. I promise," he said softly.

"No, I need you. I don't understand why they're doing this."

"I'm sorry, but I'll call you as soon as I can. Stay with your parents or Aiden, okay?"

The sheriff tugged at Ben's arm. "That's enough. Get in the car."

But she wouldn't drop her hold of him.

"If they grab you again, I'll lose my control," he said once she found his eyes. "You have to let go."

She nodded and finally dropped her hands from his shoulders.

She took a step back, and Ben relaxed his stance.

"I can get in myself," he said gruffly to the sheriff and lowered himself into the car.

He mouthed something before the door was closed, and she was pretty sure he'd said *I love you.*

* * *

"WE HAVE TWO MORE DEAD BODIES. SIX IN TOTAL." THE SHERIFF rubbed his palms up and down his face.

Would he believe the truth?

She wasn't sure.

"Let Ben out of jail. He doesn't belong in there." She was sitting in front of his desk this time, which was better than being in that little interrogation room.

"He belongs in there. I gave him direct orders not to enter the house . . . or kill anyone. He knew what would happen, and he did it, anyway."

"It was self-defense!"

It'd been four hours since Daniel had been killed, and she'd spent the last two hours at the hospital.

As soon as the ER doctor cleared her, the sheriff had taken her straight to the station.

"Daniel had a gun to my head. What did you expect Ben to do?" She fought back the tears that loomed once again. She'd been crying on and off since she'd left the farmhouse. And when she'd seen her parents at the hospital, she'd flat-out broken down.

She figured Aiden and Ava hadn't shown up at the ER because they were working on a plan to get Ben out. She hoped so, at least.

"Did you tell Ben's parents, yet?" she asked when the sheriff didn't respond. He was on his computer now, and he wouldn't even look her direction.

Her fingertips bit into her quads. She was mentally and physically tired, and all she wanted was to go to sleep and then to wake up and have this all be over.

"Let's worry about you right now." He leaned back in his chair, appearing almost as exhausted as she felt.

"And what about me?"

"Tell me from the beginning what happened." He turned on the recorder, and his hands settled in his lap.

"I was with Mandy at O'Hanlon's. When I went to the bathroom, she came in with a scalpel and stabbed me in the neck with a needle." The memory of what happened was much clearer now. "The drug made me super drowsy, but I didn't lose total consciousness at first. Mandy shoved me out the back door, and it was like I couldn't seem to stop her, or even scream. I was in some sort of daze."

"And then what happened?"

"I finally blacked out because I woke up in a basement some time later. She confessed to killing Ralph, Lydia, and Patrick."

"But not Beth Stanton?"

She pinched her eyes closed as she tried to remember. "No, she didn't say anything about her. She said she'd been trying to help Daniel, but then realized I didn't deserve Daniel, and so she wanted me dead."

"Hm." He scooted closer to the desk and eyed his computer again. She wondered what the hell he was looking at. "And after that?"

"Daniel showed up and shot her. At the time, I thought he was saving me, but then I realized something was off." A quiver darted down her spine and branched out like spider webs into her limbs.

"And that's when Ben came?"

"Yeah, and Daniel put a gun to my head."

"How'd Ben get such a clean shot?"

The sheriff finally looked at her, and she knew she had to swallow the truth and let it die. Ben protected his friends, and he'd probably rot in jail to keep Aiden out of it all.

"Ben was a Marine. Daniel's a doctor. You do the math," she answered as calmly as her nerves would allow.

He gripped the edge of his desk. "Well, it looks like the information Ben emailed us just checked out." His mouth pinched tight.

"Information?"

"We matched Mandy's and Daniel's prints to Natalie and Calvin Grey." He shifted back in his seat. "Since they're supposed to be dead, it's interesting, right? Not to mention the fact that they were linked to the investigation of a serial killer right before they died."

She did her best to remain steady, to not break down again.

"Lucky for Ben, he had a government friend obtain this information, and so I can't hold him for illegally procuring the records . . . even if I feel something is off."

"You'll let him go, then?" She sat up taller, feeling hopeful.

"Not yet. He shouldn't have gone into that house, and I'm still not certain he didn't break a few other laws. He'll be staying locked up until a judge decides his fate." He stood.

"But that's not—"

"Go home and get some sleep. You and I are done here for now."

She sucked in shallow breaths. "No. I'm not leaving without Ben." Her eyes sealed tight.

"Then you'll be sleeping here, and it's not all that comfortable."

"I don't care," she said. "I'll leave when he does."

CHAPTER TWENTY-SEVEN

RILEY WAS STRETCHED OUT ON A BENCH OFF TO THE SIDE OF THE sheriff's desk.

The morning sunlight poked through the blinds, and despite the noise from the deputy moving around the room, she stayed deep asleep.

Ben nodded his thanks to the officer who had walked him over to her.

"Sorry we had to lock you up. If it had been my girl, I would've smoked the bastard, too," the officer said, and Ben forced a smile before redirecting his attention to Riley.

He knelt before her. Her hands were tucked beneath her face, and soft breaths floated from her parted lips.

Seeing her alive and breathing—it was the best sight of his life.

"Riley." He rested a palm on her hip.

She stirred but didn't wake.

"Ri—"

Her eyes slowly opened, and she blinked a few times. "Ben." She closed her eyes again, but only for a moment. "Ben!"

He stood upright, and she flung herself in his direction a moment later.

"You've really been here for twenty-six hours?" He held her as tight as possible without breaking her bones. But it felt so damn good to have her in his arms.

"I wouldn't leave without you," she cried, and he threaded his fingers through her hair. "How'd you get out?"

"They said they couldn't handle how bad you smelled anymore, so they let me—"

"Ben." She pulled back but left her arms draped around his neck as if it were the most natural position in the world.

"Aiden made some calls," he said with a smile in his eyes.

It'd been a difficult and painful journey to get to her, but the woman standing before him was his.

She'd always been his.

He just hadn't accepted it until now.

"I was hoping that was why I hadn't heard from him." Her brows lowered with concern. "Are you okay, though?"

He brushed the pad of his thumb over her bottom lip.

The woman's ex-boyfriend had been shot next to her; blood was still smattered in the strands of her hair . . . and yet, she hadn't left the station to even shower.

"As long as you're good, I'm good." He released a shaky breath as unexpected emotions caught in his throat.

"I'm sorry I didn't believe you before." Liquid filled her eyes. "I should have trusted you."

He pressed a quick kiss to her lips and held her face between his palms, but he couldn't find the right words to say. Everything he'd held pent up inside of him threatened to rush out, but it wasn't the time or the place for that.

"Let's get out of here," he said.

He didn't let go of her, though. He didn't want to ever let go.

He was afraid that, once he did that, he'd lose her all over again.

* * *

"THEY LET BOBBY OUT OF JAIL THIS MORNING," AIDEN announced.

"Took the sheriff long enough," Ben grumbled, thankful about the man's innocence, but still hating how all of this played out, possibly scarring Riley for life.

Of course, Riley was strong. She could get through it, and he'd be there to make sure of it.

He'd never let her down again.

"So, the official theory the police are working with is that Mandy killed Ralph, Lydia, and Patrick without Daniel's knowledge. And she intentionally framed Bobby from the start." Aiden took a sip of his coffee. "We're pretty sure Daniel didn't know, at first, since he became a suspect. He would've been more careful if he'd been in the know."

"And what about Beth Stanton?" Riley stared at the half-eaten plate of food before her. It had been her idea to get out of the hotel after spending the last twenty-four hours there. But now that they were out, he wondered if she regretted it.

Yesterday morning he'd been in jail, and now they were sitting together, eating bacon and eggs. Maybe she wasn't ready.

"Daniel killed her. Mandy knew all of the victims, except Beth. There were even signs of forced entry at the Stanton residence, unlike the other three murders. And, upon close examination, Beth's stab wounds were slightly inconsistent with the other victims," Aiden explained. "The police believe Daniel murdered Beth and planted evidence to cover up for his sister once he realized what Mandy was doing."

"So they're both guilty?" Riley asked.

"Yeah," Aiden answered. "When Daniel figured out what the hell was going on, he tried to put a stop to it, to protect both you and him. And he did it in the only way he knew how—murder."

"I wonder why he chose Beth," Riley said softly.

"Sheriff's report says Bobby dated her a few months prior. Daniel must've known that," Aiden replied.

Riley closed her eyes, as if in disbelief. Ben didn't blame her. It was a lot to take in.

"I can't believe he shot his own sister." Riley tucked her hands into her lap.

Ben reached over and laced his fingers with hers.

"Guess he loved you more," Ava said. "Well, in his own twisted kind of way."

"I'm glad they're both dead." Ben tightened his grip and cleared his throat.

The animal was a killer, and he'd dated Riley for over a year. It made him physically ill thinking about it, so he couldn't imagine how she was coping with the knowledge.

"The Feds linked Mandy and Daniel"—Aiden paused for a moment—"or Natalie and Calvin . . . to another small-town killing spree that happened seven years ago. We just learned the man on death row for those murders is going to be released."

Riley's eyes opened, and her lips parted in surprise. "I hate them," she murmured as her shoulders sloped down. "Given my line of work, I should feel differently maybe, but I just don't."

"Hate isn't a strong enough word for what I feel," Ben said.

Four innocent people were dead, and Riley blamed herself. It gutted him.

The chatter from around them became white noise as they sat in silence as heavy as molasses. The clinking of dishes and the opening and closing of doors faded into the background.

"You sure you're okay with us leaving tonight?" Ava's voice broke through Ben's thoughts. "We can stay."

"No, you need to get back to your lives. I can't thank you both enough for coming through for us," Ben said.

"Yes, thank you so much." Riley pulled her hand free from Ben's and reached across the table to lay her hand over Ava's.

"Well, it took a lot more than my help, but it's over now." Ava forced a smile.

"I'd love to see you next time I'm in Boston," Riley said,

surprising him a little.

"Do you come often?" Ava asked.

"No, but now I have a reason to."

"Maybe we could all try and get together soon," Aiden suggested.

Ben's phone began to ring. "One sec." He answered it when he saw his admin's number on the line. "Hey, everything okay?"

"One of our guys was shot this morning," she replied.

"Shit. Who?" Ben's stomach tightened at the news.

"Brian. He's in surgery now."

"I'll be right there" was all he said before ending the call.

"What's wrong?" Aiden asked.

"I have to go back to Vegas." He looked to Riley and noticed her visibly tense. How the hell would he leave her? "One of my men took a bullet, and he's in surgery."

"Sorry. I hope he's okay," Ava said.

"I don't want to leave you, though." Ben squeezed Riley's thigh.

"I'm an adult. I'll be okay." She forced a stiff smile. "Besides, my parents would love to have me."

"You sure?" He tipped her chin up, not caring that his friends were across the table from them.

"Of course," she said, but Ben didn't believe her.

He didn't have a choice but to go. He couldn't leave a man down and a job unfinished.

But leaving Riley had killed him the first time.

And even though he had every intention of coming back, he worried it'd still sting, that it would be like rubbing salt in an old wound, especially for her.

"I'll be back," he said in a tight voice, noticing for the first time that Aiden and Ava had slipped away from the table, leaving him alone with Riley.

"I know you will," she said without looking at him, and her lack of eye contact nearly broke his damn heart.

CHAPTER TWENTY-EIGHT

BEN: *I MISS YOU.*

> **Riley:** *It's been 15min since you boarded the plane.*
> **Ben:** *After not seeing you for 14yrs, 15min is too damn long.*
> **Riley:** *You'll come back.*
> **Riley:** *... Right?*
> **Ben:** *Nothing could stop me this time.*
> **Ben:** *I hate leaving you. I don't like you sleeping alone at night.*
> **Riley:** *Good point. I can find someone to keep me company while you're gone.*
> **Ben:** *...?*
> **Ben:** *Ri!*
> **Riley:** *What? ;)*
> **Ben:** *You want me to make a scene and get off this plane before it takes off, huh?*
> **Riley:** *I wouldn't mind a second chance at saying goodbye.*
> **Ben:** *It's not goodbye. It's bye for now. I hate goodbyes. We said our final goodbye a long time ago. From now on, let's try something like "until next time."*
> **Riley:** *Hm. You sound like a character from a Hallmark movie.*

Ben: *What do you have against Hallmark? Those movies helped us get through some tough times at the base.*

Riley: *You're full of shit.*

Ben: *Scout's honor.*

Riley: *You were never a scout.*

Ben: *...*

Riley: *...*

Riley: *Your ellipses are always so packed full of meaning. How do you do that?*

Riley: *I'm going to miss you.*

Ben: *I shouldn't leave. I need to get off this plane.*

Riley: *No!!!*

Ben: *I love when you use those shouty exclamation points. It turns me on.*

Riley: *Ben...*

Ben: *What? I'm serious. Do it again.*

Riley: *Ben, I mean it. You need to go. You're always there for your friends, and I love that about you. Don't change. That's an order.*

Ben: *You were my friend, too. I wasn't there for you.*

Ben: *I'm not sure if I can ever forgive myself for that.*

Ben: *Also, when you give orders—it's really hot, too. Do it again next time we're together.*

Ben: *I was never great at taking orders in the military. Can you believe that? I used to get myself into trouble. A lot of trouble, actually.*

Riley: *Yeah, that's hard for me to imagine. You . . . being bad? Never.*

Riley: *By the way . . .*

Ben: *Yeah?*

Riley: *The past is the past. I made mistakes, too. And you're here now, and that's all that matters.*

Ben: *Well, I'm not technically there, but if I get off this plane right now, I can be.*

Riley: *You want another order, huh?*
Ben: *Please. ;)*
Riley: *You'll have to wait to see me to get it.*
Ben: *You play dirty.*
Riley: *I learned well. I had a good teacher growing up.*
Riley: *Have a safe flight.*
Ben: *I should've asked you to come with me. I'm an idiot.*
Ben: *Shit. I have to go. I'll call you as soon as I land.*

He switched his phone to *airplane mode* after the flight attendant silently scolded him. In all fairness, she'd already asked him three times.

He tucked it in his pocket and reached for his wallet to retrieve a photo.

Once unfolded, he stared at the faded image. It was the last picture ever taken of Nate, Riley, and Ben together.

Riley stood in the middle, with her arms over both Nate's and Ben's shoulders, and a gorgeous smile graced her face.

He'd give anything to go back in time and make things right—to force Nate to use a rope that day.

Ben had kept the photo with him since the day he'd left Alabama. He'd kept it on him while he'd trekked the rough terrain in Afghanistan. And he'd probably keep it on him until the day he died.

Fourteen years hadn't softened the damage of what Nate's death had done to him.

And he still believed the better man had died.

He'd spent years trying to save lives since he couldn't save his friend that day.

And maybe he did stop terrorists, and maybe he did protect not only soldiers but American civilians . . . but did any of that change the fact that he was alive, and Nate wasn't?

In his mind—*no.*

* * *

BEN: *I'VE BEEN CALLING FOR HOURS. WHERE ARE YOU?*

Ben: *I'm worried.*

Ben: *Your parents aren't answering the house line, either.*

Ben: *Are you okay?*

Ben: *Actually, I'm more than worried. I'm about to call in a government favor and have the Feds show up at your door.*

Ben: *I'm not bluffing.*

Ben: *My guy pulled through surgery. He's going to be okay. He's quitting, though. I don't blame him.*

Ben: *The man who shot him, well, he's not doing so well.*

Ben: *I might have taken my anger out on him.*

Ben: *He deserved it, though. Scout's honor.*

He couldn't handle the silence anymore.

Something was wrong.

He hadn't spoken to Riley all day; he'd been busy wrapping up the case his crew member had been working on before taking the bullet.

He and Riley had kept in constant contact during his stay in Vegas, though.

So, where was she now, and what if something had happened to her?

What if—

A knock on his front door jarred the *what-ifs* from his head.

He pulled up the security camera app on his phone, and his pulse quickened at the sight. He rushed to the door.

He wouldn't have to go back to Alabama, after all.

She'd come to him.

He flung open the door, and a slow smile teased her lips.

"Well, you going to let me in?"

CHAPTER TWENTY-NINE

AFTER HE LIFTED HER INTO THE AIR AND COVERED HER MOUTH with his for a good five minutes, he finally released her and closed the door.

"What are you doing here?" He rushed a hand through his hair.

She eyed him nervously. Had she made a mistake in coming?

"I couldn't wait to see you. I would've come sooner, but I had a few things to wrap up back home first."

He was in jeans and flannel, and he looked so rugged and casually sexy at the same time. She wasn't sure what to do with her hands, and the desperation to touch him again banded tight in her chest.

"You should've told me. I would've picked you up at the airport." He motioned for her to enter the living area and sit down.

His place was smaller than she'd expected, and it had a rustic feel to it. Warm and soft tones layered throughout the room.

She sat on the brown suede couch, which faced a long, expansive window that offered an incredible view of the sun kissing the ground off in the distance.

"You ruined my plans, by the way. I had every intention of making a grand gesture when I showed back up in Alabama."

She lifted a brow and smiled. "Grand gesture? Like flowers and chocolate?"

He remained standing off to the side of the couch and tucked his hands into his back pockets. "It's not Valentine's Day." He half-laughed. "But, I don't know, I would've thought of something."

"All I need is you. No gestures."

They'd spent hours on the phone each night before bed, and each time, he'd calmed her nerves and stayed on the line until she'd fallen asleep. It was his way of being with her, even from afar.

They'd caught up on years of memories between texts and calls over those days. And now that she was physically with him, she wanted to catch up on so much more.

She'd been impatient and couldn't stop herself from booking the flight.

Plus, she'd needed to get away from the sadness that hung over her small town like a dense fog that didn't seem to have any plans on going away.

Too many people had died there, and the bleak feeling of responsibility clung to her skin, no matter how much she scrubbed at it.

Part of her never really wanted to go back, even if escaping wouldn't solve her problems.

Ben had tried escaping, and she'd hated him for it.

She couldn't do the same, she supposed.

"Ri?" He waved a hand in front of her, but his gaze swept to the scar on her neck, and his face hardened.

"I closed my practice," she rushed out, not sure how he'd take the news. "I called all my patients and referred them to another doctor."

He quickly sat down and reached for her hand. "Don't run," he said in a low voice. "It doesn't solve anything. Believe me, I know."

"I'm not running. I want a new start. It's actually what Ralph wanted for me. He used to talk my ear off about how he wished I'd move and make a name for myself in a new city."

"Yeah, I can almost hear him now." His hard expression softened, as if similar memories of the man they'd lost were moving through him, too. "But, does this new beginning include me?"

"If you want it to."

"And what do you want?" He edged closer and palmed her face.

"You. You're all I've ever wanted."

He nipped at her lip and pulled back only enough to look into her eyes.

"Do you remember what I told you when we were kids—what I said I wanted when I got older?"

He tightened his hold on her hand and looked at the ceiling for a brief moment. "A house that was always filled with noise."

She nodded when their eyes re-connected. "But I'm scared."

"Why?" He kept his hand on her face, and his thumb made small, calming circles on her cheek.

"Because I'm afraid you won't ever truly be able to forgive me for keeping the truth from you when we were younger . . . or that you'll never be able to forgive yourself for wanting me."

He stood and crossed the room to the window. His palm flattened against the glass.

"With everything that happened and the heavy guilt weighing me down, I keep telling myself this isn't the right time to be worrying about my future."

Ben shook his head. "Don't. We've talked about this. Ralph wouldn't want you blaming yourself for his death." He glanced back at her. "Only two sick people are responsible."

"I can't help it. When I close my eyes, I see their faces. Every person who was killed . . ."

"Me, too," he whispered and fully faced her. "But in my case, it's every guy I couldn't save. Their faces come to mind before I go to bed. And they're there when I wake up."

His pain was so strong it emanated from him like it was visible to the touch. And she'd take his pain if she could. She'd do it in a heartbeat if it'd help him.

"It doesn't ever go away. Not for me, at least. I'm not sure that I want it to, either," he said somberly.

Her eyes watered as he approached and crouched before her, gathering her hands between his palms.

"Thinking about whether there will be a me-and-you helps keep me from totally breaking down." Her voice trembled. "But then, I worry I'll lose you again, and—"

He leaned forward and captured her mouth, taking her by surprise. His tongue twined with hers, stealing her breath.

Against her mouth, he said, "I'm not going anywhere. Not this time."

"And what about Nate?"

He closed his eyes and pressed his forehead to hers. "He'd want us to be happy. It took me a long time to realize that, but it's the truth."

"How do you know?"

"Because if it had been me that fell . . . that'd be what I'd want."

* * *

SEVEN DAYS IN VEGAS HAD BEEN GOOD FOR HER. RELAXING.

The nightmares were nearly gone. She didn't know if it had to do with sleeping in Ben's arms every night, but she'd take whatever ounce of peace she could get.

From behind, Ben wrapped his arms around her, and she relaxed against him. She focused on the small, but perfect, Christmas tree. They had gone shopping two days ago for decorations after it'd dawned on them that the holiday was around the corner.

"You weren't supposed to buy me a gift," she said, noticing the single present beneath the tree. She tried to turn around to scowl at him, but he kept her tight against him.

He brushed his lips against the shell of her ear. "I didn't *buy* anything."

The feel of his breath sent chills down her shoulders and into her arms. "Hm." She eyed the red square box that was a little bigger than letterhead in length.

He swept her hair to her other shoulder and kissed the side of her neck, his lips brushing over her scar.

"Keep doing that, and I'm going to forget about the box and give you your present now."

"So, you did get me something. You broke the agreement, too." His laughter tickled her neck, or maybe it was his beard. She'd decided she wanted him to keep the rugged look.

"Well, it's more of something I planned on wearing for you later." She tucked her lip between her teeth, and he finally dropped his hold on her, but only long enough to spin her around to face him.

"Red or black? Silk or satin? See-through or—"

"Patience. You'll get a chance to unwrap me." She smiled. "But maybe I should open my present first."

"No, it can wait." His eyes dropped to the faded Beatles T-shirt of his she wore, and he skimmed her bare thighs with his fingertips, bunching up the material. "And you're not wearing any panties."

A hard breath fell from her mouth as he teased her with his fingers.

"You're going to stand in front of me practically naked and tell me to wait?" He continued to torture her, and she bucked against his hand. "No way."

As much as she wanted him, she was way too curious about the box, so she tugged at his wrist. "I need to open it."

"I've changed my mind, though. I think the gift might be a mood killer."

Her mouth rounded in surprise. "What the hell kind of gift is it?" Her heartbeat kicked up in her chest as nerves set in.

"Unique."

She looked away from him and to the tree, to the red gift that was now like a bright beacon flashing. "Ben, you've got me scared." But she went over to the tree and lifted the box, anyway.

"Honey, you're not wearing panties, and you just bent over . . . what are you trying to do to me?"

She faced him with the present in hand.

He adjusted himself, shifting the material of his gray drawstring pajama pants.

"What is it?" she asked.

He crossed his arms over his naked chest and leaned against a wooden beam a few feet away. "Guess you'll see in a second." A touch of a smile met his lips.

She sat on the floor, with her legs crossed like an eager kid, and set the box in front of her.

Her fingers trembled as she removed the top.

"I don't understand," she said as she stared inside the box.

"Emails," he said quickly.

She reached inside for the top sheet and swallowed hard.

"The emails you wrote me but never sent? You saved them?"

There were so many.

At least a hundred pages or more.

Was he serious?

"I saved them as drafts." He knelt next to her and pressed a hand to her shoulder.

She held the stack and flipped through the pages in total shock. "These aren't just from the military." She pointed to the last page. "This one's from a few months ago."

He nodded. "Once I started writing you, I couldn't get myself to stop. It was my way of talking to you, of staying connected." His voice was nearly hoarse as he spoke, as if the same emotions choking her up at the moment were hitting him hard, too. "You were there for me, even though you didn't know it. You got me through some of the most challenging times of my life."

"I wish you'd sent them. I wish I could have known over the years how you felt."

She wanted to read every email.

Every single word.

Every admission, thought, or feeling from him.

"Why'd you save them?"

He glanced at the pages. "Not sure. You're the brilliant doc. Why do you think?" A quick smile met his lips.

"Well, in my professional opinion, I think it's because you loved me."

He shook his head almost immediately. Her shoulders sagged, and her gaze dropped to the floor, but he tipped her chin up, demanding her eyes meet his.

"You said *loved*. That implies past tense. I thought you did better in school than me." He lifted a brow and edged his face closer to hers.

She lowered the papers, and he reached for her hands. The walls of her heart shattered.

"See, the thing is, I never stopped loving you"—he continued to hold her eyes—"because, like Ralph always said, you only get one soul mate."

CHAPTER THIRTY

SIX MONTHS LATER
   Colorado Springs

BEN REACHED THE TOP OF THE HIGHEST PEAK AT THE GARDEN OF the Gods and viewed the surrounding landscape. The mountains jutted so high as if they soared straight into the sky.

He was as close to heaven as he could get at that moment.

He was as close to Nate as he could get.

He peeked down to see Riley standing at the base, holding the rope tight in her hands.

She hadn't been resistant to the idea of taking the trip. She knew how much he needed this moment.

She knew that if he were to ever truly be at peace with what happened when he was eighteen, he had to come back, he had to come here.

"Miss you, buddy." A slight breeze carried his words, hopefully bringing them up and to his friend.

If heaven was real, and he believed it to be—he knew Nate could hear him now.

Ben brushed his fingertips over his tattoo, and a hard knot fisted in his stomach as memories of his youth seized hold of him.

He lifted his chin a few minutes later and allowed the sun to sweep over his body, going straight to his soul.

"Goodbye, Nate."

And as he made the descent back to the woman of his dreams, he knew everything would be okay.

EPILOGUE

"IT'S LOUD." RILEY COVERED HER EARS AND SMILED.

"You said you wanted a house with a lot of noise, didn't you?" He laughed but turned down the volume on the new surround-sound speakers he'd had installed earlier that day.

"Yeah, but I was talking about noise from having a lot of kids running around." She playfully smacked him in the chest.

He dropped the remote on the couch and scooped her into his arms. "Okay." He found her eyes. "You want to get started on that now?"

"You just want to have sex." She rolled her eyes.

"What's wrong with that?" He nipped at her lip, softly biting it.

"You already gave me three orgasms this morning."

"Well, shit, that's not enough." He carried her down the hall of their new house and gently tossed her onto the king-size bed.

Her long blonde hair fanned out behind her, and she stared up at him as he peeled off his T-shirt.

"Of course, there is one thing I'd like to do first," he said.

She narrowed her gaze and eyed him suspiciously.

"Be right back." He left the room, and when he came back, he found her sitting upright on the bed in only a bra and panties.

"I knew you were eager for a fourth time." He patted the envelope he held against his outer thigh.

She wet her lips and traced her collarbone with a pink nail. "And a fifth."

"So, you want to wait on this, then?" He lifted the envelope between them, and she leaned forward and snatched it.

"You know I'm horribly impatient."

His nerves jammed up in his throat as he watched her remove the two plane tickets.

"Hawaii? In a week?"

"But I start my job in D.C., and you're about to begin your new career." Riley accepted a position with the military, where she'd be working specifically with soldiers dealing with PTSD. It had been something she'd always wanted to do, and he was so damn proud of her.

He, on the other hand, had closed down Logan Securities to pursue a much more exciting, albeit dangerous, profession.

"Is this a vacation?" She took a long breath, confusion evident on her face.

"Sort of." He cleared his throat, held her eyes, and then slowly dropped to one knee and reached into his pocket. "More like a destination wedding."

Her lips pursed, and then her palm landed on her chest, her eyes widening as he opened a small black velvet box.

He took a deep breath, hoping to hell he was doing this right. "This was my grandmother's ring, and she told me when I was eight that I was going to marry you." He reached for her free hand, his heart pumping hard in his chest. "And I want to do exactly that."

She dropped the tickets and covered her mouth.

"I was thinking next week in Maui."

"Next week? How?"

"Well, give me your answer first, and then I'll tell you."

She gave a sharp nod.

"That's a *yes*, right?" He needed to hear the words from her before his heart exploded in his chest.

"Yes. Yes. YES!"

He placed the ring on her finger, and she leaped off the bed and circled her arms around his neck. "I love you."

"I love you so much." She pulled back and gripped his forearms for support. "And you're serious about next week?"

"I've spent the last six weeks planning everything. Well, I've had help." He grinned. "Your mom, Ava, and others—"

"My mom kept this a secret from me?" She stared at him in disbelief. "You were pretty confident I'd say *yes*, huh?"

"If you'd rather wait and plan everything yourself, I'd understand. But I—"

"No! This is amazing. It's perfect. I don't even know what to say, I'm so shocked." She took a step back, bumping into the bed, and then she reached around and unclasped her bra.

"What are you doing?" He angled his head, his body growing hard and ready.

"I want to make love to my future husband wearing only one thing." She raised her hand, eyeing the ring. "You object?"

"Never." His body continued to tighten, and he shoved down his jeans, ready to make love to the woman who'd finally be his wife in seven days.

Seven days too long.

After spending a decade and a half without the love of his life, he didn't have it in him to even wait a week.

He wanted to give Riley everything.

He wanted to give her that house full of noise . . . of love and laughter.

AFTER THE EPILOGUE—BONUS SCENE

*Features the cast from the Hidden Truths Series

Riley

My pulse throbs in my neck, and every fiber of my being nearly explodes with joy.

Mrs. Riley Logan. I keep repeating it in my head over and over again.

I'm Ben's wife.

Eight days ago, I never would have imagined it'd happen. Well, not so soon, at least.

But this incredible man continues to surprise me.

He awed me when he closed down his business in Vegas to move to D.C. so we could be together, and then he surprised me by boldly climbing at the Garden of the Gods two months ago to make peace with the past.

And now, we're on a beach in Maui, beneath the stars twinkling as husband and wife.

"He's a great guy."

I look over at Kate Maddox, Michael's wife. I quickly learned that Michael is Ben's genius friend, the one Ben told me could never turn his brain off and who suffered from PTSD. Hopefully, I can help such incredible men, such as himself, once I begin my work.

I'm not gonna lie. Michael's a bit intimidating, and it's not because he reminds me of the actor who played in the new Superman movie. It's the pensive look he wears all the time, and I'm pretty sure he scares a shit-ton of people. But Ben assures me he's a teddy bear.

Jury is still out, though. I'm sure I'll see the softer side of the man eventually.

Kate—well, she's like the sister I always wanted. And now, I basically have four sisters: Kate, Ava, Alexa, and Olivia. The wives or fiancées of Ben's Marine friends.

I only just met most of Ben's friends this week in Hawaii, but I can tell they're going to be like family.

I'm so grateful Ben has had these people in his life when I couldn't be a part of it.

"Which guy is great?" I smile and observe the group of five former Marines, mysteriously huddled off to the side of the dance floor. "From what I can tell, they're all pretty amazing."

Kate smiles and leans back in her seat, and then glances over at the other women sitting with us. "You're right about that. But, we're all so happy Ben found you." Her forehead creases for a moment. "Well, I guess he already had you . . . he just lost his way."

I release a long sigh as memories of my childhood tear through my mind, and this time, a sense of comfort fills me, instead of pain.

"Ben has always been the wild one of the guys. Did he tell you that?" Alexa smiles.

"I'm not exactly surprised."

"Are you nervous or excited about Ben's new line of work?" Alexa asks a few minutes later.

I think about her question and stall by taking a sip of my drink. "Well, I'm both, I guess."

Ben will be working with some of his friends again, which he seems pretty stoked about. Jake and Alexa, along with a few others, began a security company not too long ago. It's apparently different than the kind Ben had previously run.

It's more meaningful, Ben had said. He'll be rescuing women from human traffickers, stopping terrorists, and working with the government as needed for special operations.

So, yeah, Ben is pumped.

Me? I just got him back, and so, I can't imagine losing him again.

But I know in my heart I couldn't ever be selfish and ask Ben to change who he is.

He is strong enough to carry the weight of the world on his shoulders. But I'm strong enough to carry him when needed, too.

We make a good team.

"Jake will make sure he's safe. I promise." Alexa reaches over and pats my forearm.

"Connor, too," Olivia says.

"Have you guys thought of a name for the agency yet?" I ask. "You can't keep calling it *The Agency*."

Alexa shrugs. "I don't know. Having no name almost makes us seem even more covert and interesting." She chuckles. "That, and the guys can't seem to agree on one!"

I glance over at our men and catch Ben's eyes from across the way; he shoots me a mischievous and lopsided smile.

He's up to something.

"So, uh, when are you guys tying the knot?" I direct my

attention to Ava first and then look at Alexa. They're the only ones who haven't walked down the aisle.

Ava and Aiden have been engaged for a while, but from what Ben told me, they haven't made any actual wedding plans.

Kate and Michael, as well as Olivia and Connor, both have children. And at the rate Ben seems to be going—more like flying —I assume I'll be the next to get pregnant. But we both want lots and lots of kids, and so, Ben thinks we should get a jump start.

"Aiden and I aren't all that traditional, so we're not in a rush," Ava says.

Alexa finishes off her champagne, now taking the so-called floor. "We've been so bloody busy that we haven't even had time to talk about it. But I get to fall asleep next to him every night and wake up with him every morning, and so I can't complain."

Olivia nudges Alexa in the arm. "Hey, the pastor's still here. Why don't you go for it now?"

Alexa chuckles. "Yeah, I think Jake would have a mini heart attack."

"Nah, I'm betting he'd love it," Kate says and checks her phone for the third time in the last five minutes. It's her first time away from her baby, and so she's been a nervous wreck.

I'll be the same, I'm sure. I'll probably be one of those crazy moms who implants some sort of tracking device in my kids to monitor them at all times.

Hell, who am I kidding? Ben will beat me to it.

"They must be ready." Ava points to the dance floor.

"Oh." Kate stands and grabs my hand, and I stare at her, confused.

"Ready for what?" I rise, and Kate ushers me to a chair that's now positioned in the middle of the dance floor.

All five of our guys are standing side by side in front of the DJ, with their heads down and their hands tucked in their back pockets.

"What's going on?" My eyes widen, and the moment I sit, the

music starts . . . and so do the men. It takes me a minute to realize it's *Uptown Funk* by Mark Ronson and Bruno Mars playing.

Ben's in the center of the group, and these strong, tough men surprise the hell out of me by beginning to dance—Ben mouthing some of the lines from the song.

They loosen the bow ties around their necks, and Ben holds my gaze as he tosses his.

I tip my head back and laugh, watching in total awe as Ben, Michael, Aiden, Jake, and Connor begin a choreographed routine.

I have no clue how, or when, Ben managed to pull this together, but it doesn't even matter.

The girls flank my sides, and they're clapping and cheering them on.

A warmth creeps up my neck and into my cheeks as I watch my husband turn around and shake his ass.

Ben hates dancing in public, but he loves the hell out of me—that much is clear.

"How'd Ben get them to do this?" I ask Kate, and she lifts her shoulders and smirks.

She had to have helped. There's no way these five guys came up with this dance on their own.

My heart races as I watch them continue to move—messing up some parts, and bumping into each other at others, which only makes it more ridiculously incredible and humorous.

And when the men stand in a line next to each other a few minutes later, they each crook a finger in our direction, beckoning for us to join them.

I rush to Ben as fast as possible, and he takes my breath away by lifting me up, nearly above his head.

His strong arms hold me up, and I'd swear he's trying to pull off a move from *Dirty Dancing*, one of the movies I used to force him to watch with me when we were kids.

And so, I go with it and open my arms like I'm the female star of the movie.

Only, Ben doesn't need to be Patrick Swayze.

I want him exactly as he is, forever and always.

He'll always be the main lead and hero in my life . . . and I'm right where I belong.

I have a feeling our story has only just begun.

BONUS SCENES, CONTINUED- EMAILS

Riley

To: WildClimber1986
From: AlabamaGirl86
Subject: You're both gone

Ben,

Nate's gone. Like sand. Or dust. Particles that float through the air.
That's Nate now. A pile of ashes inside an urn. It doesn't make
sense. I can't handle it. I just can't . . .

And you're gone, too. Please, don't be gone, too.

-Ri

To: WildClimber1986
From: AlabamaGirl86
Subject: How are you?

Ben,

I heard you're doing well in the Marines. Your mom sent my mom a few pictures of you in your uniform. You look healthy. Strong.

I miss you. I was hoping we could talk.

Can we please talk? I know you can call – because you call your mom. Please call.

-Ri

To: WildClimber1986
From: AlabamaGirl86
Subject: It's me again

I'm guessing you didn't call because you're mad at me. And I get it. I'm so sorry if I blamed you for his death. I never should've said what I did . . . or maybe it's what I didn't say.

You're not to blame. And the kiss—that was an innocent mistake. Please call. I really need you. I'm falling apart over here. I just need to hear your voice.

-Ri

To: WildClimber1986
From: AlabamaGirl86
Subject: We both need you

If you won't forgive me, I guess I understand, but Ralph is struggling. Maybe your mom told you, but I'm taking a year off from school so I can get my head together. Also, Ralph needs me. Maybe we need each other. It'd be nice if we had you in our lives, though.

Well, Mom said you were deployed yesterday. So, I don't even know when you'll see this message. But when you do, can you please call? Or even write back. I miss you.

Stay safe.

-Ri

To: WildClimber1986
From: AlabamaGirl86
Subject: Doctor Carpenter

I've been seeing a therapist to help me talk through things. And I've decided I'd like to become one. I feel a little better now that I know what I want to do with my life.

Well, I hope you're okay. I heard about some Marines getting hurt in Afghanistan on the news. Talked to your mom, and she said it wasn't you. Sorry if you knew them.

And I'm sorry again about how things ended between us.

I miss you. I miss Nate. I miss us.

-Future Dr. Carpenter

* * *

Ben

To: AlabamaGirl86
From: WildClimber1986
Subject: The Euphrates

I was knee-deep in the Euphrates yesterday with the smell of cordite all around me. The thunder of guns blasting round after round. Our camp came under attack. It'd been unexpected. Fortunately, the TEAMs guys were across the way at Camp Ramadi, and they helped us out. But I remember being in that water with my rifle in hand, my NVGs on (night-vision-goggles) . . . and all of a sudden I thought: *if I die tonight, Riley will never know the truth.*

I never think about dying. I never worry about whether I'll leave this world. And so, it shook me up when it happened.

I finally manned up and read your emails. Of course, this message
will probably sit in my outbox until I either delete it, or I get the
balls to send it.

But I needed to tell you something. I needed to tell you how much
I love you. I've been in love with you forever. I carry your picture
around with me. You're why I'm still alive today. You give me the
strength to make it through each and every day.

I hope someday I can tell you in person – I hope someday I have
the guts to see you again.

-Ben

To: AlabamaGirl86
From: WildClimber1986
Subject: Baseball

I did it. I'm a pitcher. I made it to the pros. You're the first person I
wanted to tell when I signed the deal.

I hope you're doing well. It's been forever. I still think about you.
I'll always think about you.

-Ben

To: NatesDad55
From: WildClimber1986
Subject: Hey

Hey, Ralph,

Just checking in. I almost did it. I almost called Riley. But it's been ten years. How could she ever forgive me after 10yrs of silence? So, I chickened out.

Miss you, Old Man.

-Ben

To: WildClimber1986
From: NatesDad55
Subject: Some days…

Some days I think about driving out to see you just so I can kick your ass.

CALL RILEY! You won't regret it. She'll forgive you. I promise.

-Ralph

To: AlabamaGirl86
From: WildClimber1986
Subject: I'm an idiot

13yrs, 6mos, 5 days – since I've seen you.
Not that I've been counting . . .

I had a shit day today. I was sent to rescue someone from a drug cartel down in Arizona. I didn't get there in time. I really hate failing. I hate when people die. HATE IT.

Every time someone dies I think about Nate. I think about you. I think about what an idiot I am for having left you.

I wish I could come home. I wish I could tell you how damn sorry I am. I wish so many things that will probably never come true. I still love you. I can't seem to make it work with anyone in my life because you have my heart. I gave it to you when you were fourteen, you just didn't know it.

How can I keep living without my heart, though?

-Ben

Music Playlist on Spotify

Author Note:
I hope you've enjoyed this story as much as I have writing it. I'm not sure if this book has meant so much to me because Ben's based on a Marine I once knew - or because my brother used to climb (and free climb!), and my family was so nervous those 10+ years whenever he was on the cliffs.

Whether this is your first book of mine, or you've been with the Hidden Truths Series from the start, it's bittersweet to say goodbye to this series - but you never know - these characters could show up again. And I am excited to introduce you to a new world later this year (Fall 2018) - with a brand new set of military heroes.

Thank you for this journey, and be sure to check out my latest romance suspense novel, *My Every Breath.*

x Brittney

(P.S.- people ask how to say my last name & phonetically it sounds like: Sha-heen) ;)

EXTRACT FROM MY EVERY BREATH

Synopsis

Cade King has fallen for the wrong woman. She's the daughter of a hitman, and he's the newest target.

After ten years of living in the shadow of the Irish mob, Gia Callaghan wants nothing more than to escape the darkness of her life. Her burning desire for answers about her past has her constantly plotting new ways to flee. When she comes face-to-face with the one man who might be able to help her, she'll have to decide exactly how much his life is worth.

Cade King's past is littered with questionable choices. He's made more mistakes than he can count, but he vows to be a better man.

When he meets Gia, his structured life turns upside down, and he must decide whether he's truly worthy of redemption. Can he protect a woman whose guard is even higher than his own, or will she end up saving him from himself?

As the tension and chemistry heat up between the two, they'll discover that life isn't always black and white.

A sizzling and suspenseful romance. This book can be read as a standalone.

Chapter 1

Cade

"You couldn't think of anything more original than a strip club?" I glance at my brother, the perpetrator of this cliché bachelor party, as a smirk stretches across his face and meets his eyes.

Jerry, the groom-to-be, smacks my brother in the chest and winks. "He's a smart man." He flicks his wrist, motioning for our group of five to head toward the dance stage.

It's three-tiered and glittery like a birthday cake. The dancer's leg curls around the pole as the candle on top.

"Come on, bro. You need to lighten up."

I exhale through my nose and look to where a woman wearing only silver stilettos gives a guy his own personal show.

"Why this place, though?" Strands of green beads dangle like partitions between the booths around the outer rim of the club, and the Irish flag is positioned on nearly every wall. This isn't our typical hangout.

Corbin directs his attention to the blonde dancer with her ass up in the air on stage. "It was Jerry's idea. Maybe he didn't want to be recognized."

"No one should recognize him here. Well, other than maybe a few criminals he put behind bars and are now out on parole."

"He's a homicide detective. Let's hope none of those assholes are back on the streets," Corbin says.

True. "Just try and stay out of trouble, okay?" I warn.

"Hey, I haven't gotten arrested even once this entire year."

Laughing, I tip my head back and squeeze my eyes shut for a moment. "It's January sixth." Having friends like Jerry has had its perks for my brother.

"What? That counts for something."

Corbin's only thirty. He hasn't managed to tame his wild side yet. Maybe he never will.

"Come on. Tonight is for Jerry." He casually strides through the crowd toward the stage, already reaching into his pocket for his wallet.

I need a drink if I'm going to survive tonight.

I head to the bar and move a stool out of the way so I can remain standing.

The bartender takes a shot of whiskey straight from the bottle, then fills a glass to the brim. He slides it to some guy a few feet away with a thick neck displaying a tat of a serpent darting through the eye hole of a skull.

"Jack and Coke. Light on the Coke," I order a minute later and turn toward the stage while I wait.

I honestly don't have anything against strippers. A lot of them are dancing to pay their way through college. I respect people who work hard. Period. But this particular blonde on stage isn't doing anything for me. And I assume she's wearing a wig. The almost-white hair reaches the small dimples on her back, and every time she bends over, it slips out of place.

At the sound of a glass sliding behind me, I start to pivot, but I stop dead in my tracks at the sight of a woman walking through the crowd, heading my way.

My gaze slides over her, assessing. She's in a classy black, fitted dress that hugs her body but isn't too tight. It falls just above her knees, showing off her long, tan legs. Legs that go for fucking miles.

The lighting is shoddy, but she still looks pretty bronzed for this time of year.

But Jesus, it's her eyes. They're narrowed as if I'm not someone she expects to see here.

Yeah, I feel the same about her.

The closer she gets she sucks me into her orbit almost to the point where I don't feel in control. And I'm always in control, so it rattles me.

She stops in front of the bar and tips her chin up, her beautiful pouty lips tightening.

"Your usual, love?" I hear the guy ask, a faint Irish accent evident in his voice.

Her eyes land on mine, but it's only long enough for me to catch sight of the color. A gorgeous hazel.

She shifts a barstool out of the way and remains standing like me.

Her fingertips drum on the counter as if annoyed or impatient. The color of her nails matches her black hair.

I can't help but eye the small angel wings tattooed on the inside of her wrist when she reaches for whatever the bartender is offering her.

There's something eerily familiar about her, but I can't quite place it, which is strange for me. My memory is crazy. I remember the play-by-play of every moment in my life. Important and useless information is stored in my head, even when I try to forget it. So, there's no way I know her, right?

"Ahem."

I inhale her scent as I drag my gaze up. She smells like freshly cut orchids, the kind my mother always had in every room of our summer home.

"Is there a problem with your eyes?" Her dark brows go inward as she lifts her cocktail. "Perhaps you should change your focus to the stage." She tilts her head that way.

"Say that again."

"Say what?" Black eyeliner wraps around her almond-shaped eyes, making her irises appear lighter.

She's unbelievably stunning. What the hell is she doing in a place like this?

"Say anything." I take a swig of my drink, the warmth hitting my chest. "I like your accent. I can't quite place it, so I need you to talk a little more."

She surprises me with a smile, flashing me white teeth. "Well, you're in an Irish club, so . . ."

I shake the drink in my hand, knocking the cubes around. "Your accent is not Irish. Not even close. Although, if you've been hanging out in this bar"—I raise my glass—"maybe some Irish has rubbed off on you."

Her lips purse for a moment. "I'm from Brazil."

"But . . .?" I smile, enjoying myself a hell of a lot more right now than I was five minutes ago.

"I'm half-Irish."

"Portuguese and Irish, huh? It makes for one hell of a combination."

"One point for you." She lowers her tumbler and sets it on the counter. "At least you know I speak Portuguese."

"I didn't realize I was collecting points."

A small chuckle escapes her lips, but her hand immediately darts to her mouth, covering it.

"That will be the only point you get."

She starts to turn, but I touch her forearm, and she stops moving.

"What's your name? Do you work here?"

She faces me again, and I release my hold. "No, but I can introduce you to a dancer if that's what you'd like."

"Not interested." I take a step forward, and she takes one right back. "Your name?" I ask again, my voice deepening, my intent clear.

I want this woman in every way possible. I've known her for a few minutes, but Christ, I need her on her back and in my bed, pinned beneath me.

She's probably only in her mid-twenties, which is way too young for me, but right now, I can't seem to care.

"My friends call me Gia, but I'm not available, Mister . . .?" Her palm presses to the counter.

"King," I say. "But you can call me Cade."

She rolls her tongue over her teeth, which is entirely too damn distracting. Her eyes sweep over my black dress shirt before settling on my mouth. "Hm."

"Are you married? Have a boyfriend?" I have one rule: I don't get involved with anyone who cheats. My father's string of affairs left a bitter taste in my mouth, and as much as everyone assumes I'm like him, I'm not.

I watch the movement in her throat as she swallows, her gaze cutting up to my eyes, and although I sense confidence in those irises, fear is overshadowing it.

"I'm not the kind of woman you want to get to know, Mr. King." The tone of her voice changes as my last name edges off her tongue.

"Shouldn't I be the judge of that, Gia?" I'm saying her name like I know her, like I already know the curves of her body, the way her hip feels against my palm, and the touch of her tongue in my mouth. But there's something about her, and it's not just her looks; there's something beneath the exterior that I need to get to know. Now.

"Walk away from me. Please. I'm the wrong person to hit on." There's a slight tremble to her bottom lip as she talks, and it has my hand rushing to cover hers that rests on the bar.

"Gia, I don't know who you are, but that's something I'd like to change." In bed. Preferably sooner, rather than later.

She's looking at the bartender instead of me now. The man tips his head to the right.

Her eyes widen, and she retracts her hand from beneath mine, stumbling back a step in the process. "I have to go," she says in a rush and brushes past me.

"Do yourself a favor, mate. Don't pursue her." The bartender refills my glass but leaves out the Coke.

"Who is she?" I ask without touching the tumbler.

He leans forward, crossing his arms, and his green eyes find mine. "She's like a pot of gold at the end of a rainbow: un-fucking-attainable," he says, exaggerating his accent.

He straightens and pulls on his red beard before wiping down the bar counter.

I ignore his comment—or maybe it was a warning; who the hell knows?—and turn around to see where Gia hurried off to.

The place isn't all that busy, and most people here are either crowded around the center stage or tucked away in private booths. Of course, even if the place was packed I doubt she could ever go unseen.

She's standing alongside an empty table twenty or so feet away, and she's with some guy in a suit.

He's clutching her forearm, tight enough that even from where I'm standing I can tell something isn't right.

The guy jerks her toward him, and her palms land against his chest. When she steps back, she looks my way for one fleeting moment, and then he urges her by the elbow to walk with him.

I start in their direction as they head toward the back of the club, unable to think twice about it.

There's one thing I have zero tolerance for, and that's abuse. My father smacked my mom one time—well, once that I know of —when I was eleven. I stood stupidly, frozen in place after seeing it happen. I should have done something. But I couldn't get myself to budge. I may not be my mom's greatest fan, but no woman should ever be hit.

This woman from the bar is no exception, and I'm getting the feeling something shitty is about to go down.

"Yo, you good?" Corbin swoops in front of me from out of nowhere.

I don't want him getting mixed up in anything. That's the last thing he needs. "Bathroom."

"Jerry got himself a private room. Just meet up with the rest of us at our booth near the stage."

"Sure." I nod, my body on fire, worry drilling through me.

Once Corbin's back is turned, I head to the hall where Gia disappeared.

"Please, let me go."

It's her voice. The accent . . .

But the hall is empty.

There's only one door and it's cracked open, so I shove it inward without thinking.

The guy in the suit has her pinned to the wall near a desk, his palms pressed over her shoulders.

I enter the room and hiss, "Back away from her." My heart pounds and climbs up into my throat.

He looks over at me. "And who the fuck are you?"

"Who the fuck am I?" A humorless laugh floats from my lips, and I start at my sleeves, rolling them to the elbows, exposing the tattoos I normally hide on the inside of my arm.

I cross the office with slow and purposeful strides. The need to hit the son of a bitch is overpowering right now. "I don't think you want to find out."

Another strange sensation of familiarity crawls up my spine

and splinters out, but it's not like the feeling of a good whiskey as it spreads warmth through my chest—no, it's more like the woozy feeling from too many shots of bad tequila.

What the hell is wrong with me? Why is this son of a bitch, and even Gia, giving me the feeling of déjà-fucking-vu?

"Are you the arsehole who was hitting on my woman at the bar?"

"Your woman?" I snap back to the present, to the prickly sounds of this man's Irish tongue grating on my ears. "Sounds to me like she isn't yours at all." I've always liked the Irish, but this bastard is leaving a bad taste for the country in my mouth.

"She's for sure as hell not yours." His jaw is tight, a slight tic in his cheek.

I glance over at Gia. She tugs her lower lip between her teeth as she studies us.

I'm standing a few feet away from them both, waiting to see if the asshole will make a move.

He cocks his head, and his green eyes tighten to thin slits. "Do I know you?" A long finger stabs at the air.

Yeah, the feeling is mutual.

"I do, don't I?" He taps the side of his skull.

"I'm pretty sure you and I don't hang out in the same circles."

My arms loosen at my sides in anticipation, but he doesn't look like he's ready to charge at me yet.

"Gia, come on, let's go." I hold my hand palm up, offering her the chance to leave, but she doesn't even flinch.

She stares at my hand like she's in a trance.

"Are you that ballsy that you think you can waltz out of *my* club with *my* woman on your arm?"

"She's not yours. I thought we cleared that up already." My body remains ready, poised for action, as he strides my way. "She comes with me and no one gets hurt."

God, I feel like I'm in some bad action flick right now.

He stops moving, leaving a few feet of open air—more like

tension—between us. He rubs his thick beard as his eyes focus on mine. "I think you know as well as I do that if you even try to walk out of here with Gia at your side, you'll end up with a body full of bullets. And since you walked through a metal detector to get in the club, you're not packing heat."

"I'll take my chances."

"No." At the sound of Gia's voice, my attention sweeps over his shoulder to her. "Leave, please." She's got a gun in her hand— aimed at me.

"It's okay. I'm trying to help." I keep my voice low and smooth, trying to calm her. Why the hell is she pointing that thing at me?

The guy smiles. "Told you she was my woman."

"Go." She removes the safety, her elbows locked, her arms stiff. There's not even the slightest bit of a tremble.

"Please, put the gun down." I try one more time, not sure how the hell this situation turned out like this.

The guy continues to observe her with a hint of a smile on his lips, not saying anything.

"Go!" she cries again, and I note the break in her voice.

Why is she doing this? And how the hell can I leave?

But she's not giving me much of a choice.

"I'll be seeing you around," the guy says as if he really means it. But none of my plans include ever dealing with this son of a bitch again.

I finally start for the door, guilt clawing its way through me one inch at a time.

I check my impulse to steal one last glance at her before leaving.

Learn more

ALSO BY BRITTNEY SAHIN

Hidden Truths

The Safe Bet

Beyond the Chase

The Hard Truth

Surviving the Fall

Stand-Alones

The Story of Us

On the Edge

Someone Like You

My Every Breath

COMING SOON

SEAL TEAM SERIES

CONNECT

Thank you for reading Ben and Riley's story. If you loved the book, please take a quick moment to leave a review.

Sign up to receive **exclusive excerpts** and **bonus material** for my novels, as well as take part in great **giveaways**, which include gift cards, signed paperbacks, and e-books by some of your favorite romance authors. **Subscribe.**

For more information:
www.brittneysahin.com
brittneysahin@emkomedia.net